Runner Mack

BOOKS BY BARRY BECKHAM

Runner Mack
My Main Mother

Barry Beckham

RUNNER
MACK

William Morrow & Company, Inc., New York   1972

This one is going out
for
Dennis Watson

Runner Mack

This is how it would be, he thought, and his wrists were hot, his underwear felt sticky, for he wasn't sure it was true, what they were saying about opportunities and straight to the top. He was going down the plank and he didn't know what to expect. How would Momma Lou advise him? This was worse than trying to steal home, it was a larger dilemma than being run down between second and first, and far worse than guarding the bag when a cleat-spitting runner was heading toward you. Scared as scared could be. Pilot, oh pilot me.

1

THE DENTIST was holding Henry Adams around the neck with one hand while the other hand held the medicine dropper.

"Come on, it won't hurt. What're you scared of?" Then he squeezed the dropper and a tear of water plopped on Henry's forehead. The water was boiling, and Henry grabbed onto the arms of the dentist's chair as the pain bore into his forehead. "It doesn't hurt, what are you jumping for? Take another drop." And he squeezed one more quarter-ounce of the liquid from the dropper, and it too was scalding hot as it landed on the middle of Henry's forehead and felt as if someone were hammering a straight pin into his head. And then, in the dark of his twenty-five-foot-square office, no windows, "I can't control it," said the dentist, and the drops were falling down onto Henry's forehead and cheeks and nose and mustache, and the pain was so severe he fell unconscious.

And woke up with something brown and wet running over his face. Henry Adams jumped up in bed and heard Beatrice turn over. Henry looked up to the ceiling with his mouth open and his tongue caught another drop. He spit it out.

Beatrice said, "What's the matter?"

On the ceiling was a brown ring as large as a saucer and drops of water were falling from around the ring. "The ceiling's leaking," he said, and leaped out of the bed, adding, "stay over on your side."

3

From the bedroom Henry went into the kitchen, which was also the bathroom, the toilet in one corner and the tub on top of the sink. He came back with a bucket and placed it on the bed. The water dropped in, *ping, ping, ping.* Henry stood by the bed, he was yawning and scratching himself through his pajamas.

"Is there any heat?" she asked, rolling to the edge of the bed and shivering, pulling the two blankets and the spread up to her neck, her back to Henry.

"No," he said, and watched the smoke shoot from his mouth. Then, "I'll go see Alvarez." He reached for his shoes and pulled from them the socks he had worn the previous day; then his underwear, the undershirt with a hole under the arm; then his shoes, and soon he was dressed. On his way to the kitchen and the door, he put his hand on the cold radiator. Nothing. He opened the door, stepped out, turned around and came back into his apartment. Too cold. Better put on a sweater. He went back out, wearing his black cardigan, and was stepping down the hall toward the steps, was just about to put his first foot on the cement step, was just about to put his hand on the iron rail, when he heard the giggling behind him, so he withdrew his foot quickly and looked down the hall.

"Tee hee hee. Tee hee hee." It was the Hurts' child. He knew her only as a fresh, nasty-mouthed little girl. "You got a hole in your sweater right here," she said, pointing at her elbow. She was leaning out the doorway of her apartment, cut off at the waist. Then she waved five fingers at Henry, teehee'd and closed the door. Stepping over a cracked eggshell, Henry proceeded down the steps, calling Betty Hurt a nasty name to himself, and when he got to the landing, smelling the odor of the hallway. In 3A Henry heard the loud music of a rock group, the bass vibrating against the door. He knocked on 3B.

He stamped his feet and flapped his arms around his chest and whistled. He could hear the footsteps and voices of Alvarez and his family inside; why didn't someone open the door? He lifted his hand to knock again, but brought his finger down softly on the bell. He had forgotten the bell.

Alvarez standing at the door in pajamas, rubbing his hand

through his shiny hair and looking straight at Henry Adams' waist. "Yeah?" A drowsy, unwelcome smile on his face. Henry felt the heat come out of the super's door. Figures moving in the background.

"No heat and my ceiling's leaking," said Henry, then felt that it was an obstacle he would never overcome as Alvarez spoke in Spanish, and it sounded to Henry like:

"*Ariba ariba comprendo no ariba—*" and so forth.

"Can you come upstairs and look at my ceiling? My ceiling"—pointing upward with one finger—"ceiling . . . roof . . . top . . . water . . . drip, drip, drip . . . water pieces come down . . . wet. . . ." And he was acting out an interpretation: he trickled his hand down from above his head to the floor to demonstrate how the water was dripping; made clicking noises with his tongue to illustrate how the water was dropping in the bucket; put an imaginary glass up to his mouth and pretended to drink it to get across, *water*. Then, stepping back, he huddled his arms around his waist, said, "Cold, no heat, brrrrr," stomped his feet. Come on, Alvarez, he thought, please understand me just this one time. Please. I've gone through this with you so many times. Just a break is all I'm asking for—just give me some sympathy once. You must understand some of this. Don't you?

"No . . . no heat? No nothing?"

Henry's mind came to attention, his heart lit up, he smiled broadly.

"Water . . . ceiling leaking?"

Now Henry was ecstatic. "Yes, yes, that's it, Alvarez, you've got it, my man! No heat and the ceiling's leaking." He grabbed the super in a congratulatory hug, and in that instant glanced behind the Puerto Rican superintendent and got a quick look at the apartment and something ghostlike moving in white. His wife in a nightgown? But it was something at knee level flashing and shiny. White teeth?

"Know nothing. I can do nothing until tomorrow. The office she is closed." He whispered. And now he closed the door on himself more and there were only three inches of Alvarez showing.

Henry was subdued. If the office was closed, the office was

closed, and there was nothing he could do, nothing Alvarez could do, so the water would come dripping, dripping down into the bucket until tomorrow, and he and Beatrice would be huddled up in pounds of blankets tonight. What could he do, standing in front of the superintendent's door (was it closing more, down to two inches now?), the super's black hair dangling out like a rag mop? Henry was disturbed, angry, defeated. "Damn," he said, almost a whimper; and trembling. Alvarez smiled, then grinned, two rows of shiny teeth popping out. This was even tougher on Henry. Alvarez was smiling and he was about to cry. Something was out of kilter. *Beat up the goddam spick!* He didn't like black people anyway. Wait a minute, I don't really know that. Get myself together. Still, they couldn't fight. Alvarez was small. He couldn't fight—maybe. But if he could. Suppose he knew judo? Suppose he had a knife? Probably had one stuck in his pajamas . . . pajamas . . . pajamas. From the few inches or so of Alvarez's pajamas that Henry could see, it seemed that . . . he squinted. The flowery design. The green and blue colors. Henry forced open the door by kicking it.

"What the hell are you doing in my pajamas!" He was trembling. Alvarez's eyes widened, his lips were moving but no sound emerged. "Give me my pajamas, you bastard." Grabbing at the front and ripping, tearing, pulling.

Alvarez screamed at him in Spanish and began backing into his apartment, was flailing his hands at Henry Adams. Henry kicked Alvarez in the leg and was amazed and frightened at his surge of violence, explaining to himself, I just kicked that bastard; oh, Lord, I didn't mean to do that, I didn't mean to hurt him. Alvarez spit out two words in Spanish and Henry could see that shining, glinting whiteness again and also heard a scratching on the linoleum floor, then heard the growling, then saw the German shepherd (mouth dripping foam from a long red tongue) lunging at his arm, and Henry Adams jumped back in time to see the door slammed in his face. He was glad and not glad, but mostly glad that the door was now between him and danger. He heard the dog barking and his claws scratching against the door, so he walked backwards to the stairway and took the steps two at a time, dropped his key, started to leave it but went back for it, and charged through the safety of his own door. He stood in the kitchen, listened to his heartbeat knocking against his chest and tried to steady his shoulders.

"Henry?"

He was breathing too hard to speak clearly, was barely able to squeeze out, after holding his breath for seconds, "Yeah," as if someone were choking him. He came to the doorway separating the kitchen from the other room, was out of breath, stood and looked around at the bed now made up, the television, the sofa, the dresser and that was it. Beatrice, wrapped up in two blankets, sat on the sofa. The bucket, resting tilted on the bed, was almost half-filled, and the droplets were still plunking down into it.

"What did he say? Is he going to fix it right away?"

"Uh, he won't be able to do anything until tomorrow, the office is locked—I mean, closed today." Now he was getting to the meat of his recital, and his voice took on a tenor quality, his words were mumbled since his lips were trembling and he said, "Alvarez got my pajamas. The ones that were stolen from you in the laundry. The green ones with the flowers. He's wearing them and when I tried to get them back this great Dane came attacking me." Voice leaking with pain.

"He can come up here and do something," she said, and her voice was strong, direct. "Why didn't you ask—"

"It's no use, Beatrice, he ain't gonna do nothing until he wants to. I should call the manager, but it ain't worth it."

"You'd better get ready for work. You are going to that new job?" Rising and stepping into the kitchen.

"Yeah."

"If you don't like it, you just quit and come home. I can always get a job doing assembly work."

"I don't want you to work, you know that. I'm the man of this house. I can take care of us."

"But we don't have much money left, Henry. Suppose this one is as bad as the others?"

"It can't be. Even if it is, I'll take it."

"Well, your clothes are all washed and I ironed out a new shirt for you. It's seven-thirty now."

7

He gathered his clothes from the dresser and went into the kitchen to wash. Thinking back. Two years. The day Henry joined the usher board at Bethany Baptist. Oh, she was twitchy, was fly, was loose, holding out her hand to him. "I welcome you to the usher board of Bethany Baptist. Brother's been talking up a storm about you and him on the baseball team together. Say you might go on to professional ball."

They had laughed and looked in each other's eyes and Brother had left them in the foyer. Then they went up to the balcony to get their assignments and their purple-and-white armbands, and soon the organ was playing and they took their stations in the aisles. After service he saw Beatrice waiting by the water cooler at the door. Should he go over to her?

He did. "Hey."

She had turned. "Oh, I thought you had left." Reverend Fuller was standing at the door, shaking the hands of the last parishioners. "Nice sermon, huh?"

"Um hum."

She had fanned at a fly, missed, and it circled around Henry's head, and they both swatted at it, missing and laughing. "That's a big one; I ain't never seen a fly that big in a church before; have you, Henry?"

"No. That's as big as the ones I catch when I play center field. I think the reverend is waiting for us. Uh, which way might you be walking, Beatrice?"

So she had got him to walk her home and they started courting. Henry came out of the kitchen.

"The water's cold." He started dressing. The ceiling water was still dripping, and now the ceiling was vibrating and he knew the upstairs tenants were moving furniture or dancing, and soon it was a conglomeration of dripping, plunking, banging, knocking. Almost a year of this and now he was used to it.

"You'd better leave now, honey, it's near eight. Kiss me good-by."

He eased into his overcoat, had to push and juggle his shoulders; it was a size too small and a fabric too thin. Then walked over to bend stiffly and kiss Beatrice's cold cheek, expelling clouds as he opened his mouth.

He went down the steps carefully, having slipped before on

Popsicle sticks and chocolate bars. He was steeling himself for outdoors, for the great outside and then the job itself. Downstairs he checked the mailbox: nothing. Opening the door.

Outside, the cold and the noise; the grayness of the sky. And the people packed together. There was barely room, he saw, standing on the steps of the building, for him to move. People, pedestrians, were huddled together, stepping down the street, owning every inch of sidewalk space, sometimes slipping off the curb into the street. Their heads were bowed, their elbows were sticking out and catching sides and ribs of other pedestrians marching in the cluster. There was an opening. Henry jumped in, was bumped in the shoulder and turned like a spinning top, then he himself turned to say, "Excuse me," and had to take a deep breath to keep from crying out after a pointed heel had dug into his toe. Now he was limping to keep the weight off that toe and had to swing his arms, had to half-trot as the velocity of the pedestrians accelerated. He thought the scene very similar to his inching his way through the bleacher crowd at the end of a game; except here there was no end, was there? The streets were always crowded like this; always presented to Henry some unfathomable obstacle that had to be entered into with great reluctance. He couldn't see too far ahead. Now he was walking almost sideways, having been jostled. Nor could he see behind him. He knew only that he was part of the mass of charging mass.

Also there was the ear-stunning, bellowing pandemonium of car horns; the artillerylike barrage of machines banging and echoing, banging and echoing as if nearby some steel building were being dropped and hoisted, bounced continuously from a derrick: as if the city were being bombarded by drumfire. To Henry it was painful but acceptable, too loud but necessary.

And from home, little consolation. "I told you the North was going to be hell," Beatrice's father had written. "You thought things were going to be easy, huh? Peaches and cream?" So the din, the swell, hung cloudlike over his ears.

Not owning gloves, his hands were in his pockets (big holes in each so his hands stuck through to his pants pockets); and the November air nipped at his ear lobes, stung them, and his eyes were watering. His toes were curled up. He couldn't ignore the odor either, and it seemed as if he were directly following a trail of rotten eggs, emptied garbage cans, dripping human perspiration, dead mice, disturbed skunks. A swift breeze (cold) cleared the air briefly, and the odor disappeared and reappeared. But the bleak grayness of the sky bothered him the most. It was cool and somber as if something had died in the air and melted, then spread, distilled itself molecularly throughout the atmosphere. No trace of sunshine. To breathe freely as he had in Mississippi was to punish his lungs.

This was the condition of things that day (and had been the condition since his move up from the South), the situation at the moment, as he was soft-shoe dancing over the sidewalk sleet, bumping into and being bumped against, cold and shivering, accepting and not wanting to accept. But what else was there? Back to the 'Sip? No good. His future was here, had to be.

He checked the address. Henry Adams at the corner, nervous that he might be late his first day, burst from the pack of pedestrians encircling him near the curb ("'Scuse me, please? 'Scuse me?"), was pushed on the hip by somebody and suddenly found himself in the street. His arms were up high for balance and he was up on his toes doing a jig on a patch of sleet and just couldn't get off it. And the light was red. And he wasn't near the center line yet. Traffic was roaring toward him. Henry tried jumping, but was only able to jump up and land on the same piece of ice, at once falling to his hands and tearing a swatch of pant leg at the knee.

Somebody yelled from the crowd, *"Port de bras."*

He pushed himself up to his feet again and the blood was burning his cheeks and again he was waving his arms and bending his legs and—he thought it was a different voice this time—somebody shouted, "Steppin Fetchit."

Another citizen: "Hey, Pegleg Bates, here comes a truck. You better stop that."

Also: "Is that the buck and wing?"

Henry Adams—he thought he shouldn't have turned out of his name like that (the hell I look like some Pegleg) but this could be serious—Henry turned one side of his face to

10

look over his shoulder and suddenly . . . oh, Lord! His imagination told him he had been dropped on a stage in some movie
house and was facing the screen. On the screen was a truck—
a very, very big truck, looming toward him with a grille
(smiling) of steel meshwork and headlights (winking) like
two glass basketballs. It was right on top of him, seemed to
be pouncing, falling from above, about to land on him and
swallow him, and it was just too close for Henry to do anything but turn his head and. . . .

He opened his eyes. Faces were everywhere above him now
as he looked up, squinted, tried to roll from his back to his
side but was stabbed back by the pain in his hip. He couldn't
feel anything in his ankles. He eased himself up to his elbows
and rested on them, blinked his eyes and stared at the honey-
comb of facial features staring down at him, making him feel
like a fish flapping in the sand. In the back of his head a
persistent, thudding ache was easing down to his neck. He
put a hand on the top of his head: blood. And then, *What
time is it?* He scrambled, reaching for the curb. His shoes had
been knocked off and were lying on their sides a few feet
away. He scrambled up on his knees and then gained a rickety
stance, looked around. The citizens, moving back from the
ring they had formed around him, said nothing. He bent to
reach for his shoes and then heard the alarming chimes of a
public clock announcing nine. Late. Must hurry.

Henry Adams burst through the ring of people, crossed the
street, stumbled and fell along the curb, hands outstretched to
break his fall. His nose and teeth thumped against the gravel
of the street as his palms and knees were scraped again. His
lips were pushed open by the fall and he was still sliding on
his belly, and the edges of his upper teeth scraped along the
gravel. His lips were scorched. Unsettling grating sound of
tooth enamel against the cement. The tip of his tongue was
hot with pain.

Henry pushed himself up from the ground and ran blindly,
aware of only two facts: he was late and he was aching.
Finally, by the outskirts of the city where he was able to pick
up speed, he reached the bridge connecting his part of the
city with the suburbs. On the other side of the bridge, resting

on a hillock of gray stone, imperious, ringed by an ashen fog, a fortlike architecture of towers, was the building, a giant flag waving from the highest tower: Home Manufacturing. Across the sidewalk of the bridge. The tires of the passing cars sounding against the wooden planks of the bridge. Now on the other side and up the road, dying weeds and brush directing his path. But as he reached the gateway of the building, his ankles gave in, he collapsed. Crawling. Climbing over the gate, untied shoes unsteady on the rungs. Easing down on the other side, turning and running toward the main door that was almost as wide as his apartment building, leaning his weight sideways against the wood, falling as the door creaked open. Facing him as he picked himself up from the floor was a desk. Higher up, a guard with a rusty star propped on the chest of his blue uniform, three strands of uncombed white hair, like bird feet, centered in the middle of his head.

"What the hell is this? Who the hell are you? Where the hell—"

Henry supported himself by leaning on the desk, went into his pocket for the card. Found it. Unbelievable, it's there, he thought. Gave it to the guard.

"You have an appointment with Mister Peters at nine?"

Henry, half-seeing, half-awake, feeling half-dead, summoned what he thought might be his last reserve of strength, said— nothing; breath expiring, he just nodded his head.

"Are you with the company?"

He shook his head no, sighing loudly.

"Well, let's see if we can get Peters—Mister Peters—on the phone."

Henry leaned on the desk and lost consciousness while the guard dialed. Henry still leaned on the desk, supporting himself with his elbows, and his face was a foot away from the guard's face, and the guard pushed out his palm, indicating that Henry was too close—pushed it straight into Henry's face and he fell to the floor.

"Okay." He clamped down the phone and stood up, looked down at Henry. "What the hell . . . what are you doing down there? Get up. Can't you get up? What's wrong with you? Looks like you been hit by a Mack truck." He came around to the front of the desk, bent over—"Oh, my back"—clipped a badge on Henry's shirt collar. "I'll let you in, go straight down the hall until you see Personnel, turn left, then to the water cooler and a right, and past the elevator until you see New Personnel, take a right, go down the steps one landing, make three half-rights and wait there." He pulled out from his belt a ring of keys, strode to the door behind him, stood on his tiptoes, stretched, unlocked the top lock; worked the combination on the second lock; knelt down to his knees—"Oh, my back"—to unlock the bottom lock; standing again, put a key in a lock near the center. He turned the handle and the door opened. "Go ahead."

2

A LONG HALL stretching forward from him
and stretching and stretching longer and farther from him until
at the end where it was small there was solely the clear rectangular screen of space, silver sparkles of dust dancing.
The tile walls were gray and had finger smudges. Henry was
on his hands and knees, the sole of one shoe still against the
door, and he was thinking, it looks like one long dugout, one
long, unending dugout. And then he sighed, put the fingers of
both hands (trembling) on the cold, tile floor, attempted to
push himself up; was suspended above the ground like a
sprinter fitting into the starting blocks, all weight on his fingers
(trembling), and the legs now bending forward, kneeling; and
now he was going to push up from his fingers and attempt to
stand, and his fingers and thumbs were swaying, shaking from
the weight of his body. He pushed up but fell on his knee,
and the thump echoed and traveled away from him—as if it
had feet—down the walls. And then he slipped to his side because the pain again grabbed his ankle, the pounding was in
his head, the muscles in his shoulders were being pierced with
needles.

In the game against Hattiesburg, his ankle puffed up like
this after he had tried to get a break on the side-arming
southpaw, Wilson, and went hook-sliding into second at the
bottom of the second. Stealing on a lefty! His left toe had
caught the tip of the bag but the slide's momentum took his

14

right leg past the sack, bending his left ankle and it stuck into the base, twisted so that he could do nothing but lie there, one leg outstretched, the other bent and unmoving—unable to move—as the ankle throbbed, throbbed. . . .

There were no sounds at all, just the echoes of his scuffling, crawling, half-walking down the corridor as he bumped limply against the wall. Six feet later, he was on his hands and knees again, and crouching, he peered toward the end of the hall and squinted: a contour of a figure, contracting and expanding in its haziness as if it were underwater. Scarecrow? He blinked, shook his head and regretted that, because the pain coursed from the back of his head to his forehead. Hallucination? Tackling dummy? Then the figure's arm was raised and it beckoned Henry Adams. Realizing now that he was late, knowing he had to get this job, Henry panicked, attempted to walk briskly, snappily down the hall, but was forced to smack the cold wall with his palms to gain balance. The pain again. Now the shape, outline, impression—Henry still wasn't sure—moved toward him with alacrity, water arms swinging, rubbery legs shaking closer, closer, feet clicking and echoing, reverberating off the walls until soon Henry was able to make distinctions in the form and was sure it was a man, a tall man. He stopped over Henry, who was now kneeling, squatting. The figure stopped with a final, authoritative snapping of his heels. Adams looked up at him. Gray, pin-striped suit. Bushy, raccoon eyebrows, crewcut. Hands behind his back.

"Henry? Henry Adams?" The voice was light, childlike, high, bouncing off the walls.

Henry whispered, "Yes," but it was inaudible, so he tried it again, clearing his throat this time and smoothing over what to him sounded like an embarrassing hoarseness. "Yes, I'm Adams."

"Peters. Personnel. We've been expecting you." Henry watched the arm swing from behind Peters, watched the five white, open fingers expand, pointing down, and Henry reached to clasp the hand, had his fingertips touching Peters' when again his shoe slipped on the tile and his fingers went falling away, the fingers just sliding away from Peters' and Henry falling to his knee again. Echo.

"Glad to met you, Peter," Henry said. And then, " 'Scuse me, I slipped." Would he get the job? God, please let him get the job, please.

"My name's not Peter, it's Mister Peters, M. A. Peters, Personnel. You're late." He snapped his arm, checked his watch. He was looking straight down at Henry, who suddenly remembered Momma Lou's saying, "Don't turn your eyes from no white man when you wants something, 'cause he'll think you lyin' just as natural as you breathin'," and Henry was straining, breathing hard, his jaws were tight—he *must* look Peters in the eye. "What happened to you?"

"I was hit by a truck on the way here. That's why I'm late, Mister Peters," looking him directly in the eyes. Now, Henry. Did that sound right? Why didn't I say somebody beat me up? He won't go for that. I won't get the job.

"Oh, I'm so sorry, Henry. The streets are damned crowded, though, aren't they? Did you have any trouble finding the place?"

Henry shook his head. A mistake. He could feel those midget workmen inside his head hammering and chiseling, warning him not to irritate them. The pain shut his eyes, he was drifting off into blackness, into blackness. . . .

"Henry! Uh, Henry, how's the weather out, cold?"

"Not bad, sir."

("Don't be uppity when you lookin' for a job," Momma Lou used to tell them. After Little Stuff finished his lessons in the second bedroom where Joe Boy, Sissy Linda and Henry slept also—Henry and Sissy had beds to themselves and Stuff and Joe Boy shared a third—he would go skirting out the back door and run all the way, a quarter-mile, to the motel off Route 218, where he changed beds, emptied wastebaskets, carried luggage, hoisted the rebel flag, cleaned the showers. "You gotta learn to be a man early," Momma Lou would say, "and fourteen ain't too early to begin." Joe Boy, two years younger, worked on Saturdays at Manny's garage and kept rolling tires home and leaving them in the backyard, where he would hop in the circles and somersault, stand on his hands. He had hitchhiked to Jackson once to see the circus and declared he would be an acrobat and visit the world. Sissy helped

16

Momma with the laundry she took in, plus sewed and stitched up holes, tears. And Henry? At that time he was sixteen and didn't have a job. He was to be a great ballplayer. Had to practice every day, couldn't work.)

"Well, would you like to come with me to my office so we can talk?" And he had already turned and taken two loud steps, was now looking back at Henry, was looking with his arms waist-high, palms up, face smiling with the eyebrows, Henry thought, joining the hairline.

"Yes," he answered, now scrambling, bent over as if he were a cotton picker, arms dangling to keep his balance—traveling on one good leg, and the other tucked up. Three footsteps echoed down the hall.

"This way, Henry." They had reached the end of the hall and now were turning into a swinging steel door with a red glass rectangle of an exit sign over it. So Peters held the door open for Henry, and then they went down the landing, Henry's shoes clopping down the cement steps. "What do you think about those Swans—some team, huh? I never thought they'd take that game yesterday. What a fucking pass that Broozy threw, huh?"

"Yes, sir." Wait a minute. Broozy didn't throw any passes. Broozy is an end. Should he tell Peters that Broozy is an end, that McFarther threw that long one? Would that be the thing to do, should he do it, and should he do it now, before he was sure he had the job?

"I never miss a game—this way, Henry, into this door—never. The wife is always complaining, you know, on Sundays. I make up a batch of whiskey sours and get into my slippers and just lie on the rug, relaxed in my khakis and an old Dartmouth sweatshirt. Never miss a game. That Broozy is fantastic, really a great player."

Better let it go. Be careful. You've gotten this far—here we go in the door—and there's no sense in messing up now.

"Please sit, Henry." And now there was more light and he could see Peters very well, moving across to the desk, banging a pipe in an ashtray, now sitting behind the desk, and just his body from the chest up was visible. Henry noticed the wall-length window to the left of Peters. Outside it was gray. He could see one building in the distance, near the top of the window, and it discharged circles of smoke. "Take off your coat, Henry, relax."

"Oh, no, sir," said Henry, remembering the elbow hole in his sweater, plus thinking that Momma Lou would frown (he smiled, remembering he had bright, even teeth) up to her eyes until they were almost closed, like the time Joe Boy had come home with a failing mark in fourth-grade geography. She had met him on the porch. Joe Boy held the card out to her and studied the planks under his feet and pulled his hands inside the sleeves of the overcoat worn the previous winter by Little Stuff and two winters previously by Henry. So Joe Boy was patting his shoe tip on the porch, his arms hunched up, broadening his shoulders, while the tip of his cap slid over his eyes, and Momma Lou, forewarned by Sissy ("Momma, you gonna have the surprise of your life when you see Joe Boy's card, you wait"), was going over the mysterious markings with a fastidious, black pudgy finger and voice trailing off into the delta wind, "B . . . B . . . C-plus . . . F." Henry and Sissy had peeked from the side of the house. Oh, she could frown. And say nothing. Joe Boy moved his feet. Peters banged his pipe again. "No, sir," repeated Henry, "I'm just comfortable as I am, thank you." He did have to go to the men's room, though.

"Henry, I do want to review your files before we begin the group interview with several of the section, department, group, class and area heads, so why don't you look over the annual report from last year to get an idea of what we're up to here at Home." He handed Henry a thick brochure with a color photograph of the building on the cover, three secretaries standing, broad grins, by the front gate. On the first page was a message from the president. Henry rolled up his eyes to note that Peters' head was hidden by papers, so he put the book up to his nose. He liked the smell.

"Five-ten, huh, Henry?"

"No, sir—" Then he hesitated, then the pain in his ankle surged as he thought, should I have disagreed? But I am five-eight, and two inches is a big difference, especially if I'm going to get a uniform.

"No?" Peters' hand grasped the telephone, his eyes jumped from Henry's head to his waist, back to his head down to his waist again, up and down. "No?"

"No, sir," said Henry, "I'm five feet eight inches—I'm sure." There, that didn't sound uppity—I'm sure—that allowed for the possibility of Henry's not knowing *precisely* how tall he was. Momma Lou always said that they didn't like to be wrong—ever; or you to be right—never.

"Of course. We have your height. I was referring to your weight at birth—five pounds ten ounces. Sorry about the interruption."

Henry recrossed his legs, decided his bladder could hold out just a little longer. He squeezed his thighs together tightly, refocused on the president's message. It said that the last year had been one of moderate growth and expansion for the Home Manufacturing Company, and that orders had increased a certain percentage over the previous fiscal year. Henry didn't understand everything but continued reading. The president, Newberry Clay (pen in hand and sitting at his desk), who smiled from the top of the page, mentioned the long tradition of quality and efficiency for which Home had been noted. He wrote that he was "indeed proud" of this tradition which began when his great-granduncle had married the daughter of a rich merchant one hundred years ago and started the firm with two employees in the attic of a friend who was suffering from an unknown disease and hence rented out that upper floor to pay the medical bills. Clay continued:

> I am indeed proud of this continuing tradition carried on by our employees of today. It was people who were important in the founding of this dynamic company and it is you people, you employees, who are the backbone of our progress today. Without you, Home is nothing, and we have indeed attempted to illustrate our appreciation for your fine efforts by continually improving the benefit package so that you will feel we have a home-team advantage. We always want you to feel at home at Home.

On the next two pages Henry's eyes scanned over pictures of machinery, pipes, gears, bearings, and the headline read:

"Our Machinery—Backbone of Our Efforts. Pictured below are representative samples of the tools we work with to make Home go." He focused again on Peters at the desk.

"So you've been in the city for almost a year now, huh? You like it? . . . Up from Mississippi . . . um hum . . . married . . . three jobs so far . . . one hundred sixty pounds . . . size ten shoe . . . two brothers and a sister . . . live downtown . . . yes . . . umhummmm . . . referred by the Alert Agency . . . very good. Just wanted to refresh myself, Henry, on your file," said Peters, smiling what to Henry seemed to be a sick, painful smile, like the time the captain of the Hattiesburg Hitters had stepped off first to take a lead and was tagged out, the ball hidden in the first baseman's glove. "Came up North to strike it rich, huh? Get a good job and make something of yourself."

"Well, no, sir . . . well, yes, sir. I really came up to play ball—baseball."

"You came up here to play—to fool around?"

"I was drafted by the Crowns when I was in high school three years ago," said Henry, his voice straining now because he was holding in his stomach and he knew he would have to go soon. "I hit four-fifteen for them. I played the outfield."

On his left Henry noticed three interconnected globes of smoke entering the room. Then three men marched in single file through the door, pipes in their hands. The globes melted into each other and formed a mist, rising toward the ceiling. Henry took in the definite odor of cherries, lowered his head to cough and noticed they were all wearing shiny, tan, flat shoes.

"Hi, Peters," said the tallest, shoes squeaking as he moved to the side of Peters' desk.

"Morning, Peters," said the second, taking a place beside the first greeter and flicking a spot of lint off his coat sleeve.

"Peters," said the third, lining up too so that now Henry was staring at these three men at attention with their starched white collars, their gray suits (white handkerchiefs peeking out of their breast pockets), their cheeks smooth and pink, their lips tight over the pipes. Parts in their hair. Henry looked at them, and hands behind their backs, rocking on their heels, they stared at him. Grinning and staring. Peters looked up.

He nodded, said, "Men," then cracked his pipe against an ashtray. "Henry Adams." Peters' arm went toward Henry as if introducing him on the stage.

"Henry," nodded the man closest to Henry. His hand went inside his jacket. He fiddled with his tie clip, smoothed his tie.

"Henry," said the middle man, drawing on his pipe and saluting Henry with it.

"Henry," said the one with the squeaky shoes, and he tightened the knot on his tie.

Henry greeted them. He really had to go now. How long would this take? He put his arms between his legs, sat forward.

"Henry, this is A. L. Klein, section head of international company parts and international company gears. Been with us for five years now, straight from business school. He's murder on the straightaway, but can't putt for shit."

The three giggled. Henry smiled, then snapped his mouth shut when he caught himself in Peters' glance.

"In the middle there, is B. J. Kind, area chief of identification and recovery, just got back from a survey trip of Japan, huh, B. J.? And last, but not least, we have M. O. Baby, department boss of process instrumentation. Guys, Henry here is the new man I told you about—sent by the agency. I thought we should give him an idea of what opportunities there are at Home so he can decide which area he'd like to work in."

The three men advanced toward Henry, pipes in their hands, and soon he saw them exhaling smoke, the spheres forming again, hiding their faces from him as they stood above him.

"Let's see your teeth, Henry"—voice from behind a screen of smoke—"open up."

Henry stretched his mouth open. His heart beat faster. Strange men staring at his face, in his mouth. Should he spit? Growl? At least frown?

Another executive, shoe squeaking as he advanced one step from behind the cherry-flavored wall of smoke to bend down and grab Henry's biceps and alternately squeeze and contract

21

his fingers around Henry's arm, said, "He's got strength," and his breath fell into Henry's face, curling around his nose and spreading over his mustache. It was a breath raw and stale of tobacco. Bad breath. It went down to Henry's stomach and he thought he would sicken. He really had to go in the next few seconds or he would definitely wet his pants.

"Do you believe in . . . do you believe in God, my boy?"

Henry turned to the left to answer but a voice interrupted him on the right, still a screen of smoke preventing Henry from seeing clearly the three shapes mixed in the mist—

"Of course, A. L., don't be stupid. They all believe in God. Of course he does. Uh, have you been sick lately, Henry? I mean, are you healthy and fit? Have you had the smallpox?"

From his right: "What can you do best, Henry—work with your hands, huh?"

From the middle: "Have you ever stolen, Henry? You wouldn't take any of our machinery out of here, would you?"

And from farther back, so far he knew it had to be Peters, for the voice was high also (more evidence), he heard: "Oh, he looks honest, men, but Henry, answer me this—would you run away if you didn't like the work?"

So his head bobbed back and forth, confronting each inquiry shooting at him from the haze, and the questions were coming so fast he was reminded of an auctioneer's verbal magic and he never had enough time to reply to any one question. He kept jerking his head this way, that way, confused by the voices that, strangely, asked *and* answered; insistent voices descending upon him from a nowhere land of cherry-smelling grayness; shaking him, punching his legs, biceps, opening his mouth, sticking in his ears; bad breath strangling him. And he was scared. Gray faces barking behind grayness. He was in the same confused state that he had been in after being hit by that truck and getting up, facing that collection of legs and arms and feet and eyes and noses. Then the little workmen started acting up again, this time taking a very tender side of his left temple, and it seemed that they were just jumping up and down with football cleats this time—that they had rested their hammers and were now just jumping, jumping like Joe Boy used to do on those tires in the backyard, with his arms

22

bent upward as if he were a surrendering cowboy. And hell, he couldn't take it and couldn't hold it back any longer.

He jumped up from the couch, waved away the haze, waved himself through it, turned left and tried to run out the door until the pain broke him into a limp. But he was limping fast, hobbling through the doorway, through the reception area, opened the door and was in the hallway. He heard their steps patting against the carpet behind him. They were coming. He limped along faster, his palms easing along the cold, gray wall for support, but he couldn't go too fast because he was straining at the groin. The bathroom. The bathroom!

"Come back here!"

Henry turned. With his palms flat against the wall and his cheeks resting close to the wall, he looked down the hallway and saw them: their three faces peeking out the door like two pumpkins piled on a third. They opened the door and came out, then started runing down the corridor, slipping on the slick floor, jerking sideways like unbalanced ice skaters.

"Don't try to run away, you can't escape!" They caught up with him before Henry was able to take three limps. Their faces were shiny. Their shirts bulged outward from the waist. Hands on hips, puffing so that their ties lifted and eased down with their out-of-breathness.

"Tried to . . . get away . . . huh?" the high-voiced one said slowly, even stopping halfway through the sentence to get his breath.

"Bathroom," said Henry, for he was losing consciousness, and what—did he feel a trickle down his leg? Now his face was hot and something in his stomach was flipping. "Bathroom," he repeated, adding, "which way . . . quick . . . which way?"

They understood. They dragged him down the hall, then turned left and went down more stairs, then took a short right and kept making these turns until Henry convinced himself of two things: he knew he would wet his pants in four seconds if he didn't reach the urinal, and he was sure that there was no way—*no way*—he himself could find his way back to Peters' office. He pushed open the door, at the same time lowering his fly so that it was out by the time he limped up to the porcelain bowl, and he breathed with the biggest sigh he could ever remember emitting. And it felt so relieving, as if his insides had been puffed up with fluid and now someone had stuck a pin in him, puncturing him, and the loss of each ounce was like a single, pleasurably separate experience; so he was standing there, holding it and making designs—circles, X's, zigzags, and neither the pain in his ankle nor the drumming in his head seemed as severe now. His eyes were closed and he was enjoying it. But he felt uncomfortable. He opened his eyes, glanced to his left. The three of them were leaning over, looking at it. They jerked themselves back to attention when Henry stared at them. He shook it, zipped up, washed and dried his hands, placed the tips of his fingers together and smelled the soap on them, looked into the mirror. Henry ran his finger along his mustache. Then he turned to face the three executives. He had no idea what he should do.

One stepped forward—shoes squeaking in that one sliding step—and he smiled with his hands together by his belt. Henry recognized him as the one with the bad breath.

"We didn't mean to frighten you, Henry. We thought you were trying to run away. You didn't say you had to take a leak."

Henry shook his head to show understanding.

"Uh"—looking at the other two—"we decided, Henry, that it would be best for you to join my group: identification and recovery. That's where your talents lie, we think, and you can go far—it all depends on you. Plenty of opportunities for our employees. You can go straight to the top," he said, finger shooting up to the ceiling, which echoed the shouted last word. The other two shook their heads stiffly. Each of the three held a pipe with the first two fingers of his left hand, and Henry was reminded of a pitcher preparing for a slider. "Follow us," and they marched out single file, each holding open the door for the following marcher.

Henry's limping was less noticeable and the little men inside his head were taking a rest. Down the hall again with its hard tile and colorless walls and chilliness, and although he had never been on a big boat in his life, Henry imagined himself being shepherded down the gangplank to place his foot on some bizarre strip of land where men would again pat and feel him and one would press a dirty thumb against his front teeth, testing them, and they would ask questions of him and never allow him to answer. This is how it would be, he thought, and his wrists were hot, his underwear felt sticky, for he wasn't sure it was true, what they were saying about opportunities and straight to the top. He was going down the plank and he didn't know what to expect. How would Momma Lou advise him? This was worse than trying to steal home, it was a larger dilemma than being run down between second and first, and far worse than guarding the bag when a cleat-spitting runner was heading toward you. Scared as scared could be. Pilot, oh pilot me.

IDENTIFICATION AND RECOVERY was the black-lettered sign on the glass upper panel of the door, and the three of them led Henry Adams inside. To Henry it was almost as large as a baseball field, and there were rows of desks stretching from a few feet of where he stood to a point so far back that those desks seemed like dots. So much like the rows of cotton back home, he thought. Nothing but desks—gray steel desks with men and women bent over them, green visors sticking from the tops of their foreheads. They all looked toward the door when Henry and the executives came in—all the visors snapped sideways at once, then jerked back to their former positions. And the odor was of machines—an oily, greasy, ironlike smell, but there was no machine in the room. Yet Henry heard a loud, pumping sound clanging and rumbling through the air, but there was no machine, just the thundering boom, boom, boom. Dust, smashed cigarette butts, extinguished matches, tiny cellophane wrappers cluttered the cement floor, and since the booming was coming from up high, Henry gazed toward the ceiling, noticed the fluorescent lights, also in rows like giant egg cartons. His head was up like that when someone tapped him on the chest.

The white face with pink pimples on the forehead; the little rise of hair in the front like a miniature tent; the lips separating and saliva spilling over the teeth and forming thin-as-pin secretions from the lower to the upper teeth as he smiled; a gray shirt, collar stiff with starch, open at the neck where the cleft of undershirt showed.

"Hi, Henry, heard you were coming. I'm Mister Boye, the supervisor," shouting over the hammering. His right hand came out of his pocket and took Henry's hand. He looked down and said, "Big. You play basketball?"

"Baseball."

"Well, come with me." He turned and took some steps and Henry hurried behind him, but then the supervisor stopped and Henry bumped into his chest as the supervisor turned.

" 'Scu me," Henry uttered, frightened that he was making too many mistakes and he hadn't started work yet.

But the supervisor just nodded, looked over Henry's head, waved to the three executives now behind Henry—they each slapped or punched Henry on the shoulder and told him to work hard, they knew he could do the job, then went back through the door—waved and turned again. On Boye's right hip, hanging from his belt, Henry noticed a leather case with some pens and pencils sticking in it. On his left hip was another long, thin leather case.

"I'll take you to your desk and explain what your job is," he said, turning so that Henry saw only the side of his face, and some of the words were lost in the clanging, but Henry cupped his hands and shouted an okay. Henry's head was light and easy now, without pain at all, and he was walking without that stabbing pain in his ankles—walking as he liked, a slight bending forward of his torso and his arms swinging, head down, his whole body slicing through the air. And a little bounce and tip on the toes. During the last year he hadn't had the chance to walk like that much—a walk developed through many innings of trekking from the outfield to the dugout, from the dugout to the outfield. But he was on his way to a job! A new job! He was almost to his desk—almost there, and when he got there he would work his hiney off, obey orders, listen, smile, keep his head to his desk. He was walking in step with Boye now, right in step, keeping his eyes on Boye's flat, high behind and not worrying about the trash on the floor he stepped on occasionally or the furtive, invisibly fast glances-up thrown at him by the other workers at their desks. He would get to know them, but right now, he had to work. He would write Momma Lou and Beatrice's father and say he was working for a *manufacturing* company. He would send Momma Lou a few bucks. Doing good again. Maybe they had a company baseball team? Oh, he was back in the money again and this time he meant business. He was in the ballgame to stay —listed on the roster. Boye was still moving with that stilted, stiff-behind way, and Henry could see the ants of dandruff dancing on the back of Boye's shirt as the supervisor nodded to one of the seated workers or tapped his knuckles on a desk or gave an okay sign with his fingers. Henry looked down the aisle: they were still a way from the end of the row. He might become foreman some day. He noticed a few black faces; so he wouldn't be the only one—good. He hadn't noticed it was so hot. He took off his overcoat.

Boye was slowing down now, and then he stopped and Henry stopped in time to avoid another collision. His hands on his hips, head high and tilted as if he was testing the breeze, Boye squinted, then fidgeted with the leather case on his left hip, pulled out a white plastic instrument and squinted again and looked up to the egg cartons, then licked his lips and frowned. Henry edged closer. He had seen that before—a slide rule, wasn't it? Hadn't Thomas Washington, the only dude in the class who went to college, used one? Thomas got a scholarship to one of those rich white schools in the North—in Pennsylvania. Ooh, that nigger was smart, and the girls loved him, too, but he didn't pay them any mind. Wonder where he is now, thought Henry, I know he went to . . . lessee . . . Schwartzawald . . . Schwartzmore . . . Swathmore—something like that. Joy Boy'll be getting ready—

"Henry," smacking the middle of the slide rule into place, Boye turned, slipped the rule into its case, clicked shut the metal clasp, and mumbling to himself before addressing Henry ("Lemme see, the square root of thirty-six desks is six desks lengthways . . ."), he continued, "I think I've found your desk, Henry. It's number one thousand five hundred and seven," and he turned in a circle. "It's seventeen rows down; let's go." Again, as he marched down the aisle, careful to step

27

over the strewn trash and dirt, Henry noticed the heads (green-visored) jerk up and snap down again, and he smiled as each head jerked up, but it always fell down again without acknowledging the greeting. The blasting still covered the room. Henry perspired. "Here we are," said Boye, stopping in front of a gray steel desk. Henry had seen them before—but never had he owned one. To sit behind? His own? His own! "Have a seat."

Henry sat in the chair. It rolled back squeaking, and his hands and legs went into the air. Wheels. The seat also turned circularly, and Henry whirled himself around, legs stuck out horizontally.

"My office is over there," Boye said, turning, nodding toward a wooden door that had OFFICE printed in black letters. It's at the end of the row, about seven desks away from where I am, calculated Henry. "Come on over for a few minutes,"—his voice dissolving into the hammering and pounding. So Henry looked at the desks surrounding him—again the heads snapped down as his eyes fixed on their faces—stopped his chair with his heels and rose, following Boye into the office.

He took a seat. It was quiet, cool, the walls were cement, painted gray, and Boye seemed pushed against the wall as he squeeezed into his seat and now he was sitting behind his gray desk and was facing Henry Adams, who was looking just above the rise of hair on Boye to a framed photograph on the wall. "It's the president," said Boye, leaning forward now, picking up a trophy, a bronze-figured trophy that Henry had not noticed when he entered. "He presented me with this trophy for winning the bowling tournament last year, and threw in the picture, too."

"That's nice," said Henry. That's it. Make him feel good, like when the pitcher strikes out the side and you pat him on the way into the dugout.

"This is a great place to work," said Boye. "I've been here for over forty years. I love it." His hands went behind his neck and his elbows stretched to either side of his head, and he was smiling—but with lips closed so Henry couldn't see any saliva—and although he had just said that and he was smiling and Henry believed that Boye had been there for forty years and Home was probably a good place to work (hell, he was damned glad to be working there now), he felt a warning surge through his mind; something from another part of his body had taken control of his mind and was directing it away, *away* from that conclusion. Henry had the sudden vision of lying under the covers and Beatrice's shaking him, *wake up wake up*, and she was pulling the covers from around him so that every few seconds a corner of sheet or blanket would disappear from under his chin—but he wouldn't get up, wouldn't rise, wouldn't heed, wouldn't even *look*. He wouldn't, didn't want to wake up. Boye uttered, smiling, "I love it. Henry, just give me a brief rundown on what you've been doing since you came to New York last year. Your jobs and so forth. I've seen the forms on you, but I'd like to know how you felt about them—the jobs."

Henry Adams started by relating how he got to the city by himself to check things out before he would send for Beatrice, and he ran into Alvarez standing outside the building, and it was raining (why was Alvarez standing in the rain?), and Henry stood under the protection of the door frame, his black traveling bag by his side. He could see the rain falling on Boye's desk.

"You look for apartment?" Alvarez had asked. Henry had answered, was ushered upstairs, shown his apartment, accepted, paid a month's rent and security with traveler's checks. His first job was obtained through the newspaper, and he reported to a big hotel and was told to enter at the back door. And feeling as if he were being dragged through a film that was projecting too fast, he found himself with an apron on, surrounded by steel machines in a cage, a clanging rumbling above him, and dishes moving along a conveyor belt in wooden pallets, moving, cups jumping up at his fingers, forehead wet. He did it for three days and was fired after the dinner shift on a Friday after he had gotten sick to his stomach from seeing a pallet of dishes—the dishes holding triangles of fish, some custard, a cigarette, tomato bisque. The steam in his face and his being tired from having worked since breakfast—these were the reasons, he knew now. And he had blown lunch, had turned bent over, holding his stomach and spurted it all over the coffee cups he had just pulled out of the rinser—just as the manager had come by.

So he was out of work and had just sent for Beatrice and had enough for another month's rent. He got a job driving, something to keep him out of doors; the truck had a heater and it wasn't hard work, delivering fish to retail customers. Pushing through the crowds from work every day, though, Henry received frowns and turned-up noses and some pedestrians would stop, stand toe to toe facing him and say, "Phew." Beatrice arrived with two suitcases, didn't like the apartment, didn't like the city, didn't like the smell Henry brought in every day; said Alvarez peeped at her all the time as she went to the basement laundry. He was late for work frequently after the first two months—just couldn't wake up, and he would get sick to his stomach on Fridays.

Again, facing Boye, he could see part of his past, and this time he could see the gulls flying over Boye's little tent of hair—the gulls who had floated over Henry's head on Fridays when he had to empty the garbage cans of fish heads at the dump. He would be dragging a twenty-gallon pail from the panel of the truck up to the mound, and sometimes before he got to the top of the mound a gull would slam into the pail, or four of them would flap around it, picking out fish heads, squealing, beaks long and too menacing for Henry to raise more than a weak "Get outta here" of an objection, and he feared their dark, threatening eyes, too; so he would be dragging one of eight pails he'd have to empty, trying to close his nose to the dump's filth, while his one pair of shoes slid down the muddy mound (once he lost his balance and the pail fell on his lap and left pounds of fish heads on him, plus an assortment of stringy entrails) and the gulls picked over him, making it difficult to keep his balance, and other gulls would swoop past his ears. Farther up the road where the sun would be setting, the other trucks were dumping rotten fruit, old shoes, wrapped magazines. Henry would stand resting on top of one of the mounds, would stand there knowing he had three or four more buckets to empty, and think, this is crap, and then bend over, sick again.

He was late more often, too often, and so when one day he

barreled through the streets to the door of Agnes' Fish Market, stopping with a hand on the handle to regain his breath and then walking in cleanly, Agnes was standing there with her hair unkempt as if just back from a fishing voyage, her smallness of frame (the blood-spotted apron like a blanket) stiff. She had a check in her hand. Henry took it and turned, and as he was going out the door her voice followed him: "Don't use my name for a reference!"

Now it was spring. The pimples on Boye's forehead reminded Henry of spring. Henry was into his third job. Selling the *New Encyclopedia of Real Knowledge*. He could still remember sitting in the back seat of the convertible, speeding up to the suburbs, a week's training behind him.

"Oh, hello, how are you?"

Smile. You gotta smile. They will not let you in the house if you don't smile, dammit!

"My name is Henry Adams, and I work—"

Grab the hand! Shake the hand! Look into his face!

"I work for the New—"

Don't say work! Say, "I'm doing research for"!

"I'm doing research for the *New Encyclopedia of Real Knowledge*. May I come in?"

Put your foot in the door. Move forward! Okay, now you're inside, Henry; what now? What now, huh?

Move toward the television, try to turn it off. Get the children into the conversation. Talk about the lifetime referral service. Let them feel the binding. Show them the full-color illustrations. Remind them of the free bookcase. Mention the payments spread over seven years.

Yes! Yes, Henry, you've got it! Now we go out tomorrow. You're ready!

Six of them were in the convertible, and they all got out at an intersection where a dirt road met the highway they had driven up on, and they looked at the map of the area, accepted their assignments, agreed to meet at the intersection before sundown. It was about noon.

Henry walked up the dirt road and then took a left. He saw this house, a small, common-looking structure with a porch and a front yard—much like the houses in his home town—and

31

shiny packed briefcase swinging and banging against his right calf, he went through the gate, up the steps, rang the bell.

"Hi, I'm Henry Adams and I'm doing research for the *New Encyclopedia of Real Knowledge*. May I come in?" Give him your best smile. Stick the hand out.

"We gave already," was the answer, then the door slammed, and to this day—sitting in Boye's office thinking back—Henry could not remember the shape, color, size of the face that greeted him. The door had opened as if he had stepped on one of those automatic supermarket door mats, the answer had been thrown out, discarded like rubbish, and the door had been slammed again and there he was, standing like a recently discharged hitchhiker on a dark road. He went down the steps, through the gate, then spied another house, a large one; it might buy two sets of the encyclopedia to compensate for this first inauspicious contact. So Henry Adams, salesman, former dishwasher, former fishman, former center-fielder-slugger for the Crown nine, tramped up the road. Another set of stairs, to a porch, heads popping by the side-window curtains, a lady in curlers and a robe; three-fourths of her hidden by the partially closed door; and Henry, keeping a respectful distance and consciously trying to smile professionally, courteously, and definitely not romantically or suggestively, noticed rings under her eyes.

He introduced himself, tipping his baseball cap. He was also wearing a cardigan and a tie, a white shirt and pressed dungarees.

She said, no, he couldn't come in.

He went farther up the road, and the dust was covering his shoes. He tried a half-dozen more houses, but he never got to utter the second sentence of his soliloquy. They—whoever opened the door to greet him—always interrupted his first sentence with "No." No, you can't come in.

Henry Adams, after an hour of unsuccessful climbing up unfriendly porches, decided that he had had it for the day. His feet were aching, his shoes had a thin skin of road dust, and now he remembered that he hadn't eaten before meeting the car; and he had no money. *He had no money.* His insides moaned and tumbled as he turned a corner, and at the end of the block there was a Little League baseball field. He took a seat in the stands on the third-base side, stayed there for the first and most of the second game, guessed at the time, and hustled toward the corner where the car was to meet them. A few of the salesmen had sold a contract. Henry sat silently in the back seat as the convertible staggered with the going-home traffic, and when they let him off in front of his building and said they'd see him tomorrow, he smiled, waved, while in his mind he was saying, the hell you will, crackers. He dropped his sales bag down the incinerator.

Of course he did not tell Boye everything as he remembered it. Henry embellished his account so that it seemed as if he were a fastidious, concerned worker who had been outdone by a complication of heartless titans who would decide whether he was to have a job and how long he should have it. When he finished, Henry watched Boye click shut his slide rule, clear his throat. He said, "Henry, we're glad to have you with us. There's plenty of opportunity here if you just do your job." He was standing up, bending his forearm to look at his watch. "Time to quit. See you tomorrow." Henry pushed back his chair as Boye stood, patted his hair, then seemed to be suspended in thought, dangling in a dozen indecisions which were finally resolved by his smacking his lips and bending down and pulling out the desk drawer. Henry sat back down also, thinking, maybe an advance? "Henry"—he was pulling out a manila envelope and undoing the clasp—"I just have to tell you something . . . I mean . . . well, look . . . don't get uptight about you being black and me white. . . . I understand, Henry, and I don't have anything against you people. Look," he said, almost choking out the word as he pulled the photo enlargements from the envelope, then moved toward the door to secure its lock, then slammed down the photos on the desk.

Henry bent forward from his chair to look. Boye was leaning over, sifting and arranging the photos for Henry, who glanced at the saliva spilling over Boye's teeth. She was a thin, angular black woman wearing only an off-centered wig, loop earrings and garters. In one photo (Boye giggling, "Look at that") she lay on top of the blanket and her legs were widespread so that most of the photo space was filled with the inside of her thighs, and just about in the photo's center, her finger in her vagina. Boye slapped another one on top of it. In this one, the black woman was sitting on a rug and she looked strangely domestic, with a pole lamp to one side and curtains in the background. This time she was sitting up, holding the handle of a baseball bat with two hands and directing the fat of the bat between her legs. Henry looked closer to see if indeed the bat was— was entering her. Boye laughed, "You like it, huh?"

"Very nice," Henry said, rising and glancing at another photo of the same woman in a wrestler's hold with a chair, her tongue stretching for her pubic hairs. "Not bad," he added, confused, face stinging with shameful pleasure and anger. Boye could call a black woman up to his apartment and encourage her lewd modeling, and then he could show these photographs to him, Henry, to prove that he, Boye, understood black people. Always, that they could take these pictures of *his* women, but he couldn't. . . .

"Well, it is time to go, isn't it, Henry," said Boye, and now he was scurrying around to the side of the desk, his slide-rule case banging against the desk, his hands shuffling the photos back into the envelope. "See you tomorrow, right?"

3

AS HE CLOSED the door to his apartment, and
before he scraped his hand up the wall for the light switch,
Henry, in the dark for an instant, stood there and felt like
kicking himself. "Gotdam!" he said. "Gotdam!" How could he
have been so stupid? Here he had a new gig in a big place—
not some small-time fish market or some lightweight meat-and-
potatoes restaurant—and in his excitement he'd forgotten to
find out what the pay was! *Are* they going to pay me? Of
course. Much? Weekly? He walked into the other room and
slapped his palm together when he heard the radiator banging. "Good man, Alvarez," turning on the lamp and picking
up the small triangles, pentagons and other shapes of chipped
ceiling from the bed sheet. He looked up at the brown ring of
water on the ceiling, then sat on the bed. Then he leaned over
to turn on the television and noticed the folded note. He lay
back on the bed and unfolded it.

Dear Henry,

I went out for a walk and to make a phone call to my
folks. I left some ham in case I'm not back before you.

Love,
Beatrice

Henry propped himself up with two pillows, rested the note
in his lap and stared at the television. A woman in a gym out-

35

fit was smiling through exercises, her thighs up near the screen's top. He went into the kitchen and made himself a sandwich with one slice of boiled ham and pulled out a beer from the refrigerator and sat on the edge of the bed, and (the tip of the can to his lip), watched the lady go through her exercises.

He didn't think she was very good; she was without grace, like some players he'd seen who would swing at the ball with puffed cheeks and frowns, and if they missed, their follow-through would be so awkward, instead of bringing the bat around to the top of the other shoulder with the lead knee bending nicely so they looked good even though the ball was in the catcher's mitt (or if the catcher was fast enough and wanted to make you look bad, he'd be throwing the ball back to the pitcher before you had straightened up), they'd lose balance and bang the bat against the ground, grunt "Umph," stumble, kick up dirt as their cleats went sideways, even fall. She reminded him of one of those "killer" hitters who had murderous intentions toward the ball (and he'd heard them warn the catcher: "I'll knock the shit out of the next one"), lacked smoothness and ease, precision and order. She did knee bends too quickly, not up and down easily as if it came naturally. When she rolled on her back for the "bicycle" she fell into trouble, rolling sideways and getting up, out of breath, hair in her eyes (Henry considered how they loved to throw their heads to the side like that, even if they had a crewcut), she smiled a forced, apologetic smile that begged for patience. She stood for a moment, perplexed, eyeballs skipping horizontally, as if forgetting the next exercise, then said, "Well," quickly, as if the word had only one *l*, and started running in place, and from above a microphone on the end of a pole was lowered and hit her in the head, then disappeared up again, and Henry thought he heard faint laughter in the background of the set as the gymnast stood there again doing nothing, face pointed to the side, off-screen, looking for directions.

Beatrice could work out on these exercises, he thought. She was so smooth, so naturally graceful. The way she walked, the way she moved, as when she stepped from one side of the room to another to pick up an ashtray and turned, catlike; unconstrained, all of her; *everything* compliant, facile, from her hips to her shoulders, and her neck and stomach, too.

Now the exerciser had her back to the screen. Shouldn't he tell her tonight that he loved her walk and was going to make her walk around the room for him at least once a week? With no clothes on? Her mom and pop would call him obscene. They didn't like him that much anyway, especially because he was so dark. (He had heard her father refer to him twice as "that blue nigger," and once her father had asked Beatrice, "Why you dealing in coal, girl?") And she was tan, almost yellow. The exerciser was spreading herself out on toes and fingertips, feet toward the screen, and began push-ups, her head bending over her shoulder in an attempt to address the viewer, and she went down three times. On the fourth one, as she was suspended near the floor, not going up or down but suddenly in abeyance, there was a light ripping sound. Again, light laughter from somewhere in the television studio. Henry finished his beer and looked closer. There was a split in the rump. A narrow fillet of white ass showed. She put her hand over half of it (and Henry thought, to keep out the breeze), then she jumped up, turned around, disappeared from the screen, and a commercial appeared.

He wasn't really there, wasn't really concentrating on the show, so that the muffled snickering coming from the back of the television soundtrack didn't seem unusual, nor did he find the microphone's falling on the girl's head out of the ordinary. His eyes were on the screen but his mind was on his past, and he kept seeing another screen behind the television screen, and this one was flashing scenes on which his mind was fastened.

A toilet flushed, startled him back to his apartment—he had been way down in Mississippi, had been going back for a long fly ball—and he saw coming on the screen a show that he and Beatrice watched frequently. It was that quiz show for newly marrieds, and this time there was a black couple sitting behind the booth, and Henry thought he might watch it, but he got up, thinking one of those girls might still be in the bathroom. He dashed on his toes into the kitchen and pulled down a glass, tiptoed back to the other room, put the glass to the wall in back of the television and put his ear to the glass. He could hear the water running and guessed one of them was washing her hands. And he imagined her hands were soft and manicured. Sometimes both girls would be in the bathroom— the toilet seemed to flush every hour—and if Beatrice was out shopping on a Saturday, Henry would listen to them. He had accumulated facts on them: they were older than he, in their mid-twenties; worked as secretaries in a big firm; were black but sometimes dated white men; giggled a lot; were not looking for husbands; loved to stay out late; hated Alvarez; had lived in that apartment for two years. But he couldn't find the apartment! He had been all over the fourth floor and would walk slowly down the tiled halls, ears pricked, trying to catch a trace of one of those porcelain voices he had heard in the bathroom. To know what they looked like, yes, but suppose— they were free, young—who knows what he would get into?

But the insidious design of the floor. Although the bathroom of those women was right behind Henry's television wall, their apartment's front door was nowhere near Henry's apartment. And there were only four apartments on the fourth floor. And he had never seen a woman aged twenty or so enter or leave the apartment building since he and Beatrice had lived there.

He had been frightened by the first toilet flush, because the first night he slept in the apartment he had lain on the bed with the lights out, reviewing his trip up from Mississippi and his prospects for the future, and there was just the blare (like a faraway parade) of car horns in the air, when suddenly—the flush. He jumped off the bed, his heart was up against his chest, his hands were clenched. Then the voices, hollow, metallic, spoke from the flush, and he was certain that the pressure of looking for an apartment had driven sense from his mind:

"Can you see my slip?"

"No, but how do my eyes look?"

"Okay. Hum hmmmm hmmm."

"Hmm hmmm hmm."

It took him a half-hour to conclude that it was someone's bathroom, and the first week he had walked up and down the hall very slowly, putting first his heel down, then his toe; stood outside the door of each apartment on the floor, squinted his eyes to hear better. No one ever seemed to be in any apartment (except the Hurts'), or at least ever made any noise, and once, working ingeniously and smiling at his ingenuity, Henry was able to look under the crack at the bottom of one door—his nose scraping up dust on the hall floor—and could have sworn that the apartment was empty. Nothing but light. But hadn't Alvarez said that there were no vacant apartments? Still, credit his genius. Walking down the hall another time in his patented, quiet, heel-and-toe manner; stopping outside the apartment door; bending over and throwing a penny under the opening; complaining loudly, "Dammit, I dropped my key"; then bending down so he could look under the door. A beautiful maneuver, beautiful, until one day, his ears and right cheek burning from the scraping on the dusty floor, balancing fingers shivering as they supported the upper half of his body, knees aching a little, he heard this voice. Someone was in the apartment! The voice was light, floating and indistinct, and he squeezed his nose closer toward the door, and he was anxious. Maybe one of the girls. Then a harsh, grating noise as if someone was scraping the floor near his ear, then a giggling, tittering. The little girl from the end of the hall! His eyes traveled up her height, from the dirty white socks to the diagonal scar on her knee to her eight-year-old face, covered now with her fingers. Her eyes were half-closed from the broad smile. Henry, getting up, bumped his forehead against the door. She laughed out loud this time, bringing down her hands from her mouth, and the laugh's echo danced down the hall, and Henry had terrified visions of heads popping out of the doorways as he straightened himself out, brushed dust from his knees.

"I dropped my key. It rolled under the door. I was looking for it." His face felt hot and a vein in his temple was enlarging.

Then little Betty Hurt laughed louder. She leaned backwards, her hands back over her mouth; next, bending forward, cackling like every little eight-year-old Henry had ever heard laugh: undisciplined sputterings of glee, strange blend of innocence and mischievousness. He looked over his shoulder down the other end of the hall—no one. He leaned over and brushed off his pants at the knee, then started walking backwards, explaining, "Well, I guess I've just lost the darn thing," and scrambled back to his apartment. That was the last time he had tried to find the women's apartment. But he had his dreams, and although he was (he knew, he insisted he was) insanely in love with Beatrice—why not a little adventure? Those women—he could tell by the many conversations he had overheard with the pressed glass—were venturesome, unreserved, loose. He might meet one in the hallway, strike up a conversation, and she might invite him in for a drink one evening. And that would be the start. She wouldn't care if he was married—no—in fact, would probably be attracted to him more.

"I didn't tell you no such a thing," she said, and Henry's attention was drawn back to the television screen. The black woman was beating her new husband over the head with a shiny pocketbook, and he was leaning away from her as if he were moving away from a flock of pigeons, and smiling, grinning between a crisscross of arms and elbows like the boxers against the ropes Henry had seen in the gym back at home.

"Wait, honey, wait. I just said what I thought was true," he said, poking his head up and over an armor of arms.

And the audience was jeering, whistling, clapping. A buzzer rang.

"And now, contestants," said the emcee, wearing a jacket and turtleneck, "couple number two is ahead by seventeen points and we move into the third round."

Henry was off again, back into Mississippi, then his mind fluttered, the focus turned, and he was somewhere else, thinking about Beatrice without a time and place, just her looming in his mind like a giant kite on its way skyward.

Yes, yes, he loved her, he did very much. Her father was the one. He would be so glad to keep Beatrice away from Henry. His restless stump of a mustache that wiggled when he spoke from the side of his mouth, as if he was always pulling one in to share a most recent dispatch. And rarely did he look you in the eye, but focused those stony, black eyeballs that danced mysteriously up and down—focused them on your chest; or, your neck. His hands were behind his back, always. He rocked on his toes and heels or stood straddle-legged. Always Henry had the feeling that Beatrice's father was challenging him to make a move, the way he would stand in front of Henry with his head down, widow's peak forming a devil-like point at the tip of the forehead, and always a short haircut.

They had been sitting on the porch that Saturday playing war, and Spot, a trio of flies stinging his ears (flicking), was lying sideways in the shade of Leon Mark's truck, his tongue resting on the ground.

"What this Petula say about you and Beatrice tying up, huh?" He threw down an ace and grabbed up both cards when Henry gave him a seven of hearts.

"We'd like to do it, Mister Mark—get married, Beatrice and I. We been thinking about it for a long time since we met in church. She'll make a good wife."

"I *know* she'll make a good wife, ain't worried about that at all," and his voice rose and Spot lifted his head, then grunted, let it fall back to the ground. Henry was looking through the screening surrounding the porch, staring at Spot and the pickup truck behind him and the flat, even fields of cotton beyond it all, meeting the sky far away. He had only two cards in his hands. He was going to lose. He put them to his nose. They smelled like Spot. Looking straight ahead through the screen door, he knew Beatrice's father was looking at him but not really looking at him; actually, looking at Henry's chest or his shirt or his waist. "What I'm worried about"—now he was on his feet—"is you," and his back was to Henry, he was looking out the other side of the porch. They still had two cards to go. Henry wondered when or if they'd finish the game. His hands were clasped behind his back, his legs were straddled. "How you gonna take care of my little girl? That's what I wanna know—how you gonna fix her up?" Henry thought Leon was speaking loudly, but since his back was to Henry the voice came to him evenly. "I don't want my baby to have nothin' but the best. Can you give it to her? Can you give my baby the best? Or will you be runnin' around chasin' other women like the rest of your gang?" His hands were at his sides and the fingers of the right hand were clenching into a fist and unbending, clenching and unbending as if diseased, and then he whirled around, face glaring, the eyeballs sparkling and glinting now because the sun was visible for a while, so that half his face was illuminated, the other half covered by shadow, and he refused to move sideways, fully into the shadow, but stood there squinting both eyes at Henry, the diagonal line separating sunlight from shadow, running from the tip of his widow's peak to his waist. So half in sunlight, half in the shade, fingers twitching, upper lip twitching, he stared at Henry.

"I expect I can take care of her pretty well," Henry said, staring at the squat figure immersed in more darkness as the clouds covered the sun more. "I believe in taking care of one woman and only one."

"How you gonna do it? How? How? You got a job? No! Going on to education? No—ain't even finishing high school. I don't want my baby living in no mess, having to take in laundry for the rest of her life, then have a bunch of children who live in poorness. She deserves a real life being . . . living! She ain't going through what we did, look"—and he turned in a circle, his hand guiding Henry's eyes—"broken-down porch, old pickup truck, shack cold in the winter, better not have a storm, rickety old boards will fly away. No, Henry, no!"

"I'm taking her up North where I can get a good job," said Henry. He had an ace and a queen and he slid one end over the other continually. His throat was dry, the words not as loud as he would want them.

"What kind of job? What kind of money? You'll be running after other women. I know it. You wild young things don't know how to protect our women."

"I had a tryout a couple of years ago with the Crowns, did pretty well. They want me to come up North to play for the big team."

"What kind of tryout?"

"To see if I make the team."

"Team?"

"Baseball team—the Stars."

"Now I know you a dumb black nigger! You actually sitting there on *my* porch taking up *my* time trying to tell *me* somebody's going to pay you to mess around with a baseball—a white baseball at that?"

"You heard of Jackie Robinson, ain't you?"

"That's right, and Willie Maze and Hank Iron. They don't need no more. You think they gonna take another one?"

"They said if I make the team I'll get twenty thousand dollars for the first year."

"And you dumb enough to believe it."

"I know I can make it. I can play. I can hit any pitcher they got. I can play better than them all," Henry said. He threw down his queen. "You still playing or what?"

Beatrice's father took two quick steps, kneeled down and let a ten of spades fall from his palm. "Don't make no difference no more how good you are," he said, talking again out of the side of his mouth, "you still black. Come on around the back with me." He pushed open the screen door, jumped over the one splintery step, said, "Stay there, boy," to Spot and turned toward the side of the house. The sun was coming out again, but by the time they reached the back of the house, it was overcast. Beatrice's father undid the board latch from the outhouse and closed the door behind him. His voice came out hollow, and Henry was thinking that Leon could have been cupping his hand around his mouth, could have been stuck in the bottom of some valley, the way his voice was far away.

"Suppose you don't make the team—then what?"

"I'll make it. I been planning for this all my life, Mister Mark—"

"You know I can't hear you in here, speak up."

"Been planning for this all my life, sir, since I was twelve and they had to let me play in the Little League because I was so good. In high school I hit a home run almost every game."

"I want my girl to have the best, Henry. I don't want her up there frettin' about you not taking care of her, you hear me?"

"Yes, sir."

"You'll see she gets to church every week?"

"Yes, sir."

"You better not put your big hands on her, or I'll come up there so fast and shoot the shit out of you"—he banged against the wall—"you'll think I'm a patroler."

"Yes, sir." He heard Leon Mark wiping himself. A clicking and knocking of the door. Now Beatrice's father was standing by the door of the outhouse, hands on hips, legs straddled, staring at Henry's chest.

"Henry"—he was looking up at the clouds—"tell me this. Is . . . is she . . . pregnant?"

"No, sir, not at all."

Then Leon Mark fell into a walk toward the house, stopped, turned to face Henry who was still standing, staring at Leon Mark's back; went into a pocket of his overalls, held out his last card so Henry could see. "Can you beat it?"

Henry showed him the ace.

The screen was jumping vertically, pulling Henry's consciousness back to his apartment. It cleared up, two vertical lines coming together in the middle and then spreading, separating out toward the top and bottom of the screen. The camera focused on the black couple again, and the woman, a kerchief around her neck, was screaming at her new mate: "How can you say that? I never said no to you during the first week of our marriage!"

And the audience was hooting, and the camera focused on the emcee, who was covering his mouth with his hand, and then the camera showed back to the couple, who were gesturing at each other, glaring at each other (their noses almost touching), shaking their heads at each other, and Henry was reminded of Punch and Judy.

"You always wear flannel pajamas." The audience hooted again.

"You don't wash your face in the morning." Now the hooting was wild, uncontrolled, and it sounded metallic and inhuman, as if the laughing voices were not the voices of the spectators in the audience, but voices from another time, another, larger, more risible assembly. So the chuckling continued, but it did not die out gradually to end in a few stray, energetic voices and then a halt; instead, Henry observed, the audience stopped abruptly, as if following a conductor who had just signaled with his baton that the audience should close its mouth.

Henry watched these shows frequently, with a dispassionate neutrality. He never laughed when those in the audience laughed. He never thought about what was happening or why it was happening or if it was good that it was happening.

Then there was a blank screen, blinking black; in an instant two women were standing around a washing machine. A commercial. His mind automatically suspended itself so that it hovered behind two visions: the movements on the screen and the other movements—the vision in his mind. He saw the screen, yes, but the registerings—those jerks, flits of gray and white movements—were hazy and indistinct now, as if superimposed over that view was another landscape, cleaner and more demanding of his consciousness. He had experienced this frequently—the apprehension of two visions, two settings, one more lucid, sharper than the other.

So his mind was going back, and the voices on the screen were distant now, the gestures of the characters were minuscule; and larger, more imposing was another scene.

Beatrice and he last spring—he couldn't remember the exact time, except it was spring, wasn't it? He wasn't sure anymore, time seemed to pass so quickly and mysteriously there just weren't that many things he could remember about specific scenes. Yes, he could recall the events always, but *when* they occurred; he could draw up within his imagination the shapes of people and how they moved and the voices and how these sounded. But the day, the month, the year? —No. So Beatrice and he were holding hands and carefully picking their way—they had just climbed the incline of grass leading from the park's entrance—and he could hear the voices of ballplayers drifting toward them from the top. When they reached the level stretch of grass, with his free hand he dropped the picnic basket and tugged on Beatrice's arm, and for a moment —for a brief, scary moment when he had a vision of her toppling down the incline and falling over as he had seen the Indians tumble in so many Western movies on Saturdays (sitting in the balcony)—he thought he wouldn't be able to hold her. They were suspended for that instant, her eyes wild and fathomless while his heart thumped—and then he pulled her up with a heave and soon they were at the top of the plane, laughing about that moment.

"Let's spread out right here," she had said. The wind was pushing against the front of her hair so that it appeared as if she had just combed it back, and it stood high and flat in the front and bushy around her face like a shadow. Now she was shaking the blanket she'd just taken out of the picnic basket, her eyes were wild and frontal again, but this time Henry knew she wasn't frightened. "Grab on," she laughed, and Henry was fighting the wind, trying to tighten his fingers on the ends of the blanket. He grabbed onto the two ends and took a step back, then another. Suddenly, he was facing the sky. He was on his back. He had dropped the blanket in a frantic attempt to gain his balance. He looked up at Beatrice. Her hand was over her mouth and she had dropped her two edges of the blanket also, so now it was skipping away from them over the grass like a fallen kite, billowing and tumbling. "Henry, are you—" Her moving toward him was suddenly halted and now she was frozen, bent over him, her arms outstretched as if she were treading water. "Look what you walked into, Henry." She stepped backward, then began looking around her footsteps to see if she had stepped in any of it.

"Damn," he said, resting on his elbows, now curling himself sideways to stand up. He scraped the bottom of his shoes against the grass. "Damn dogs don't belong in the park anyway," shuffling his shoe and turning it sideways to shave the edges, banging his heel into the turf. Henry Adams balanced himself on one leg. He lifted the other, and holding onto his ankle with two hands, examined the bits of fresh, tan dog manure that was still clogged in the little space between the beginning of the shoe heel and the sole. He wanted to place his nose closer, just to get a whiff of it. But Beatrice was watching. He knew the odors varied somewhat with the color and even with the animal, for cows and horses always had a slight greenness circling their smell. A peculiar oddity, he knew, to be concerned inordinately with smells, odors, whiffs;

and even stranger that this eccentricity should extend to offal. He had always wanted to smell things. His strongest curiosity.

He dropped his ankle. "Give me a stick, please, honey, a small one." That was the only way to get it out, he knew, unless you had a toothbrush or were crazy enough to run your finger through it, and he watched the ridges of her slacks squeeze her thighs as she bent now, several feet away from him, to pick up a twig. When she stood, she shook her legs and then had to stoop over to smooth down the lower part of her slacks, for the cuffs had risen almost to her knees.

"Here's one," she said, and she had that sometimes annoying lassitude in her voice as if she were weary already of the picnic, Henry's accident, everything. But that was her principal attraction. The lack of excitement in her eyes, the slow sway of her hips: he translated it as controlled enthusiasm, ardor. He was accustomed to the contradiction: when she spoke slowly, she was often most irritated, fascinated, thrilled; smiling gaily, talking so that short, quick monosyllables fluttered from her mouth—these gestures frequently covered up a coolness that was yet unstirred. So as she was now holding the stick in her hand and standing tilted so that one of her hips was larger, higher than the other, he took it and looked at her and thanked her and knew that really, she was excited about the picnic.

Always, that had been her nature, her style—an easiness, casualness—as far back as he could remember. A grin spread on his face. How had he ever gotten to talk to this fine mamma? Why hadn't he been turned off by her seeming disinterest? And oh, the craziest thing he was remembering now, sitting in his room, the smaller screen still flicking and gray and white, was the—*the craziest thing*—was that dance. She had driven him in her father's pickup to the dance at the Come On Inn. Even when she whirled in the yellow and black darkness of the Come On's giant hall, where the other couples were jerking themselves in a sweat, and Henry was also, she was the only one not perspiring, but she was *moving*. She seemed to be swooping gull-like with her arms and shoulders while Henry, bending and dipping, turning and darting, felt that he was expending twice as much energy as she. And was he as graceful? he wondered. His feet, too, though perfectly in time with the music pouring from the small band on the stage, seemed to be accelerated in their sliding, tapping, scraping, as if he were moving progressively faster than she. But she was moving, and she was moving very, very fast. It was the smoothness, though, the ease with which she controlled her movements, which suggested an illusory slowness. She wasn't slow at all, he knew; she was agile, expeditious, brisk, winged; and the circles of gold-plated wire—her earrings —twisted and jiggled against her face, the simple chain necklace with its heart-shaped, imitation-ivory pendant jumped up and down and around her neck and collarbone. If he wasn't sure of her motion, the evidence was there in her accouterments, for they were uncontrolled and free, answering to the speed of her body. Yes, she was moving, all right, just deceptively so. But there was no stopping the earrings and the necklace, and also her three bracelets, which clinked and twirled around her wrists as she lifted her arms upward or pushed out with them for balance. When they had finished, when the saxophone soloist, standing on the edge of the stage, had leaned over like a man sick to his stomach to blow those powerful, culminating notes, and they all were standing still, clapping, Henry noticed that he was out of breath and that his shoulder, which was against Beatrice's now that his arm was around her waist, was moving up and down, rubbing against hers, and a cool line spread across his forehead. Perspiration. His armpits felt moist too and he imagined his jacket was at war with him as it tightened around his chest. He unbuttoned it and patted his cummerbund. Some of his buddies were unclipping their bow ties so that the little black cloth hung from one collar, and they had their wrists up to their brows.

But Beatrice—she didn't even seem to be breathing hard. He knew she had just put down some steps and had kept up with him and perhaps—he could allow for it if it was true— perhaps she had *outdone* him.

"A tough band, huh?" He pulled her closer—more out of reflex than from necessity or tenderness, as if that gesture had some connection to the words and would therefore add author-

ity and strength to the question. Somehow he couldn't just
ask her a question. He had to do something at the same time
—pull her closer, squeeze her hand, even scratch his own head
if necessary. But something to tone down the awkwardness
of the naked, unprotected question.

She tilted her head, answered him so that only half her
face seemed to point up toward him, and he had to lean down
to distinguish her words, which were rapidly mixing with the
buzz of other couples' chatter and laughter.

"Not bad."

"Not *bad?*" His hand slipped from her waist. He faced her.
Her lips were pushed out in a half-smile and her brow, in-
quisitive, challenging, was raised (he noticed a wrinkle, too—
one line in the exact middle). "Not *bad?!* Do you know these
cats came from Atlanta? Do you know they may make a
record soon? Not bad! Come on, you can do better than that."
Someone tapped him on his shoulder, he turned to chat.

They began "Li'l Darlin'." Now she had that look of resignation, leading him to accept one of several conclusions: the
matter was closed; or, was this important enough really, to
argue about? Or, you probably wouldn't understand if I went
into it anyway. So he weighed interpretations and she was
looking at him like that and pulling him toward her and soon
he could feel her hips—her substantial, warm hips—moving
against him as her chin touched his neck (her hair mashed
by the side of his face), and her hands—he missed a step;
could he be mistaken?—her hands, *both* of them, were inside
his jacket, one against his shoulder blade, one around his
waist. His left arm dropped at his side as if he didn't want to
own it, although he did have his right arm around her waist
(and it was wider and more solid than he had imagined;
much wider, something to hold, to grasp).

"Hold me with both hands, Henry."

His imagination tripped. Was this the night? She was giving
him the right commands, why couldn't it be? They *had* been
seeing each other regularly for two months, she *was* holding
him tightly and her thighs were possessively firm in their press
against his legs, he was positive she could feel, wanted to
feel, everything. "This Could Be the Night," a song by a group

he had seen long ago in Atlanta (The Dubs, was it?), flashed across his memory, and he was singing in his mind the lyrics he could remember:

Couldn't you, couldn't I
Fall in love tonight?
Wo oh wo oh
This could be the night
To hold you tight
Wo oh wo oh wo oh
This could be the ni-i-ight.

"Do duht duht, duht duht doo dee doo wha." She was humming in his ear to the band's tune. All the other couples were locked together, Henry could see, as he pressed his other arm into duty against her back.

It was always a command—that's the way she worked, he thought, but now the command was encouraging, inviting, suggestive, and as his right hand relaxed against the soft, graspable layer of skin around her waist (he had never felt that before either), he raced over the evenings of all those negative rulings. In the balcony of the movie theater during an especially romantic scene which moved him, moved him to place his hand on her knee; she, staring more intently at the screen, said loudly, firmly and without even a twitch of the knee, "Take your hand off me, Henry Adams." Petrifying, guilt-causing glances. He concentrated unseeing on the rest of the movie. On the porch of her house one night, the moonlight too bright, and mysterious bumpings and rumblings inside although the lights were out and he knew the Marks should have been asleep at that hour, he tried to place a hand on her larger breast as he advanced to kiss her good-night and had it slapped to a sting with: "Keep you hands to yourself, Henry Adams." Immediate yellow illumination in the front window followed by a masculine clearing of the throat. And invariably, when he tried a long, hard kiss accompanied by both arms around her waist, she would squirm, declaring, "You don't have to be that familiar." But now! Now she was holding out the welcome mat. Tip, Henry, tip.

The moon, the stars
Are out tonight
Wo oh wo oh

Her earring was cool against his cheek, and her white gown swished against his clothing, and Henry wasn't sure he could keep in step since his knees shook from a light trembling and he wasn't even certain he could hear the music.

"Henry, could we leave after this piece?"

"*Leave,* Beatrice?"

"You know what I'm talking about. We can drive back into the woods."

His heart was making a deafening sound like drums, footsteps against his chest; hollow, loud palpitations. Could she feel his heart banging against her breast? Hoping to slow it down, he took a deep breath. Now he was remembering their conversation of—two, three weeks before that? In the woods behind the Hide Away Lounge on a Saturday, the jukebox giving off a suggestive B. B. King tune, her back against a tree and his lips traveling up and down her neck, and she was moaning but still held his wrists in her hands so he couldn't touch her as he had wanted. "Henry, I think I'm falling in love with you—" Her voice, whispered, was charged with passion, her head rolled left and right against the tree trunk. "—I want to make love to you, but not tonight. I'll let you know when I'm ready." And that was that. He pleaded; his wrists strained against the restriction of her hands; his right thigh failed to insert itself between her legs; his lips were brushed aside each time he tried to press them down within the opening of her blouse. But now! Now she was ready, she was giving him the reins, urging him to make his move. The music stopped. She still held onto him while her fingers massaged his back and she leaned into him—once, twice with each thigh—and then slid away from him with two bouncing steps. The other couples were just separating too, although the last note had sounded twenty seconds ago.

So she was standing two feet away from him, staring at

him, bouncing on her toes, again humming the tune to "Li'l Darlin'," her eyes jumping and her forehead raised inquisitively. Then an awesome, empty floundering filled Henry, his temples flushed. Was she playing games with him? Just her style, he thought, to change her mind and go giggling to the punch bar. Now he was angry—at himself, mostly, for being so gullible.

"Hey, Slugger," someone greeted him.

He could imagine her explanation, something like she didn't even know him that well yet, or couldn't he take a joke? Or she just changed moods suddenly.

But a surprise: "Let's go, Henry," taking his hands into hers, stepping backward, then turning so they were walking side by side, and she started the swinging and they were swinging their arms together, Henry thinking, your fingers— they are so soft and long. On the porch, she knelt to take off her high heels.

"Careful you don't step on some glass, Beatrice, all those broken bottles out there."

She was down the steps, the black shoes dangling from her hand and the bracelets ringing, then she was tiptoeing cautiously. Headed for the parking lot. At the top of the steps, Henry watched her. She stopped, whirled, sending the bottom of her gown flying around her knees. Her hand reached in his direction.

"Come on, we don't have all night. I've been walking barefooted all my life. Come on. Afterwards, you can tell me about yourself."

It was another fast one. After they had reached the end of the path and were on the edge of the gravel lot (his hand in hers), he turned to stare through the open windows of the Come On Inn. The dancers, like shadows, were moving with the beat, and the horns now sounded like a chorus of faraway trains.

"Where did I park the truck?" She was on her toes. "Over here, come on."

It was in front of a tree, near the beginning of the woods. As they separated at the back of the truck to go around to the doors, Henry heard a rustling in the woods near the

52

fender. Beatrice gasped. A tall, thick black shadow emerging. Henry tightened his hand on the door handle.

"What—" He couldn't say anything else, and even that was an involuntary outburst.

"Oh," Beatrice blurted, and looking at her through the windows, Henry saw her forearm come up to cover her mouth. Then he turned to see the figure looming above Beatrice with arms outstretched as if it had a small tree limb in each hand and perhaps—perhaps this dark, large specter would come falling down on Beatrice and would crush her skull. It was leaning, tilting, and Henry felt himself frozen in his shoes as the figure leaned. . . . It was a human shape after all. A man. A black man. A black man he knew—Allport. The man stumbled out of the woods, red suspender hooks flashing in the moonlight, cummerbund up to his chest, losing his footing and diving with arms up high toward the truck hood for balance. His hands slammed down on the truck.

"Hi, Beatrice. Hey, Henry. Yawl leaving?" Pulling up his fly.

"Allport! Allport, whatch you doing in those woods scaring us like that?"

"What are you doing out here scaring us?"

"Us?" Henry moved to the front of the pickup truck, placed a foot on the fender.

"Come on out, Reola. Come on, girl, it's just Slugger and Beatrice getting ready to leave. You two aren't planning to be driving up the back path, are you?" Laughing and bending over, brushing the dirt off his knees with his hand, eyeglasses glinting.

"You ought to be ashamed of yourself," Henry said, "talking like that. What were you two doing in there, hunting? Come on, Beatrice, let's go."

After he got the truck started, Henry turned on the lights and caught Allport and Reola in the lights' path. They were embracing and her back was to Henry and Beatrice. The zipper on her dress had been pulled down to her waist, and as Allport turned her around and out of the path of the headlamps, Henry, shifting into reverse, strained to see if her bra strap was missing.

Allport and Reola in the woods, their clothes ruffled up! Allport? But he was always so *quiet*. Even he's getting over? He steered, holding tightly as the pickup tossed left and right, falling in a progression of potholes.

"Henry, I want you to know I'm doing this because"—he watched her head framed in the window, her elbow on the window rest—"because I love you."

Something hot was melting, trickling down his chest cavity. He felt chills move over the hairs on his skin. He looked at her. She stared at him. Your eyes, they are beautiful, he thought. I love your forehead, too.

"I love you too, Beatrice. I have for a long time."

She put her hand on his thigh. More chills, melting.

"Turn up here. We've gone far enough, Henry," and her fingers were pulling the studs out of his shirt, unsnapping the bow tie. Henry looked around. They were in a small patch, an opening just a little larger than the truck, and the patch was surrounded by trees. The faraway sound of the band made him think of the chatter of infielders.

"I'm a virgin, you know."

"I"—he almost slipped in his excitement, almost admitted that he was one also—"just thought . . . I just figured you were, Beatrice." He then thought back to the times—how many?—just three or four—when he had gotten some girls against trees and in the bushes, always at night, each time hastily, with his companion's dress pushed up over her waist or her short pants slid down, and his underwear and pants would be around his ankles. But these experiences, he reasoned, had been adolescent fumblings, unsure and unfulfilled gropings into the sexual unknown. After all, he wasn't even sure if he had enjoyed doing it—whatever it was. Mostly it had been something he felt obligated to try, particularly since his road partners would boast of their extravagant sexual exploits in the poolroom or in the Hide Away Lounge. Reputations fell and rose at the whim of a braggart, Henry remembered, and he himself—sure—had concocted some doozers.

"You pop Lucinda yet?" Revere had asked him one night, and three beers downed within him, knowing the gang around the scarred wooden table would break out in surprised, exclamatory putdowns, Henry lied, not yet having passed his hands up to her breasts without their being slapped.

"Sure," he replied.

"Wow," said Revere—there was an affirmative, congratulatory scraping of beer mugs across the table by the others—"everybody is gettin' some of that leg." Agreeable laughter and chuckling. Henry knew it was an invention of jealousy.

Beatrice kicked off her shoes, started pulling down her stockings. "Unzip me," she said, turning her back to him, "then unhook my bra. Are you going to take off your clothes or not?"

Hell, I won't be bashful, I'll strip down to my underwear. But how could I have ignored the signs? Was I asleep? The way she looked at me. My heart, how it cripples when I'm with her or touching her hand. The way she walks—her hips. How could he have failed to see these things? Watching her bending now and twisting; then she pulled her gown down to her waist: and then almost stood, bumped her head against the roof, eased the white (hard and noisy) dress completely off and around the black stick of a gearshift. She was in panties and bra.

Was he doing it right? What was he doing? Nothing yet. But he was feeling right. He knew that. Revere, who seemed to have the greatest knowledge of anyone in the group about technique—always dressed in tight pants, usually a hand on his crotch when sitting with the fellows and a sneaky look, an about-to-laugh-in-jest look—Revere had told Henry about the tingling glow. "If it's really good," he had said, "afterward you feel this dynamite sensation that can't be described, man. Your skin and muscles are quivering. This warm gleam shooting over your body. Your heart going haywire. Afterward, you want to be against her skin. Even your breathing feels good. You think about it all day the next day. You have to walk bowlegged." Henry remembered Revere's description like that. Allport, for proof, had walked bowlegged for a week. Now. How could it be any different from that with Beatrice tonight? He was feeling too much already, and as he undid her bra and then pulled off his own underwear at her command (she took off her panties and was apologetic, embarrassed about the hole in the back) so that they were both naked (goose pimples like miniature chicken pox on her upper arms and collarbone), he knew he would (they *both* would!) feel the glow. As he lay her lengthwise on the leather seat, his elbow bumping against the handle of the gearshift, his mind was already ahead of himself and his progress with her, and he imagined himself at bat, having stolen the signal from the pitcher, who telegraphed his curve balls by wiping his mouth with his forearm. Here it comes, high, inside, and Henry knew this time he was definitely waiting for the right pitch, knew it would break down and away. Cocked his wrists. Let go. An exhilarating contact, sending vibrations to his toes as the bat's fat part caught the ball, and it was already spiraling out and high like bait at the end of a cast line, and the feeling was all over him, a smile forming on his lips. All this from the initial contact, from just the meeting of *him* with *that?* He was already squeezing the most out of it, and now the follow-through: his arms brought the bat around to the other side of his shoulder, but suddenly his arms were going around very slowly, mysteriously floating through the air, and so the elation, the electric shock of bat meeting ball, was expanded, lengthened, and as he brought his arms around to the other side of his body for the follow-through, then lost balance and unwound himself, the fat end of the bat banging against the ground, Henry felt he had lived through an indescribably fulfilling moment, and he was shaken—gloriously shaken. His wrists tingled.

But his vision dissolved. He was back in the truck. Beatrice, forehead creased with frowns, was shaking her head back and forth as if she were in pain; and moaning; feet kicking the door; and her hands were heavy against his back, and he noticed that she didn't even stir at the crash of branches to the side of the truck.

"Oh, Henry, Henry."

He hadn't felt that good with her since they had moved. In fact, watching now the increasingly clearer figures on the television in his apartment and thinking back to that dance and that picnic, he wasn't sure if he ever would again. Maybe it only happened once. Did he love Beatrice? Of course! Did she love him? Certainly! Did they enjoy it? Yes, enjoyed . . . but . . . did she get the tingling feeling when they made love? No doubt about it, the way she wiggled and trembled during those culminating, lingering moments, sometimes punctuated by screams and other verbal declarations. Then why, he was thinking, for what reason—and he had been thinking that during the picnic as he worked with the stick on his shoes—for what reason was he being denied . . . ? Sure, he enjoyed it; but feeling cheated, deprived, for it was she who quivered and trembled, dug in his back in ecstatic frenzy, twisted and turned, moaned—sometimes screamed (she wasn't cool or aloof at all during those moments)—while his climax came calmly and satisfyingly, but not explosive and exhilarating. And actually he was positive that he was getting further away from the glow. Of course, he told himself, it's all in the mind, so he had not mentioned his dissatisfaction to Beatrice. It was obviously a temporary thing, to be worked out after they had accustomed themselves to each other.

It looked like the news. Two groups of people were on each side of the screen, one group younger, dressed like people he had seen every day in the streets; the other group, in uniforms, with rifles, advancing down a hill toward the younger people. Henry watched the encounter with a neutrality of emotion, was about to drift off into another reverie when he was startled by a sudden rush of cacophony from his right: car horns and fire-engine sirens, derricks pumping, airplane engines, and then silence, just the muffled noise of voices from the television.

"Henry." It was Beatrice. Clicking of the locks. "Henry, I'm home." Her voice, high, almost excited, freezing him for a moment, and then it registered with him: she's home already.

He ran toward her. They held each other. They kissed, then she said, "Wait," stepping back to twist and fling off her coat —she was in slacks—and then moving toward him with those large eyes half-closed. But she stopped, and her eyes were now widened and Henry felt uneasy. "Henry, what happened to you? Your forehead is all bruised." She stepped back, holding his hands, to stare at him. She looked at his fingers. "Your knuckles—the skin is all scraped off! Henry, what happened?"

Her voice brought out a fear in him, and now a strange sense of dread and fright inched over him at the memory of the morning. And the panic in her face, the wild distress in her voice, made him uneasy and anxious, as if he had forgotten the event or what it should mean; and now that he was reminded by her, realized that something awful, alarming, terrifying had happened to him.

His voice shook. God, he was glad to be with her. "I got hit by a truck."

"Oh God—" She put her hands to her face, her arms went out and she was unsteady, moving past him and toward the couch.

He went over to her. He liked her perfume. "But I got the job, Beatrice, and I don't feel too bad. Nothing hurts now"— just then a flashing ache in his head. "How's the folks?"

She had tears in her eyes, looking up at him. "Let me get some hot cloths to put on your head," she said, and went toward the bathroom. Watching her disappear from the room, Henry felt strangely guilty, as if he had taken something out of Beatrice. She came back and told him to lie on the bed while she pressed the wet, hot washcloths on his head. He told her about the new job and how he was determined to keep it, how it seemed to offer opportunities. She, gaining composure, complained about the traffic and the noise and how she was almost run over by a cab and how it was almost impossible to walk in the streets or breathe. She said that her ears ached.

"Daddy's got something wrong with his liver but he's out the hospital now."

"Good," he said.

"Little Stuff's engaged."

"Engaged?"

"Yep—to the Rutherford girl. They plan on getting married next spring. And Lucinda Garrett is pregnant. Revere is in jail for messing with a white woman. Buster Riley building a new house near the highway. Stuff wants you to come down for the wedding. Does that feel better?"

"Much better," he said, pulling her toward him and biting

her neck. "Turn off the television and the lights and let's get in bed. I missed you."

They threw their clothes on the floor, Henry thinking that with his mind at ease now he could obtain the missing link, the bothersome, worrying omission that unsettled him as much as going hitless for an entire season would.

"Henry, afterwards, I want to stay in bed with you and talk with you. I want you to tell me things you did when you were a little boy. I don't even know enough about you."

And he agreed, realizing that she was so right, that in almost a year of living together they had yet not been successful in sitting down and talking. Always, an interruption. In the park that day, just as they had finally settled on the blanket, a man carrying a portable radio stumbled, almost tripped over their beverage container as he ran between them. An old, hysterical lady, hobbling with a cane in the air, eager to strike, was on his trail. "Stop, thief, stop—somebody help me." Next, a crowd of sympathizers, police, questions, and an admission that the picnic had been ruined. When they took walks, the streets were always too crowded for them to move together, and they could rarely hear each other's comments because of the auditory bombardment of machines, cars, subways, boats, bells, screams, barks. The apartment wouldn't have heat and they would be too irritated to talk about anything. The neighbors—above them or to the side—would bang against the walls or play music loudly, anything confounding and not encouraging for a quiet talk. Annoyed temporarily, yes, but Henry never felt completely discouraged or rebellious; periodically resigned, yes, but always assuring himself that the situation would naturally improve. He accepted, agreed, consented, complied, with the understanding that these disappointments and inconveniences were only temporary—were trials actually to test his mettle, and in the end everything would be all right. So one day, if he did right and acted right, as his father would say, he was positive of success, was positive that, just through faith and perseverance and trust, he would enjoy Beatrice as he wished, would be able to sit and talk with her on a sunny day in the park—just the two of them with a jug of juice, would make the baseball team, would move to a nice apartment with heat, hot water, would live. Would live.

His face was to the side of and just above her left breast as he rolled carefully on top of Beatrice, and he loved the smell of her deodorant, and she was moving her hips into him while he started to dream again of hitting a ball with the fat of the bat and the startling reverberation coursing through his wrists, when he was stopped by the banging at the door. Alarmed, Beatrice jerked her hands from around Henry's back. Once more, three insistent, solid knocks. Some voices. The banging repeated, louder and faster—Beatrice jerked her arms, this time squeezing Henry—and he could tell from the cracking sound and the sudden strip of horizontal light breaking into the room that the door had been broken open. Soon the floor was sprayed with a rectangle of light.

Then a softball-sized circle of light pointing at them, then another. Two flashlights held at the waist. The figures, tall and bulky, moved into the doorway.

"Who is it?" asked Henry, sitting up, and then one of the figures turned on the lamp. Henry blinked his eyes; his entire chest was covered with a blanket of hot fear, his wrists felt moist, his neck was burning. Beatrice, sitting up also, pulled the blanket up above her breasts. Henry felt her body tremble next to his. His eyes accustomed themselves to the light, he could see them better. "What do you want?" They turned off their flashlights. Both were covered from head to toe, so Henry was sure only that they were human and probably men. They had white helmets and stood there straddle-legged, the flashlights replaced in their belt holders; long, complicated-looking rifles pointing at Henry. Dark goggles over their eyes, and Henry couldn't even see the eyes. White hip boots shining. White leather jackets, clean, with small pockets all over the fronts and pockets on the shoulders, too. Finally, before the one on the left began to move, Henry noticed the whistles dangling from a chain connected to the upper pocket of each jacket. The one on the right motioned with one white-gloved hand. The other, who seemed to be the same height and weight as the one giving orders, bent to look under the bed, and then Henry heard just the scratching and crawling as the

60

man disappeared under the bed. Henry made a motion to throw the covers from himself and rise, but the one standing over him and Beatrice stepped back, clicked something on his rifle. The barrel was less than a foot from Henry's nose. It was a gleaming, metallic blue, with a smoky odor. Henry covered up.

The one under the bed came out on the other side, brushing lint and dust off his white pants. Then, his rifle braced, nestled on his forearm and wrist, he opened the drawers of the dresser, rifled his hand through the socks and underwear, handkerchiefs and shirts—tossing them on the floor, examining them closely. He ran over to the closet, searched the pockets of the few slacks and a jacket in there, turned up the edges of the linoleum, looked under a chair, then came over to the one guarding Henry and Beatrice. He shook his head, out of breath, the top pockets on his jacket rising and falling with his chest, the jacket's leather cracking.

"What are you looking for?" asked Henry, not expecting an answer. He felt the words coming out in a childish, pleading tone rather than angrily demanding as he had wanted.

The one guarding Henry and Beatrice—he must be the leader, Henry reasoned—motioned for them to get out of bed. They held hands rising from the mattress, Henry feeling as if he were walking naked down the middle of the street, one hand spread to cover his privates, and Beatrice held her arms folded over her breasts. The men grabbed Beatrice away from Henry. She was trembling, her knees were together and knocking, and her breasts were flat, lacking the pointed firmness Henry had relished when they were in bed. Perspiration dripping down her arms. She was over by them now, her hands at her waist, and they began putting their hands on her—the gloves thrown to the floor—and something heavy, the size of a grapefruit, began to lift up and down in Henry's stomach. The terrible feeling of his skin—was his hair rising like the fur of a frightened cat? The pounding came back to his head. He was getting dizzy. He saw them pull on her nipples—Beatrice was weak against a wall now, her eyes closed and her head back so that her chin stuck out—then squeeze and pat her breasts, and he was furious. But he couldn't move, for one, the leader—one hand moving over her hips—kept the rifle trained on Henry. He could feel her humiliation as Beatrice winced and held her breath at every new contact—seemed to start at each new spot on her body touched by those grasping, colorless fingers between her legs, in her navel, on her legs, around her buttocks.

Exhausted with dizziness, pain, humiliation, Henry fell on his knees and yelled, "Stop, please stop." Now the leader had the tip of the barrel against Henry's forehead, and the fear was hot and active within him. But he wanted it stopped, and his hands were to his face as he pleaded and—

"Hello."

Because he was so weak and unstable, Henry accepted the greeting without looking. Then it registered with him. At the same time the two men stopped, the barrel of the rifle was withdrawn from Henry's forehead.

"Teehee hee." It was Betty Hurt, standing in the doorway with bowlegs, a red dress, fingers to her mouth, giggling.

The two made threatening gestures at her, and each time Betty Hurt would scamper away, then return to the doorway again, the frenetic giggling continuing. So the two charged toward her, and it seemed a permanent kind of departure— they were going for good, Henry hoped, but one stopped abruptly just at the edge of the doorway, came briskly back into the apartment toward Beatrice. She was against the wall still, her face against it, and the man bent to pick up the two pairs of gloves and pinch her on the fat of her right buttock, did it again, then ran out.

They were there for what seemed to Henry to be an eternity —he on his knees and she, naked, shaking with fear, face against the wall paint, hands outstretched against the wall for balance. Finally, when it seemed as though they would not return, Henry got up and put his hands on her shoulders (she jerked) and pulled her over to the bed, whispered to her and kissed her on the neck and she was crying louder now, her shoulders going up and down involuntarily. And suddenly, Henry thought, in spite of all the soothing and relaxing he was attempting for *her* benefit, *he*—he, Henry Adams, a man—was scared, petrified also, and he clung to her in bed.

4

OH, THIS IS TOO MUCH, Henry told himself, too much for me. In the last two weeks I've gotten a job and now this note. It was in his pocket, but he wouldn't take it out, and he darted his eyes left and right. Had anyone seen him smiling to himself? He stepped to the edge of the platform, looked down the canyon of darkness—no subway coming —then his eyes passed over the scatter of candy and Popsicle wrappers along the ties of the tracks. He yawned. The clock read eleven-thirty. Panic seeped up his backbone. Was he due there at twelve-thirty or eleven-thirty? He couldn't go in late. He couldn't bring the note out of his pocket either, for then he might look like a lost Southern nomad, bewildered in the big city. The note had been slipped under his door that morning—how long had it been there? He hadn't seen it, Beatrice had discovered it; and after they had thought of looking down the hallway, it was calm and empty, as if no one had even walked in the building. Let's see . . . there is a way he could get to it inconspicuously . . . yes. His hand went into his pocket, his fingers edged around the note . . . he had it. Then he turned quickly, moving toward the crowd on the platform, letting the note slip out of his fingers, heard it flitter toward the cement, whirled theatrically and bent to pick it up. He spread out the paper as he rose, and his eyes cruised over the lines until he found the time; it was twelve-thirty, so his first guess had been right. His eyes picked over other words on the page before he crumpled up the note, stood and placed it in his pocket, then shaking his head as if you just couldn't keep from dropping notes, and wasn't it a pain sometimes? It said:

> We take our pen in hand to inform you, to write you that we are willing to give you a tryout with the Stars. Be a Wide Awake when you report at 12:30 P.M. at the Sportsmen's Dome tomorrow, Saturday, taking the A train to the Sport Street stop. Be cautious in your words and in your deportment toward your superiors, avoid all suspicion of discontent and do not stir uneasiness among those near you. Heads up, keep your eye on the ball, don't let your meat loaf.
>
> Writing most cordially,
> Stumpy

Soon the walls were shaking, a rush of air came through the tunnel and the other passengers moved toward the platform edge and Henry had to turn his head away from the blast. He took his hands from his ears. The doors opened. He was pushed; he bent just in time to avoid hitting his head on the top of the door. Although he had gone in face forward, he had been spun around so that now he was sideways to the door, one button from his coat falling to the floor, and he was still being shoved and pushed, turned and bumped when the doors started to close. Someone had just stuck a shoe tip and a wrist in the inches of remaining space between the doors, and Henry watched the shoe wiggle, watched the fingers on the hand on the end of the wrist bend, beckon, point, until the doors opened completely and the owner of these appendages—a man, Henry thought, whose weight they didn't need more of—burst into the car and squeezed between two people. The train moved slowly, but there was an old, short, bowlegged lady Henry could see from the window on his right. She was hobbling along the platform, a stuffed bag dragging. She raised her fists and tried to bang on the windows of the train. Then she was gone from Henry's sight.

Now. He had one hand on the roof strap and the paper bag of equipment was held down, pressed against the side of his knee by two passengers on his left. Someone stepped on his shoe heel, apologized, and Henry turned his head sideways, nodded, smiled, as if *he* were embarrassed for the man, then stared out the window of blackness, an occasional light bulb flashing by.

The last (and third) tryout had been in October down South. They liked him well enough but thought he might be a flash in the pan. So would he come up North for a tryout with the big team? Henry and Beatrice moved up. Now in November he got his notice. This was it! He was being given a workout by the Stars in their own park! "Excuse me, miss." His elbow had caught her in the neck. He would sign a nice contract for three years or so, quit Home; he and Beatrice would move out of Alvarez's lousy building to a *home*. Then he would be relaxed, calm, free—would be living—and perhaps the glow . . . the tingling. . . .

His left hand was tiring, so he pushed the bag of equipment up under his arm. As if by signal, people on three sides of him moved in closer to fill up the extra space. His hand . . . it was very soft . . . round . . . moving left to right . . . very round . . . his hand was on . . . no . . . can't be . . . can't possibly be. He moved it closer toward himself, but now he was positive, for he looked to his left, downward, and saw the hair and shoulders of a woman. And his hand was against it again. She had moved closer. No doubt about it, he told himself, my hand is definitely against her ass, and she likes it. He turned his head, frowning, as if he couldn't read the sign on the other wall: good, nobody could see his hand. The train jerked to a stop, pushing the woman against him, and he caught her weight with his open hand this time, his palm against the coat at her hips, as if he was steadying her, and he slid his hand over the width of her rear, took in the perfume as her head went back, hair sweeping his chin. He wanted to squeeze her behind.

"Chile, we going to be late for lunch if this keeps up." The train jerked forward again. Was she talking to him?

"They ought to stop letting so many people on these trains. It's a disgrace." Aha! She was talking to someone on her side, someone Henry couldn't see. The people in the seats were nodding their heads.

The back of his hand lay easily against the cheek of one buttock, and he closed his eyes, enjoying the touch, his mind undressing a woman on the beach. She was soft. She moved against his hand and Henry let it fall downward, so now it was against the inside of her thighs and the way she moved—in time with the rolling and twisting of the train—allowed his hand to slide up and down freely. What is she doing? What am I doing? Does she know? Henry, what have you come to? You're a married man, in love, a happily married man, sensible, faithful, and here you are with your hand feeling a strange woman. Now you're—no, stop me, somebody stop me before I get myself slapped or locked up—you're going to put your *open* palm against it, work with your fingers? Oh, Jesus, why am I doing this, what is happening to me? This woman, is she as insane as me? These people, packed in here like cattle— maybe they're all doing the same thing? Suppose all the women are having their asses felt? Old ones, middle-aged ones, young ones, cripples, doctors, teachers. Maybe that's why they pack themselves in here—stepping into a, dark, anonymous world of escapade.

"This is really too much—this crowd," said the woman, leaning against and twisting her rear against Henry's palm.

That voice. How familiar, that voice. But where? He strained his memory, tried to induce her through his mind to say another sentence. He had heard that voice before. It was a voice distinct and clear, too, carrying an authority and maturity, he reasoned, and a voice that he had not heard enough of. That's why he wanted to pinpoint it, to connect it with someone, for he felt that in a way he had been cheated by that voice. It owed him something, was in his debt. Why? He wasn't sure.

The train came to a stop and a few passengers got off; several pushed their way on, scowls and frowns on their faces.

"Did you get the makeup from the bathroom?"

The woman whom Henry was massaging had been turned sideways by the new passengers, and his hand nestled momentarily between her legs. It was a shock, a pleasant, soft shock, accelerating his heart. For an instant, he was sure his hand had fallen (or been pushed) between an opening in her coat. And brushed against her dress. And felt the outline of her panties. It was only for an instant, and then she had her back to him once more; his hand rested against her with familiarity. Maybe she's enjoying it as much as I am. If Beatrice's father found out— But this woman is *making* me act this way, she's encouraging me, daring me, and . . . wait a minute . . . the bathroom . . . the makeup. Everything clicked. Just one more sentence and he would have it. One more sentence—

"My boss told me an excellent secretary is worth a million dollars."

Yes! He was positive now. He knew who they were. Amazing! These were the girls with the apartment in back of him, whom he heard flushing the toilet and running water late at night and early in the morning; whom he had never seen and couldn't even find their apartment door; who he had imagined were foxy, sly, slick chicks who might give him a play. He saw Leon Mark pointing a finger at him. But he wasn't leaving Beatrice. Just a little adventure, Mister Mark. And now, and now—and now he realized that he didn't even have a buddy with whom he could share this story, and he wanted to be able to tell somebody—and now he was rubbing (he, Henry Adams!) his hand all inside one of them as if he owned her. Getting the thrill of his life. God, would Little Stuff cream his pants when he read the letter describing this! He'd never want to get married.

After a half-hour of stops the train had reached the elevated tracks. Henry watched the passengers leaving, tired, clothes disheveled, filing out, as if this was the last stop they would ever make. The two women—his neighbors, he thought—sat down to the side of him. He had disciplined his hand long before the train had begun to empty. He turned his head casually. This was the way he looked for a seat—unconcernedly, as if he were really looking out the window or checking one of the poster ads. During his first week in the city, he had learned his lesson. Several times he had spotted an empty space on the row of plastic benches, started toward it, and by the time he was bending to sit, someone—usually a rouge-cheeked old lady—had slid into it before him. So he would be in the embarrassing position of standing up again, walking away to hang on a strap or lean against the door, sure that the unmoving, unresponsive faces of the other passengers were cloaking their assessments of him: slow, awkward country boy fumbling around; you can't get no seat like that; go back to the South if you can't get no slicker than that. There was a seat. And across, directly across from the two neighbors. He fell into it, his hands going up against the wall to keep his balance. Easing his shoulders between the other two passengers, placing his bag on the floor and—oh, no, this is too much. She, the one who had allowed him to feel on her, was staring straight at him—through him. While he had bent to place his bag down, his eyes had caught an open space between her thighs—her overcoat buttons stopped at her waist and there the coat spread to both sides, baring her legs and skirt and some of her blouse—and he was positive he had seen . . . she wasn't wearing panties. No, that couldn't be. First, it was too cold for that and secondly, no such luck would ever come his way. His heart was racing. His eyes were magnetized to a poster above her. He didn't dare look again. Check out the other one. From the corner of his eye, he saw she was beautiful also, but was wearing slacks and her light, her yellow face—thin, strong cheekbones catching the fluorescence from the train bulbs—was turned toward the woman with the skirt, and she was whispering in this woman's ear. Who was smiling, eyes focused on—on him. He looked back, something going awry in his stomach at all this beauty staring at him: her skin almost shiny black, hair falling over her cheeks, lips tight and gleaming with lipstick. Her thighs— he dared look down now, and enjoyed the widening taper as the thighs disappeared up her skirt—were larger than Beatrice's. Her knees were together, but he had never seen so much of a strange woman's legs before, and he had to cross his legs to calm his excitement, easing his back down within his seat in the process. Forbidden fruit. Now he had a better view of the dark, triangular opening under her skirt, and this time he took a deep breath, pretended to rub his eyes and stared. He kept his eyes on the spot for thirty seconds and felt exhaustedly pleased. He had violated her, infiltrated her. It was a conquest. He had looked at her, this woman whom he had heard on the other side of his wall, looked at her where very few, very, very few men had set eyes upon her, and he could write Stuff about it and talk to men about it. He still wasn't sure—the light wasn't good enough—if he was staring at her panties or something more sensuous, more electrifying: her pubic hair.

And she was staring at him still; smiling, listening to her friend, and her legs, perfectly tapered, not a scar on them, he noted, stayed in that position. Should he introduce himself as her neighbor? No, then she'd know he was married and that would be that. But wait. Maybe . . . of course . . . she wouldn't care, not her kind . . . it wouldn't matter if he was married. He remembered their conversations. Not to her kind. She might be his mistress, he could meet her secretly at the incinerator late in the evenings. Yes. He would go over, hang by the strap, introduce himself and ask her if by chance she lived in the building—but what was he saying, thinking? What was he doing to Beatrice, his Beatrice? He remembered her father's words: "When you black men goin' to learn to take care of your own women? When! Why must you keep runnin', runnin', leavin' good, honest, decent black wives sufferin' for you? When will you learn?"

"But I'm not leaving Beatrice. I'm taking care of her," he would answer. I just . . . I just want a little . . . well, hell, this woman started it, rubbing herself up against me. She, they were getting up. Wait! Let me introduce myself. Her knees went apart for a moment, and exposed everything. She shifted her weight forward. Smiling at Henry. He saw then she was wearing panties—sheer—and before he could catch his breath, they both were hanging onto the straps and moving toward the door. Too late. Now disappearing into the noise and fog, out the door.

"Disgraceful." In the brief seconds that the train had come to a stop, he heard that word, soft but clear. It was from the man sitting to his right. And then, turning toward Henry, his eyes sad, glassy, he said, before the train pulled off, "What's happening to us? Where are we going?"

Henry shook his head, responding out of respect to the

white man's age. What was the talking about? I'm going to the stadium.

He remembered that the stadium was near the end of the line. There were only a couple of passengers in the car: the old white man sitting near Henry, and another man. Henry could see only his legs, the top of his hat, his fingers around the edges of an opened newspaper which covered most of his body. He was at the end of the car, his back was against the corner. Henry pulled his glove out of the bag, and placing it on his glove hand, sniffing the fine leather, punched it with his other fist. He was getting off soon, and he didn't care what the two men thought of his eccentricity—a baseball glove in the winter—he would soon be out.

The clanging, rolling rhythm of the train; a circle of colored saliva on the floor to his right; cracked windows; empty candy boxes on the floor, airborne for a few seconds and skittering down the aisle; folded newspapers left on some seats; profane words crayoned on a sign opposite Henry. He was being taken in by the rhythm, the rolling, the hypnotic commonness of the subway car and its decor, and soon he was in a trance, eyelids heavy, chin dropping against his chest, back to his hometown, back to his mother's living room, where he had sat on many nights with his family and sung. He had felt the same rolling rhythm then as he was riding with now. His eyes would be closed, his head resting against the rocker's back and—the man behind the newspaper was peeping at Henry. He wore dark glasses and stuck his head behind the paper when Henry looked at him. But Henry's head was rolling downhill now toward some invisible, fuzzy comfortableness, and it seemed to him that he couldn't stop the descent, couldn't keep his eyes open long enough to concentrate on this man in the corner and . . . he hadn't noticed before, but the man was wearing white shoelaces; black shoes, but white shoelaces. Henry tried to gather himself together to concentrate on where he was, but the train's motion was tugging at him. He was back rocking with eyes closed in his mother's living room, in the small, crowded living room, the fat black pipe from the stove reaching through the center of the roof. His eyes, closing now, rested on the collection on Momma Lou's wall: the outdated calendars (some hanging off-balance) with their advertisements for local hardware shops, drugstores, five-and-dime stores; round, gold-plated picture frames with uncles and aunts whom Henry had heard about; a patch of Sissy Linda's hair taped on the wall, too, cut from her year-old head. And he remembered—could see—the black console Victrola sitting in the far corner, the one that required those big needles but didn't play. They couldn't throw it out because the Culpeters, a family for whom Henry's mother did day's work occasionally, had given it to them; the faded lace doily on the mantel shelf, and the prize piece of furniture, the tall chifforobe, imperious in its position against the wall, confronting you as you stepped through the front door. He would be rocking in the chair—was . . . *was that man peeping at him again?*—and Momma Lou and Daddy would be singing those songs that somehow, he thought, fit in with the rhythm and purpose of this subway ride:

> *I'm bound for the promised land,*
> *Friends, I'm gonna leave you*

He knew the words by heart—they all did—and he was nestled against the hard, plastic back of the train's chair, was imagining it to be the pine rocker at home; and now he felt he couldn't fight anymore, couldn't hold up against the seeming pulling at him from two sides. One imaginary rope was tugging at him to relax, settle into the comfortable pitch of the train's motion, sing those old songs with his family; the other pull was a warning to stay awake, keep an eye on this man with the mysterious white shoelaces and don't miss his stop. Then there was a tightening, an equilibrium and inclination when he felt he was divided between the two and could, should make his decision. The man in the corner, newspaper still in his hands, slid down to another seat almost opposite to Henry. His pants seat had squeaked as he slid. But Henry chose to fall back into the rocking chair, and he was singing again:

> *Oh Canaan, Sweet Canaan*
> *I'm boun' for the land of Canaan*

And:

I'm goin' to ride on de mornin' train
All don't see me goin' to hear me sing

And:

I'm goin' to heaven, don't want to stop,
And I don't want to be no stumblin' block

And:

Well, I may be lame and cannot walk
But I'll meet you at de station when de train
  come along

And he was rocking and singing all those songs they used to gather for, and suddenly he was filled with a rush of nostalgia for those gatherings with his family, those calm, peaceful evenings when, realizing they had little more than themselves and these songs—which were theirs, which they *owned* and could fashion and improvise as they could nothing else—their hearts and eyes met and they felt grateful for having each other, if nothing else. But he had to leave, Henry reminded himself. They expected him to leave. He had a talent that could bring him a better life, fulfillment, freedom, a chance to live, exist; breathe cleanly, comfortably. There was nothing for him down there. His father did odd jobs; his mother worked for the white folks, she scrubbed their underwear and fed their babies when the folks asked her to come to them. And poor Sissy Linda and Joe Boy and Little Stuff—what would they do? If they didn't leave, what would they do? He wanted to talk to that squirt, that sassy Sissy who would be running off at the mouth all the time with Henry, not taking anything from him, and scared the daylights out of him one day, threatening him with a rake if he didn't leave her alone. She was the strongest of the three, he believed; she might marry well—but who was there to marry? She might finish high school and should go on to college, but where would she get the money? She was smart, handsome, energetic, but what good would it do her? God, he missed them so much, missed the arguing and laughing and singing and running, and he wanted to be with them; not just be where they were, but be with them, hold their hands, follow the peculiar manner of their voices, follow the movements of their lips and the twitches of their cheeks and foreheads when they talked and smiled. Smell them; especially Joe Boy when he came back from the garage.

But more than his brothers and sisters, even more than his mother, he missed his father, his large, dark father who somehow managed, not having any education beyond grade school, to provide for and love and control his family. Oh, the jobs that man could do to get money in the nick of time: when Joe Boy needed new shoes, or Sissy Linda's dress tore on the fence, or the time Henry needed a new baseball glove. He would just go out in the morning, return in the evening with a story of how he had back-furrowed with the plow or picked two hundred and fifty pounds of cotton or fed Mr. Culpeter's mules and swine or chopped wood all day. And knowing nothing about baseball, he had encouraged Henry to become as good as he could when, at age ten, Henry decided he wanted to play ball for a living after having seen his first high-school game.

"You can be anything you like," his father had said, standing in front of the screen door, the sun working on him, and the skin on his hands wrinkled, rough, twice older than he himself, "but you must leave here, you know. All the teams are up North."

Always calm and agreeable. Momma Lou would say frequently, so frequently that it became a common putdown in the mouth of his brothers and sister, that Henry was weak and gave in all the time just like his daddy.

"You can measure the size of a man by what makes him angry," he would tell Henry. "Your grandpop told me that a long time ago."

So this, of all the maxims, proverbs, warnings, prophecies that his father had planted—and Henry thought that he, the oldest, had been singled out to carry this on as a familial proverb—this one stuck in Henry's mind.

He wondered at times: temperance always? Twice in his older years—and the picture of those events ran vividly through his mind as if they were recorded there on film—twice he wanted to speak to his father about that principle, for it seemed to him that a man *ought* to get angry when something vital was at stake. So many times those two events had screened themselves in his mind, and he had been tempted to re-evaluate his father's stance. Was it calmness, really, his father possessed in the face of a screaming, mindless adversity, or was it—the word came reluctantly each time he tried it— resignation? Each time he thought of the two events, he played with them in his mind more, introduced matter for further interpretation, reconstructed them from end to beginning, then middle to end, then midmiddle to midend. Perhaps fear, the fear of discovering something unpalatable, something he had guessed but didn't want to acknowledge, had kept him each time from coming to a conclusion. Was it resignation? And if so, why?

Now. Dreamily rocking on this train to the stadium, half-asleep and thinking back to his family, Henry went over those two important events.

First. George Benson, a neighbor down the road, had mentioned something about social security one day.

"Social security?" Henry's father scratched his head with his thick hands. Henry was sitting on the porch next to him. He had to squint at old George, standing, blocking the sun in his overalls.

"I'm retiring. No more cleaning up those bathrooms in the bus station after next year. So I found out from my niece who's smart, got a good job up North—I told you about her—sent me a letter saying I should look into this social security thing. You know they been taking money out of my pay for fifteen years?"

"Fifteen years?"

"Yeah. And now they got to give it back. Monthly. I'm gonna get *paid* when I'm not working."

"How do you find out about this social security thing, George?"

"The government in Washington does it, but first you got to go to your boss and get the slip and ask him to write Washington for you. Or you can write Washington yourself, but I'm not good at letters."

So Henry went with his father to talk to some of the people who had employed him, and they also visited the Culpeters, who had kept Momma Lou on for twenty years.

"Social security? Yeah, we took it out of your pay, but we forgot to send in the forms to the government." Henry, standing in the road, the sun steaming on him, listened to the speaker and watched him through the wire-fence squares, up there on his porch, standing sideways as if, thought Henry, he were out there just temporarily and would say that, say in other words, "I don't know what you talkin' about, nigger," and move on inside.

He heard his father clear his throat, a signal that the next words were buried within him, and Henry, who was about fifteen, sensing that already the "confrontation" was rapidly gaining in unevenness, began, searching for the words even as he opened his mouth, wiping his forearm down his neck: "Uh, uh, Mr. Culpeter, sir, do you have any papers with numbers on them or anything so we can write the government about my father's account?"

"Nope," taking a step toward the door.

And inside, "Who is it, honey?" The curtain jerked aside.

"You doing well, boy, what you want to worry about social security for? Why should the government support you people? Don't you want to work for a living?"

Mrs. Culpeter coming outside now, and Henry watched her in her clean white dress, a glass of iced tea in her hand, not even sweating up there, while his forehead was dripping.

"What's this, more of yawl talking about social security? Who started this talk, anyway? Not you, John, good as you worked for us all these years and this is the gratitude we get?"

"Hello, Miss Culpeter."

"John, you don't have to worry about a job. You can always get one here. Now, go on with that crazy talk about social security. Go on, now."

Henry wanted to ask if they would mind if he wrote to Washington just to inquire. Who knows, they might just have the name on file, but before he could fashion the sentence, he felt a tug on his shirtsleeve, and from the corner of his eye he could see his father turning. Henry thought that there should be something else, should be a few more words exchanged, some parrying, a little give and take—something before his father had given himself over to his pose of grave tolerance, self-command, inoffensiveness. But he was already clumping down the road with his hands in his pockets, and Henry followed.

The other time he recalled frequently was a day in the rain. He and his father had been slipping and rolling along the northeast road in Leon Mark's pickup, borrowed for this special occasion. Henry had spotted the dog, lying in a running position at the side of the road, and already Henry's mouth was dry, and there was just for an instant the monotonous scraping of the wipers as both he and his father stared down silently, John Adams leaning with his hand on Henry's shoulder, the truck tires settling in the mud.

"There he is," Henry said, pulling on the door handle, swallowing after getting down and out and closer to the dog, whose teeth were bared, spotted with mud and blood. Henry turned from the animal when he saw that half the ear had been blown off from the shotgun shell.

He heard his father say, "Oh, no. Why did they have to kill it?" and Henry thought that the voice was hardly louder than the patter of the rain, but certainly too calm, too self-controlled.

Henry's vision went weak from the anger he felt, and standing in that mud that day as the rain thumped against the dog's body, against the frizzled twirls of loose, wet dog hair, he was seized (he knew now, remembering) probably with more fury and bitterness and indignation than he had ever trembled with in his life. Clearly it was new for him, this shaking in the knees, red waves before his eyes, dizziness, the frighteningly refreshing urge to grab something and swing, swing, swing. . . .

"We should have given them the dog," his father said, turning again from Henry's side just as he had when they stood in front of the Culpeters' gate one day. Henry had the spooky feeling that the turning was a strange re-enactment of the same turning outside the Culpeters', that the opportunities were the same, that the failure was the same, that . . . that

76

his father's calmness was perhaps something else. But never mind, he thought, turning to get into the truck. Poor dog, hadn't been named, just called Dog, belonged to Little Stuff, given to him by Beatrice's family, and those dirty, red-neck Kings, unable to accept the Adamses' refusal to give the dog to them, finally stole him in the night, and here . . . here the dog lay. And his father—could he still accept that as the inevitable, something to ponder briefly and then retire with "We should have given them the dog"?

"You want to sell us that dog? He looks good for huntin'. Ready to sell yet? John, you being stubborn, boy, for nothing. . . . You can buy the boy another dog, we'll give you a good price. *You won't sell, huh? Sure? Okay.*" That's how it had gone for weeks. Lucifer King knocking on the door at nights, huffing and spitting tobacco, cursing, begging and begging until . . . now this.

But that was the influence, he knew, which had shaped and conditioned him—his father's ubiquitous tranquil temperament in the face of all discord, plus his unswerving faith in Henry's future. Henry would make it, would break out from the constrictions and emptiness that his father had known all his life and which, silently acknowledged by him and Henry, would probably bind Little Stuff and Joe Boy and Sissy Linda too. So that was what had made him the way he was, he tried to explain to Beatrice after the men in goggles had burst in upon them several weeks ago. He wanted her to calm down. Things would be a medley of ferment and commotion for a while. One had to expect a little indisposition. After all, this was the North, they were new here, and these events—the Mack truck, Alvarez, even the subway he was riding on now and slowly gaining wakefulness on—had to be reckoned with if they were to survive. Other people—everyone he had seen, as a matter of fact, although they did have a curious emptiness on their faces—were surviving. Why couldn't they? So hold on, Beatrice, he tried to tell her, things will work out. As soon as I sign this baseball contract, you'll see, everything will be worth the trouble. *Persevere.*

Now the rolling and pitching were jerking him, and he was fighting the pull out of his comfortable, nodding, dreamy reverie, fighting the climb into wakefulness. But one more song was clinging unaccountably to his mind, and he had to savor the lines that forced themselves upon him before giving himself up to the overwhelming draw into wakefulness:

> *Wake up, sinner, you will be too late*
> *Gospel train done pass yo gate*

"*Wake up, sinner!* Henry, Henry Adams. Wake up." Someone was kicking the sole of his shoe. A blue uniform, brass buttons, black face, mustache. Another search party? Henry jumped, sat up straight. Just to the left of the blue figure, he could see the man from the corner, now sitting almost directly opposite Henry, the newspaper spread, its middle crease up to the man's hairline. "Sport Street coming up next. Isn't that your stop, brother?"

But how did he know and where did he come from and who was he?

Then the man whispered, bending over, "I'm the conductor. The conductor?" Neck stretched forward, forehead creased into expectancy. "The conductor?"

The train slowed down, wheels squeaking and whining. Henry dropped his glove into his bag, fixed his topcoat button. He rose, said, "Thanks a lot," and legs spread for balance, took baby steps toward the door. He heard the rattling of the man's folding his newspaper and guessed that he was getting off also, but Henry didn't turn around. Now coming into the station, staring black faces on the platform whizzing by, and soon the train stopped. The doors opened. Henry turned to say good-by to the conductor and . . . what? The man in the white shoelaces was up now and tussling with the conductor, who wouldn't let him pass.

"Get off, Henry, get off before the door closes. Go on!" Henry stood confused, watching the two men wrestle and grunt, then an oncoming passenger excused himself around Henry, and Henry stepped onto the platform. The door closed, the train started off. Henry was on the platform. The man with the white shoelaces was staring at Henry through the window, and then Henry watched his face, distressed and folded in horror, slowly move ahead. The conductor waved at Henry.

78

The other man was pointing his finger, threatening, accusing, at Henry as the train separated them.

He started toward the steps, his stomach snarling. He reached the sidewalk and soon he was being pushed and shoved about as he blended in with the other pedestrians, and he had to tip gingerly along, there were so many people on the streets. He avoided stepping in a pile of sausage-shaped dog manure. Above, over the heads of the surround of pedestrians, through the red, sooty atmosphere, now coughing and feeling unstable from the noise of trucks, subways, trains (he felt they were all traveling toward him at once), he saw the clear, plastic-covered dome of the stadium with an American flag—a gigantic flag, the largest Henry had ever seen in his life—twirled around its pole. He wanted to move faster, wanted to get to that stadium and start roaming that outfield and hitting that ball. But he felt like a halfback surrounded by too slow-moving blockers: he kept bumping into them but they wouldn't move forward, nor could he edge out to the left or right. And they might just as well have had helmets on, Henry decided, for they stared straight ahead, no one acknowledging anyone, one man kicking Henry in the heel and staring straight through him when Henry turned to look at the man.

When Henry Adams fell out of the rank of pedestrians and had his hand on the gate leading to the small expanse of land on which the dome sat, he was trembling, his heart was double-timing. This was what his father had wanted for him, and this had been his goal since he had first learned that you can get paid for playing ball. And that there were black players in the majors making good money. Now, he told himself, through the gate and turning to catch the latch, he was this close to making it. He was this close. *This close.*

It was warm and bright inside the dome as if they had obtained an artificial sun and stuck it on the ceiling. Henry was standing there, just inside the dome, his package at his side, looking up at the white glare and enjoying the warmth, when from behind a wall came a man. He was on crutches. He welcomed Henry with a smile, then shook and angled his shoulders until he was able to thrust out his hand. He looked familiar to Henry, but he didn't want to ask his name, for thinking back it occurred to Henry that he had read about the man's disabling accident. He looked very young, too, to be finished with baseball for life. And the changes he had to go through to shake hands. It embarrassed Henry to wait for the man like that, and he was certain that the player himself was probably embarrassed also. Henry was taken to the locker room. He was alone so he took his time getting dressed, looked at the familiar names on the lockers, dressed, and ran through the long cement hallway toward the patch of light at the end. His cleats made a beautiful clicking, and they echoed nicely, too. He wanted to go back up the hallway and try it again, but now he was on the few feet of brown dirt, outside. The entire field was bright from the sun, and Henry was struck motionless by the impact of its beauty. The field looked like one of those color photographs he had seen in the magazines. But never, never had he imagined that it could be this way, with its blue-green grass which was perfectly separated, trimmed away from the running paths. The chalk lines were luminescent white, shining, sparkling. And the stands had red-white-and-blue chairs that looked as though they had been installed recently.

He was transfixed. This was the Star Stadium he had seen on television so many times. But never, never had he thought—

"Think fast." A voice from behind him. Henry whirled, glove protecting his face, and caught the ball at that level. "Damn. Pretty damn good."

He looked up. A half-dozen or so faces staring at him from some suspended box seats behind the batter's plate. Henry could see only the faces and some of their necks. Then they rose and started down the ladder.

"Hey, Slugger, I'm Stumpy," he said. He was balanced on the shoulders of two players, balanced this way between them, and a half-dozen escorts surrounding him at the foot of the ladder.

"I'm Rabbitt."

"I'm Lou."

"I'm Pee Wee."

"I'm Sparrow."

"I'm Lefty."

"Let me off, guys," getting down from their shoulders and walking toward Henry.

Henry knelt to shake the hand of Stumpy, a midget manager, and then his hand was grabbed and shaken by the other players. Then Henry was staring at Stumpy, who was staring at him, and for a few seconds Henry went dizzy, felt spookily unstable as he thought that somewhere in his past—was it the meeting with the executives?—he had stood on that spot and shaken hands before. He had done this before?

"I guess you received my letter?" His voice was squeaky and seemed to be coming from his stomach. Henry stared at Stumpy's chest as the manager, facing Henry, peered up at him with his hand shading the artificial sunlight from his eyes. The others surrounded Henry. He prepared himself for their questions. They just stared. "How do you like our little field, Henry? We can play in rain, snow or sleet, and we have an artificial sun. See it up there? Wait, don't stare at it, for God's sake, boy, you'll go blind. The grass stays green forever. And quiet, too. You'd never know that shit was going on outside—noise, crowded streets, red pollution, dirt and garbage."

"It's . . . it's . . . ." Henry couldn't think of the right word.

"Yep, it sure is. Tell me, Henry," reaching out and taking a miniature bat from a player, next lifting one leg and banging the bat against his cleats, "what happened to you at the try-outs in the South? You didn't do so well."

Henry wanted to say that he had done very well and that he wasn't positive why he hadn't been granted a contract immediately, but instead, feeling that this was no time for sour grapes and believing, too, as his father had insisted and insisted and insisted, that baseball was *the* American . . . he'd get a fair shake. He *had* to.

"I guess I just didn't play well enough," he said, hanging his head for effect, then bringing it up quickly, "but I'm ready to show you my stuff today, Mister Rickey—I mean, Mister . . . ."

"Call me Stumpy," he interrupted, turning, and Henry started toward him with hands out, thinking that the manager was falling. He was bowlegged, Henry discovered, and had been pivoting. And now up close he noticed rings under Stumpy's eyes, wrinkles lining his forehead, a double chin.

"Okay, let's see what you can do, Henry." The other players ran out to the field. Stumpy went over to the dugout. He pushed an aluminum contraption toward the mound. Henry thought, pitching machine. "You're up, Henry."

He got a bat. Fear trickled through him. He hadn't played since the summer. Would he be rusty? Stumpy was climbing up on the base of the machine, was setting the arms, and Henry imagined himself actually playing in this stadium; and now he could hear the crowd in his ear, it was the bottom of the ninth and they had to score and—he stared at the speed indicator, the tiny dial at the bottom of the machine. Had Stumpy turned it to 150? And did that mean one hundred and fifty miles per hour? No human could throw that fast. He knew the majors were different, but . . .

"Okay." The machine cranked and Henry heard a whistling sound like the exhaust of a jet plane. He knew he had to keep his eye on the ball, but where was it? "Strike one, Henry. Hey, wait a minute, I forgot," running toward the dugout. "We can't play," he said, leaning in the dugout and pushing a button, "without the national anthem, boss's orders." Walking back to the mound. The national anthem blared over the stadium while Henry held his cap at his heart and the others sat on the grass, yawned, picked up and threw pebbles. "Okay, let's go."

Again a whistling sound, but Henry had moved back in the box this time, had spread his feet wider, cocked his bat higher. He swung and knew he had gotten a very good chunk of the ball. He had judged the height of the ball by the height of the hole in the machine. He had calculated the velocity of the ball by swinging proportionately earlier than he would swing on the fastest man he had ever faced, rumored to have a good fast ball traveling ninety miles per hour. So there was the tenorish snapping sound of the connection, followed by the rippling vibration down the bat to Henry's wrists, and he knew it was the best hit ball that anybody would see in a long, long time. Knees bending in his follow-through, ecstatic, heart leaping, he saw the ball, still rising, shoot for the highest point . . . it was going and going, still plenty of power behind it and . . . yes! He dropped his bat and began to run around the bases. He had cracked the top of the dome.

"What the fuck . . . What a . . ." Henry, skipping around second base, heard Stumpy.

Stumpy pitched ten more balls at Henry and he sent each one to the outfield. By the sixth pitch, the other players had parked themselves in the center-field bleachers, and jumping over seats and running down aisles, tried to catch Henry's shots.

Stumpy rolled the pitching machine toward the dugout. "Okay, let's see you field some, Slugger," he said, waving the others in. Soon he was pushing another steel box-like machine, shiny, gears clicking, toward the batter's box, and Henry was jogging to the outfield. He punched his glove in center field, standing half-deep.

The first ball was a high, high accelerating fly, and Henry turned to go back, finally reaching the wall. The ball was still very high and coming down. His back was against the wall. He knew if he leaped he would still be four or five feet too short, so he began furiously to scale the wall, sticking his cleats into the wood—his glove had been thrown away for the climb—and fingernails grabbing into the tiny cracks. He would slip a foot and grab again, slip, grab some more, until he had reached the top of the wall and could climb over it, climb over the metal railing. Now he saw the ball sailing downward. There was one possibility, he thought, and balanced himself on the railing, jumped in the air toward the arc of the ball's flight, and cap in hand, stabbed at the ball. He felt it break into the cap as he plummeted down toward the grass. Dazed for an instant from the fall, he got up, raised the cap in his hand to indicate that he had caught it. Stumpy waved back.

The machine hit another ball, this one going almost directly vertical, hanging over second base momentarily before its descent. Henry played it as he always played these high flies: he waited until it started to fall. But the ball seemed to hang by a force other than its own, and then, just as he began to punch his glove and start forward (for it had not traveled far linearly) toward second base, he was blinded. The sun was exactly behind the ball, just above it, so if Henry looked at the ball he had to stare at the artificial sun which, he observed, had suddenly spurted from its position far to the left. Now the ball was falling rapidly and the sun was, too, and he couldn't look. He had trotted up to just behind second base. Standing, looking away from but keeping the sun in his view. When it was just above his head, Henry stuck his glove upward. The ball plopped in. The sun, a large, bright circle, hovered around his waist, then rose rapidly toward the top of the dome again, moving to the far left.

"Damn," said Stumpy, leaning against the machine, and Henry wasn't sure of the tone. Was it congratulatory incredulity or disappointing disbelief? "Some catch," he said, cranking up the machine again. "Helluva catch." Well, that was a compliment, Henry decided, but before he could get back to deep center field, the machine had sent another ball out.

This was a whizzing, singing line drive coming straight at him, about two feet over his head, and he knew he wouldn't have time to take more than two steps back and leap. He did. The ball slapped into his glove. Its power knocked him to the grass. He wanted to smile but gritted his teeth to hold back his pleasure as he got up from his knees. Suddenly a loud buzzing in his glove. Pain sizzling through his hand and wrist, moving up to his forearm. Stumpy and the other players bending over with laughter. Electric shocks in his glove, and he stood paralyed, his arm palpitating involuntarily before he realized their joke, and he shook the glove off his hand, the ball still sticking to it. They were still laughing, now lying on the grass, and Stumpy was jumping up and down and spinning around and shaking his stubby arms, and Henry was standing there looking at them, wondering if he had made the team. Was this their decision, this laughter, glee, that they were so happy he had excelled?

"How . . . how . . . did you like that hot ball, Henry? Look at his face, guys. Oh, hohoho. I betcha never heard of a hot ball before, huh? Hahaha."

Henry smiled uncomfortably. "That was some trick, Stumpy. I've heard of a hot foot before but—"

"Oh, hohoho. He's heard of a hot foot, guys. Hahaha."

Now Henry had moved to the batter's box, was standing within a few feet of them as their laughter dissolved into quiet coughs, catchings of breath, *whees* and *oohs*.

"How did I do, Mister Stumpy?" Quiet. Just the hum of the batting machine's motor.

"Well, you need some work. You swing kind of wild and I don't like the way you play those fly balls, but . . . well, you know . . . the guys and I have to talk it over, Henry. . . . We'll be in touch," walking toward the clubhouse, then turning, and again Henry thought Stumpy was falling over on his bowlegs, stockings up to his thighs. "What did you bat for the Crowns?"

"Four fifteen. Sixty-three homers," Henry answered, watching the players lift Stumpy to their shoulders. He tried to look serious, because usually when he divulged these figures people exclaimed so much he had to smile with embarrassment.

"Not bad for the minors." Headed for the clubhouse.

"Uh . . . when can I expect to hear from you, Mister Stumpy?"

"Soon, kid, very soon." Voice disappearing, melting into the hollowness of the tunnel, and Henry standing with his hand still itching from the shock, his shoulders aching from the banging against the outfield wall. Standing, hoping, frowning. The grass smelled good.

5

"I DON'T THINK they will call you, Henry," she said. "It's been five weeks, and I don't think they will call you."

He was on his way out the front door. He stopped. They had been discussing the tryout with the Stars since he had awakened, and now he stood in the doorway, the door open a foot, and stared at Beatrice. So this was her conclusion, was it? She had given it? She felt he would never make the big time?

"They'll call me, baby, you just wait," he said, voice almost choking from emotion, as though he was the only person in the world who believed in himself now.

"They don't want you, Henry. Can't you see that? They're just playing with you—they don't want you."

"What are you talking about?" he said, thinking that he didn't need this, not this morning anyway, not on a Monday; not this discouragement to pile on the mountain of worries and fears crushing his shoulders. His voice was choking again, slipping away from his control so that his words faltered and had little power, as if the wind had been knocked out of his stomach and he was straining to get the words out despite a deficiency of air in his lungs. He closed the door. "These are the Stars, the American baseball team, Beatrice. Don't you understand?" Her eyes caught his. They were different. They weren't bright, weren't dancing or skipping, but sadly dim and listless, fixed not on his face but lower, on his chest. And her face: was it thinner? Her cheeks: had they deflated slightly? "Beatrice"—he moved toward her, put his hands around her waist—"look, this is the American pastime, they've got to be fair with me. They've got plenty of black ballplayers on teams, don't they? It can't be what you're thinking. They have to judge me on my ability only. That's all."

"I guess you're right," she said, touching the side of his face. They kissed. "They'll probably call you very soon," stepping back from him and turning into the other room. "Don't mind me."

He was in the hallway, making his way down the steps. Soon he was outside on the sidewalk. He had forgotten his earmuffs. He pulled them out of his pocket and stretched them over his head, but the drone and banging, although distant-sounding now, were still discernible. But instead of overpowering him, the barrage was like the hum of faraway gears and pumps and rattles. It looked like rain, but he could never be sure if the sky was overcast because of meteorological conditions or because the sun was shut out by the smoke and vapor that hovered hazelike over the city. Again he was in the crowd of morning walkers, and he slowed to almost a crawl as he squeezed into a space among the pedestrians. He bent over suddenly to cough because his nostrils were burning, stinging, and his throat felt clogged and heated as if he had swallowed some hot peppers. He coughed louder and faster, with more force, tears coming to his eyes and his cheeks swelling, his stomach muscles straining. Henry was coughing when he got to work; punched his time card; sat at his desk and pulled out his visor from a drawer.

Suppose, he thought, that Beatrice was right, that the Stars might not call him. With the Crowns, he had hit like a ferocious madman, fielding like stingy itself, running like a track star. Hadn't he done the same for the Stars?

He unbuttoned his shirt and looked around him. The man sitting in front of Henry had two quarter-moons of perspiration on the back of his shirt. On either side of him was a man, and he still, now that he thought of it, hadn't had a conversation with anyone since he had started working for Home. They were bent over their chairs and tinkered with their tools from a few minutes before starting time until a few minutes after the day had officially ended. Henry's forehead was becoming uncomfortably moist from the heat which was always incomprehensibly linked to the inexplainable pounding that reverberated throughout the auditorium. They too were hot, for he saw clearly the tears of perspiration falling from beneath their visors. In back of him was a woman. He caught her staring toward the ceiling, a smile on her lips. Was this the first time he had seen one of the employees show life? He pushed against the floor with his feet to whirl his chair around, and he wanted to introduce himself. But she didn't look up after staring, startled, in his face, making him feel that he had pulled up her dress in the middle of the street or performed some similar indiscretion. Instead she jerked her head down, with an effort so intentionally physical that her chin almost banged on the desk top. She wouldn't look up. Her fingers flicked busily around her tools, her brow was creased into a serious, permanent frown.

Henry looked at his work. He had four dozen hammock hooks on which he had to assemble spring-lock washers. Then he had a drawer full of double-roller catches. On these he was to check the rubber rollers for smoothness of operation. Also, he had some tubular mortise locks, and he reminded himself of his assignment for them: to test the pins in the tumbler cylinder. He liked the tools much more than he did his assignments, and the fact that he hardly, rarely—now that he thought about it, never—used them did not alleviate his fondness for those steel pieces. He liked the way they smelled and would often pull a squeeze-type rivet or a stud driver out of a lower drawer, and peeping around quickly, bend under his desk and put his nose close to the forged steel. The metallic smell, the oil, the strength and irresistibility of the dark metal would send an exhilaratingly refreshing chill through Henry's body. These odors were somehow cleaner and purer than the greasiness and oiliness that surrounded the room, and, too, they belonged to him. These were *his* tools—as long as he worked at Home. He owned them, protected them, cleaned them, directed them. Let's see, what do I have here—thinking to himself over that pumping and clanging which still had some clandestine location, some hole of habitation that seemed to be everywhere and yet was nowhere when he tried to find it. Here, he thought, fondling the rubber handles, is my wood chisel. And he reached down into another drawer, found his jointer and his push drill; reached into another and weighed his sliding T-bevel, his surface gauge and his micrometer.

His arms were wet from perspiration and shining from the cartons of fluorescent light. His face was hot, feverish almost, and as he began assembling his pieces, the perspiration rolled from his fingers onto the metal figures. He worked for twenty minutes, but his mind was drifting, so although he was staring straight at his hooks and washers as his wet fingers slipped over them, his eyes registered other scenes: of hitting those long balls at the Star Stadium and not being given a spot on the team right then; of trying to love Beatrice and each night falling asleep with a pulling on his mind that it should have been better; of living in the North for fourteen months and feeling the occasional urge to leave this place with its cold apartments and noise and crazy women and fog and mysterious inexplainables. But where would they go? And then his mind cleared, and he began to consider the hooks and the washers he worked with every day. Suddenly he was standing up, himself surprised at this boldness. He was pushing back his chair. Visor on the desk. He was walking up the aisle. *He* was doing this? He got to Boye's office, and then his balloon of courage seemed to have suffered a small puncture as he stood by the sign, stood wiping his neck and arms of perspiration and wondering why there was an instantaneous recall of his having stood in this same spot before—perhaps when as a fourth-grader he had to visit the principal?—and knowing that he couldn't have stood here before. He took a deep breath. Knocked on the door. Was invited in.

"What are we doing and what does it mean?" Henry asked before even closing the door behind him, already feeling the chilling evaporation of the air conditioning on his arms. He felt the veins in his temples go in and out. Boye was sitting sideways to the desk when Henry came in. He turned toward Henry, faced him while the small figure of front hair tilted to the side and then sprang up again, and Henry could see

plainly the pimples on the forehead shining under the fluorescent light. Henry observed he was putting something under
his desk. Photographs?

"Huh? Oh, hi, Henry. I'm going over some production reports," folding up what was unmistakably a newspaper and
sliding that under the desk.

"What are we doing, Mister Boye?"

"I just told you, I'm going over some production reports."

"No, I mean, what are we"—pointing toward the door—
"doing? Why are we putting these little pieces together and
where do they go afterwards? Why don't we ever use the
tools?"

"Have a seat, Henry, please," said Boye, slide rule now in
hand. He pulled out the middle dial. "It may seem senseless,
but every piece of work, every operation performed by Home's
dedicated and faithful workers is an inestimably important
contribution to the progress of this company. This is a great
company, and we are great because our people are great.
Such a large organization, complex in its far-reaching foreign
and domestic influence in the economic sector, understand-
ably has a myriad of seemingly furtive and clandestine assignments. But each part fits into the whole. Each screw goes in
a hole. Every hole has two halves, and a half-loaf is better
than a whole—if you're hungry. Uh, uh, see what I'm saying,
Henry? Each part—every contribution is valuable to this company, and that's what you should know, that you have a stake,
and if you do your—if you perform your tasks proportionately
and with dedication, Home will certainly reward you commensurately—both financially and promotionally."

The words—had he read them or heard them before? *Reward you commensurately . . . dedicated and faithful workers . . . economic sector.* They had a familiar rhythm and
sound to them; even the spacing of the breath and the accent-
ing of certain syllables were familiar. Henry didn't know what
to say. How could he, staring blankly at the pimples on Boye's
face—how could he respond? He really hadn't come in here
on his own, anyway. Some specter of a presence had encouraged this display of boldness, and now that he was here, had
blurted out his question, had received an answer—now what?

Boye was tapping his slide rule on the desk. An ink spot on his gray shirt pocket. Licking his lips. Who is he, sitting here in front of me? What does he do, and why? Could he, Henry, ask him questions, make him smile, get him angry? Yes, he is white and that means automatically a distance. And did he know nothing more about us than those photographs of the pantyless black woman with her legs in the air? Did he have problems with his landlord and his heating, and did he get crushed by women in the subways? Did he want to follow the sway of strange women's hips up alleys too? Did he—

"Mister Boye—" Knocking on the door.

"Come in."

"Mister Boye—" It was one of the employees Henry had seen around, but every time Henry had advanced toward him in a hallway or even in the men's room, the man had scurried away, sometimes almost tripping down the stairs, and looking around as if he were being followed, profile of a face glancing over his shoulder past Henry. He was standing, fingers excited, twittering at his side as if they contained the urgency of his message. The top of his shirt dark with perspiration, and his green visor shaded his face. "It's Eldred Hicks, sir . . . seat . . . seat four eighty-two, and Jessie Newton, seat one-oh-five-eight. They've collapsed from the heat, lying on the ground. Call the ambulance?"

"First, see if they can get up—fan them a little. If that doesn't work, call the infirmary, but get clearance from Personnel and Practices first. Also, call Work and Time to have their time sheets nullified. Make sure you get Benefits, too, and have their files forwarded to my desk."

"Yes, sir."

"Uh, Jackson—"

"Yes, sir?"

"How many does this make for the month?"

"About thirty-two, sir."

"Damn. How am I gonna reach my quota?"

"I don't know, sir."

"Okay, that's all," Boye said, turning now to Henry, who was telling himself casually that he had just heard two more reports of employees collapsing from the choking, stuffy heat of the auditorium. And many times he himself had seen them collapse, tumble over on their desks or fall on the cement floor. A man in a white suit marching snappily from a side door would drag them to a rear door. Before the afternoon was over, the worker, perspiring and fingers working frantically, would be back at his desk.

He wanted to ask Boye about those exhausted capitulations to the heat. Why didn't Home turn down the temperature? Where was the banging and knocking coming from? Why was the workroom so trashy and the outside of the building so dull, so gray? And why hadn't Henry noticed these things before? Why hadn't he thought about them? He wasn't sure he could ask. After all, he was in this office because of some strange impulse, and not because he had bravely decided that he had to have answers. Answers!

But if he didn't talk to Boye, with whom could he speak? Then the strangest thought caught his attention. Whom could he talk with anyway? He didn't even know anyone in the entire city. The super? No, Alvarez spoke little English and would probably call his dog on Henry. The women next door? He still couldn't find their apartment. The little Hurt girl? That child! So it had to be Beatrice. But lately he could not talk with her, for she was fidgety—running from one room to the other, jumping out of bed in the middle of the night, disagreeing with him on every matter. And late in the evenings they stared at television, listened to the women in their bathroom behind the television wall, tolerated the vibrating bass of the record player in the apartment below them, woke up some mornings with the two bathroom spigots spilling only cold water; and they picked up chips of plaster fallen to the floor from the still-unrepaired ceiling. And of course, after making love, he would roll away, unsatisfied with the mediocrity of his pleasure and exasperated, too, that she through it all would be gasping and kicking and stretching her arms out as if it were the most torturously ecstatic experience she had ever undergone. He didn't want to tell her that he was envious, that he could not match her feeling.

"Henry, tell me about yourself. You promised me a whole life story," she had been saying just two days ago, "and you haven't told me. I know very little about you, Henry."

But nobody did, really, and he wanted to talk with someone today, now. He didn't even care if the person didn't listen, wasn't interested—he wouldn't mind if the person yawned in his face. But he wasn't enjoying his wife and he wasn't sure if what he wanted to do more than anything—to play ball— would be possible now. Suppose Beatrice was right? Suppose they wouldn't let him play, regardless of how good he was? But why not? Never mind why not, suppose they just wouldn't let him? Then what? What was his life? What could he do? Who would he be? A worker at Home?

"When do you think I'll be up for a promotion, Mister Boye?" He himself was startled. Had he asked? . . . did those words . . . was he . . . Henry, did you . . . ?

Boye, patting his rise of hair, surprising Henry with his calm, spoke: "Well, you have to be patient, Henry. We have to have time to evaluate your performance, and you haven't been working for us that long. You know, I started with this outfit the year Josh Gibson hit that ball—"

Henry jumped up. "Josh Gibson!" he shouted, blood rushing to his temples. "You know about Josh Gibson?"

"Do I?" said Boye. "Do you? You know about Josh Gibson?"

"Do I know about Josh," said Henry, and he was smiling, laughing out the words excitedly. Boye might not be such a bad guy after all, despite those photographs. He knows about the black baseball teams?

"What I was going to say is that I joined Home the year Josh Gibson hit that fair ball out of the stadium."

"In nineteen thirty-four," said Henry, "and he hit ninety home runs in a year."

"Eighty-nine," corrected Boye, face tinted blue by the fluorescence. Then they both laughed and Henry sat down and they stared at each other over the desk. They smiled, talked rapidly, and Henry's toes were uncontrollable, wriggling in his shoes.

"How do you know about him?" asked Henry, chin stretched forward and almost lying on the desk.

"He ain't the only one I know about. I saw Satchell Paige *pitch.*"

"Get out of here," said Henry, praying that Boye was telling the truth. "You *saw* him pitch?"

"Listen," he said (patting his hair, Henry thought, like Stuff used to pat his dog), hand circling above his head now, "I've seen him throw his wobbly ball. Goes like this—" hand churning out figure eights and circles. "His fast ball has a double hop on it, and that bat badger—that bat badger was a bitch. It was a bitchy badger."

"Where did you see him throw?"

"In Cleveland, when he first came up. But I used to watch the Elite Giants and the Homestead Grays every time they came to town when I was younger."

"Who else did you see?" asked Henry, his voice loud, excited. "Did you ever see Cannonball Dick Redding? How about Cool Papa Bell steal second base in five seconds? You ever see him?" Imagine that, thought Henry, all this time we've been in the same building and he knows about the old black baseball teams. He might not be so bad. Henry stared at Boye. His Adam's apple was pushing against his throat, he was clearing his throat, too, and Henry had the uneasy feeling that Boye was losing his composure; not quite breaking down as Henry had done when he had discovered Stuff's dog in the road, but as if the weight of something had been circling Boye's shoulders and now was descending—had descended— with an unexpected force. So Boye was trying to fight it away, was he? Henry watched Boye lift his chin forward with another clearing of the throat. Finally, he went into his pocket, and pulling out a handkerchief and complaining about a cold, blew his nose. Now what was the story? Certainly the memory of the old black ballplayers wasn't doing this to him. Henry looked to one side, became intensely interested in a gray spot on the wall, examined the frame holding the president's picture.

"I . . . I've been here for almost forty years, Henry," he said, mouth full of saliva. "Josh Gibson is gone and I'm still here. I've come a long way . . . started out as a messenger . . . now . . . now I'm supervisor."

Was this, then, what he had to look forward to? If he didn't make the team, was he to have nothing larger in his entire life than becoming supervisor in this loud, strange building? And how long would it take him to make supervisor? And what did that mean—being a supervisor? What would he be,

94

how would he feel, where could he go, what would it mean?

"Uh . . . uh, how long did it take you to become a supervisor, Mister Boye?"

"I worked hard and long for this company. I've been supervisor for thirty years, Henry."

"Where do you go from supervisor? After you get promoted," Henry asked. For the first time, he was talking with someone at Home and his questions were being answered.

"I'm not getting promoted, damn it," shouted Boye, rising, standing over Henry so that the leather case on his waist was at Henry's eye level. "I'll be here for the rest of my life," he said, slamming his palm down on the desk. "I've been here for thirty years supervising and I'll be here for thirty more years sitting at this same damn desk. I'll be a lifetime supervisor. I'm finished. Thirty years ago they decided that I didn't have it to become an executive."

Silence. The hum of the air conditioner. Boye, leaning over, chest lifting and falling from the heavy breathing, relocated the trophy on his desk. Henry shuffled his feet. Boye sat down.

"And as to your questions when you first came in, I don't know the answers, Henry. I don't really know *what* we're doing. Or what it means. Or what I'm doing and if that means anything. I'm supervising. And I get paid for it."

"What?" Henry stood now, and he had already decided not to try to speak right away because he could feel his voice slipping away from him. He blinked his eyes, which were clouding. "What?" he repeated. "You . . . you don't know. . . ."

Boye's face had turned pink, and Henry couldn't decide if Boye was nervous because he had disclosed something he should not have or if he was nervous because it was painful for him. Henry remained silent, his legs crossed. Let him go on. And as Boye continued, talking about his life at Home and how he was going to remain a supervisor for the rest of his life, and that he had nothing different or new to expect, that his life was nothing more than waking up, going to work, coming home, that he wasn't sure there was any sense, any rationality in his routine, that he was nobody, almost—as Boye continued with his delivery, Henry felt panicky. Yes, he too was scared and jittery, and now the banging and pumping seemed to be embedded within the ceiling over Boye's head, his vision seemed to be cruising away from him (Boye was a figure like the shadow of Peters melting down that hallway), and the words, Boye's words, came out indistinctly. Was Boye saying that the tools, then, the tools that every worker had in his desk, were for no purpose at all? Was he saying that he was just as puzzled about the noise, that banging and pumping, as Henry had been? And the trash on the floor? The workers fainting, too?

"I'm just here for the rest of my life, Henry . . ." Boye was continuing.

Oh, God, what was he to do? Suppose he didn't—and the possibility seemed less remote than he had previously imagined—suppose he didn't make the Stars? Just suppose he didn't? He had never thought of that really happening. And in his talks with his father, they had never discussed *if*. What could he do? What did he know? Not a damn thing but taking fish to the dump and trying to sell encyclopedias. I want to live well and take care of Beatrice and maybe be able to send some money back to the folks, he thought, gritting his teeth as if someone were contesting him. That's all I want: just for things to mean something, to make sense. But if Boye can't do it . . . can I? If he's bewildered, why shouldn't I be? I can't stay here. This is all stupid and Boye knows it, he just told me. And there's no chance for me. We were talking about baseball and then he started thinking about how long he's worked here and told me everything. If he told me, maybe he can help me. Tell him you like baseball. Tell him you *play* baseball. That'll do it. Yes. Yes, Henry, yes, dammit. Now. Clear up your head. Tell him.

"I'll probably be leaving soon anyway to—"

"Leaving?" Boye unbuttoned the top of his shirt. His mouth hung open for seconds. "Leaving here? For what?"

"To play ball if I make the team. I had tryouts with the Stars. That's why I came up North. I thought I told you at the interview. All I want to do is play baseball. That's all I want to do in my life—play ball."

"Can you . . . can you play well enough . . . to . . . ?" Boye fumbled with his slide rule, couldn't seem to keep it in his hands. So Henry told him about his high-school career, about his being recruited, about the tryout. Tell him all, he thought, tell him all. Not looking directly at Boye, Henry still could see that the man was interested, was holding on to every word. He told him about the leaks from the ceiling; about Alvarez's dog; about Betty Hurt; about the women living in the same building and how yet he had never found them. And then—Beatrice and that problem. Should he reveal that too? Maybe Boye had some weird, freakish solution. Maybe Boye knew a good doctor—a psychiatrist if necessary. It was silent again, just the hum of the air conditioner while Henry, his arms between his knees, sat thinking and looking at the scuff marks on the front of the desk. No, not now, he decided, shoulders already lighter, mind looser and unclogged.

"I don't know, Henry," said Boye. "I just don't know if it looks good for you with the Stars. They probably won't call you." Tapping his slide rule. "Um"—wriggling in his chair—"did you really hit four-fifteen for the Crowns, Henry? That's —that's pretty good, if you did."

"Sure," said Henry, "those pitchers were weak."

"Well, you might not make the team—I mean, the Stars only want the best. You might have to stay here and hope things work out, Henry. What will you do if you don't make the team?"

A knock on the door. Another worker Henry had seen before, face punctuated with perspiration blots, standing and puffing out his words.

"The president is on his way to give his annual Christmas message, Mister Boye. Mister Peters sent me in to get you."

"Be right there," said Boye, standing, bending his arm into the sleeve of his jacket, patting his hair. "Let's go, Henry," and the three of them filed through the door. "This is your first Christmas with us, Henry," he said, over his head, Henry walking behind him, "but this will give you an idea of what interest our executives take in the employees. Every year the president comes down, takes valuable time away from his work just to deliver the Christmas message. He's a grand old man, you'll see," stepping over a discarded can. "Watch your step." Henry rubbed his eyes to accustom them to the darker light of the workroom.

Several desks had been pushed away to provide an open space, and the employees surrounded this space in a semicircle. Henry and the other worker joined the group; Boye walked to the desk that had been set up to face the workers.

He sat on the desk and brushed lint off from his knee, straightened the collar of his jacket, adjusted the pen-and-pencil holder in his shirt pocket. He looked down at his shoes, then at his white socks, then pulled down his pants leg to cover the six inches of exposed leg—an odd pink color, thought Henry, and plenty of hair.

Henry had eased into the crowd with the other employees and was watching Boye now over the shoulder of one. He looked around him. Their faces were dull and gray under the dim fluorescent lights, and they stared ahead, stared through him with a heavy muddiness in their expressions that left Henry empty. Did they ever smile? he wondered. At least back home people would speak to you whether they knew you or not. He turned around. He knew they were all staring at Boye, and he knew Boye was sure he was the center of attraction. Henry shifted his feet, wiped the perspiration off his face. Looked at Boye again, who had his slide rule out this time and was performing what appeared to be an enormously complicated operation.

Then the door, the wide, black, steel swinging door without the EXIT sign over it, opened mightily. Henry turned in that direction, feeling that five hundred heads had turned in the same direction with his, almost making a single sound of motion (swishing) in the change of direction. It was Peters, pipe in hand, smile wider than Henry had ever seen it, coming through and kicking a mound of dirt out of his path, then turning, holding the door open with two hands, and announcing, "Here comes the president."

A murmuring in back of Henry. A few pushing hands against his shoulders. Boye was at perfect attention. Henry was reminded as he stood there staring expectantly at the rectangle of darkness, stood there leaning forward with the drumming in his ears—waiting, waiting—of the way that baseball fans lean forward in their seats to watch players come out of the dugout. He was on his tiptoes. Peters was still smiling, and

98

Henry could barely see his eyes because of the distance, so it seemed that, from where Henry stood, there were two splotches of black on either side of Peters' nose.

"Here he comes," said Peters, bending over and peeping at the dark entrance of the door. "Here comes our president." Voice musical, especially at the end, where he stretched each syllable of the last word, reminding Henry of the times Sissy Linda would sing out: "I'm gonna tell on you . . . ooh . . . ooh." Again Henry was pushed from the rear, and this time he could feel the expectation around him. He concentrated on the space again. The jacket ends of Peters' suit rose above his waist as he bent forward, his upper body pushed forward and invisible as he leaned into the dark entranceway. "Here he comes," he said again, this time the voice echoing metallically, and he was jumping back into the workroom, pushing the door with him as he came in again. Now, standing in the doorway, holding the large door with one hand, his other up above his head, thumb sticking out and waving backward: "He's coming." And he jumped out of the way as two blond sticks thumped the floor of the entranceway, and standing between the sticks—crutches—his shoulders leaning forward, was the president.

He came out of the darkness, the thumping of the crutches strangely in time with the banging throughout the room; came into the lighter dimness and stood in the entrance. Two men, one on each side of the president, lurked in the background, and it was only when the president decided to take one more step and looked backward that Henry understood these men to be his assistants. Each one moved a crutch delicately forward, then they stepped to the back and eased the president's back ahead so that his body was straight.

Peters, Boye right behind him, moved over to shake the president's hand. The right-hand assistant raised the president's into Boye's. Then Boye stretched his arm in the direction of Henry and the other workers. They moved toward the desk, and Henry stretched forward to get a better look. As they approached the desk, Peters faced the employees and began clapping his hands furiously. Soon Henry found himself and the other workers applauding the president.

He was wearing a bow tie, and Henry had seen bow ties before (had even worn one himself)—on his high-school principal and on a violinist who had gotten lost in town one day on his way to Jackson—but this one was thinner and shorter than those he had seen before. On the president's lapel Henry noticed a plastic nameplate, but squinting as well as he could, he couldn't read the printing. His suit, gray, was wrinkled, particularly in the pants, where around the knee Henry observed a drooping, puffy bagginess. His lips were thin and tight, his chin was doubled, and on either side of his upper lip there was a patch of mustache as large as a Chiclet. Cheeks: fluffy, saggy, like the rolls of plumpness on chubby women's thighs exposed on low subway seats. He had no hair, and even in the dullness of the weak fluorescent lighting the skin of his head glistened. But what surprised Henry was the lack of resemblance this president had to the man whose photograph was in the annual report. This president was much older. When had that photograph been taken, during his college years? Henry started to ask the man at his side if he had noticed the difference, but then he remembered that all the workers he had approached usually scuttled away from him as if being paged by an inaudible voice. So, face still stung by the heat and the drumming pandemonium rhythmically beating above him, he watched the group of men at the desk.

"Before the president says a word or two," began Peters, taking one step forward (and Henry could see much better the thick symmetrically angled eyebrows), "he just asked me to get you all in the holiday mood by leading you in a song." He unbuttoned his suit jacket. "He especially likes 'What Christmas Means to Me.' Shall we sing that? Come on, now." Arms going up in a conductor's pose, he began:

> *Candles burning low*
> *Lots of mistletoe*
> *Lots of snow and ice*
> *Everywhere we go*

But he was getting no response, and it was just his voice alone, echoing over the humming of the machines. He began to stutter and his voice lowered, his arms flapped, losing the brisk, quick movement they had originally. "Come on now, folks, this is the *president's* favorite. Come on. . . . 'Choirs singing carols, right outside my door.' . . ." Still little response except for a few voices Henry heard in the rear, but they sounded out of tune, and the different melodies sent the voices crashing into each other.

Henry wanted to sing. Back home they would gather by the stove and sing those songs; the candles, Sissy Linda clowning around, Joe Boy doing the jig, their voices . . . their voices . . . what were they doing now? Would they have a nice sing this year? God, he and Beatrice hadn't even been to church.

"Well, come on now. What kind of holiday spirit is this? Let's get into it," roared Peters, swinging his arms emphatically, taking a step forward, too, bending forward also, his eyebrows jumping up and down. "Let's *go*. Let's do 'Silver Bells,' another of the president's favorites. Come on," taking a big breath that lifted him to his toes. " 'City sidewalks, busy sidewalks' . . . Come on, now . . . 'dressed in holiday style' . . . that's it, you're getting it. . . . 'In the air there's a feeling of Christmas' . . . okay! 'Children laughing, people passing, meeting smile after smile' . . . yes! Now a little louder. Put your hearts into it now; get in the spirit! . . . 'And on every street corner you'll hear . . . silver bells, silver bells, it's Christmastime in the city' . . . yes, that's it; now another chorus . . . 'silver bells . . . silver bells. . . .' "

The voices, at first separate like the slaps of single hammers banging, were added to until they were no longer distinct, off-key, stumbling elements; they caught up with each other—and Henry had rolled back his head, closed his eyes, sang with them—so that they sounded together, single, a chorus. So there were two strains of sounds now in the workroom: the metallic drumming and hammering of the invisible machines and the resonant, lively singing of the workers. Warmed up, they sang another song, "Jingle Bells."

Peters bowed, thanked them, stepped back and whispered to the president, who was sitting on the desk, his trouser cuffs having risen to the beginning of his calves where his garters, supporters of his white socks, showed. The president smiled, but Henry noted that he didn't open his mouth; instead, he pushed the corners of his lips upward, inflating his cheeks. Then Boye came over and slapped Peters on his back. Peters came out to the front of the opening again.

"The president asks me to tell you how much he enjoyed that beautiful rendition of 'What Christmas Means to Me,'" he said. "And now, before the awards for the best service are presented, the president will say a few words." Again he clapped his hands vigorously, imploring the employees to follow his example. They did, Henry joining in the effort.

The president was eased off the top of the desk by his two assistants and Boye. Standing up, he leaned precariously to one side. One assistant, pointing his body almost diagonally, held his weight against the crutch until the president was able to control his balance again. Then, bending and contorting his arm, the president wiped the perspiration from his head and neck with a handkerchief and almost lost his balance. Henry patted his face and neck with his hand. The president cleared his throat. He opened his mouth, his lips moved, then stopped, and he looked expectantly at the crowd of workers. Henry hadn't heard a word, so he turned to both sides. The other workers were turning, too, as if to ask what had been said.

"He says the company that sings together works together," said Peters, stepping in front of the president.

And the president continued like that—speaking in soft, inaudible phrases as if he were afraid to open his mouth, and Peters, after Henry and the other workers had stood without comprehending, would step in front of the president to explain his comments. Henry soon lost interest in the talk and his mind drifted off into his own world with his own problems. Occasionally a phrase from Peters' interpretation would slip through to Henry, and he picked up parts of the speech: *When I started this company . . . dedicated employees . . . quality and control . . . Home is your home. . . .* He was trying to deal with the disconcerting jumble of his life and so, as he always found it best to do, consciously willed his mind to superimpose another vision. He wasn't asleep, no; he wasn't' unconscious either of what was going on before him. But somehow it didn't have much to do with him; had *nothing* to do with him. These men standing in front of all these people who themselves were just as enigmatic as the men—what could they give him, what could they offer? There were other things to consider, things which were swelling up inside him, boiling now, and he needed this respite, this retreat from the demand of focusing on them, to think. So his eyes were closed. The rhythm of Peters' words sent him rocking into contemplation.

Boye, the first man he had really spoken to—confessed to, would be a better word, he thought—had suddenly changed during their conversation. The initial honesty which had drawn Henry out seemed to have been reversed. There he was, telling Henry that there was no future for him at Home—if, indeed, he had to stay (and suppose he had to?)—and later, as if he had let the cat out of the bag, speaking of Henry's possibilities with the company. Boye has been here too long not to know this place inside out, he decided. He knows this place. He knows it, and he probably knows that the tools we have mean nothing, were never meant to be used. And he knows what the purpose is for the work we're doing; or knows that it has no purpose. And the change he went through when I told him the Stars might draft me: was he jealous? He doesn't want me to leave, doesn't want me to make the team and become a star. He's been stuck here all these years and to see me get away . . . of course! He'll try to keep me here. He's lonely, got those photographs of black women in his desk and thought I'd like them; remembers the old black baseball teams and that's what got him talking, and he probably talked too much—dropped a Texas leaguer, committed an error—and is sorry. Watch out for Boye, he told himself. Watch out. He wants to keep me here, and I don't like this place at all. I don't like these people.

They were applauding, intercepting him from his contemplative journey, so that now he was fully aware of what was happening in front of him in the space set aside for the president and his associates. The president had finished his speech and they were applauding. Henry clapped his hands also.

He watched Peters take the center again. "And now"—speaking slowly, pipe between the fingers of his left hand, and drawing on it after every two words—"and now we have the annual presentation of awards." His hand slid inside his jacket, pulled out and unfolded a sheet of paper. "I have the names here of Home employees . . . [draw, draw] who have distinguished themselves . . . [draw] throughout the year, who have performed . . . [draw] meritoriously and faithfully the complicated and significant operations which Home is responsible for . . . for which Home is responsible. Mister President," he continued, stepping backward, "may I have the first medal for longest consecutive number of days reporting on time." The president turned frowning, looking at Boye, who moved over to him and pointed at an outside jacket pocket. The president fumbled with his right pocket until an assistant reached in and pulled out a box the size of a cigarette pack. "Thank you, Mister President," said Peters, bowing. "I am honored to name"—snapping the paper in his hands, pipe in mouth—"Miss Lucy Taylor as the recipient. She reported on time three hundred and nineteen days consecutively, and was only late four seconds on the three hundred and twentieth day. Lucy, come forward, dear. Where are you, Lucy? Don't be bashful, Lucy. Step out here and get this medal engraved with your name."

Henry instinctively turned around. Everyone was turning around, facing the rear of the crowd. Nobody was trying to get toward the front. Henry turned back with everyone else to face the space of executives. Boye was whispering in Peters' ear, his hand covering half his own face. Peters whispered in Boye's ear. Then Peters faced the workers.

"It seems that Lucy Taylor had to go to the infirmary. Now let's get on with our second award, the special Ezekiel P. Bloomruth prize for the highest production quota in a month during the past year. This one"—drawing on his pipe—"goes to Herman Anders, seat seven hundred and twelve, for the largest production number in the month of May. Herman, come on out here—let's give Herman a hand—come on out here, Herman." Peters took another box from the president's assistant, and he opened it, smiled at it, then stood, smiling at the workers. Henry applauded with the crowd and looked around also for Herman. The clapping trickled into silence. No one stepped forward. Boye whispered to Peters. Peters whispered back. Henry wiped his forehead, felt the uncomfortable easing of perspiration down his arms. "Well, it looks as if Herman was taken to the infirmary just this morning. The president wishes me to thank you all for your participation in this impressive spirit of corporate togetherness, and he looks forward to seeing you again next Christmas. But remember, his door is always open, feel free to visit him any time. Thank you, Mister President."

He was between his assistants still, and when Peters turned to thank him, he was sitting on the desk and swinging his legs, patting his face with a handkerchief, head wagging, reminding Henry of an apple on a stick.

"Thank you, Mister President," Peters repeated, and then the president squirmed and twisted until his assistant helped him down and the three of them went out the thick, dark door. The other workers scraped their feet, turned in different directions, marched to their respective desks.

Henry stood by himself, feeling like the lone member of a scattered herd of sheep. He put his hands in his pockets. Boye and Peters stood by the desk that had been temporary headquarters for the ceremonies, and they were staring at Henry. They faced each other but were looking at him, glancing at him from the side; Peters with his pipe, eyebrows hovering low over his eyes, one hand on Boye's shoulder and his right leg crossing his left, while Boye had his hands on his hips, jacket pushed back so that Henry could see the leather holder for the slide rule against Boye's hip. They took a few steps, moving in a semicircle, still glancing at Henry and frowning, both of them. Henry decided to turn toward his desk. Boye was probably telling Peters about him. They were talking about him just twenty or so feet away and didn't even try to conceal it. Henry turned his back to them—he thought that's how they should understand his gesture—and he wanted badly to stick out his rear end as Sissy Linda had done so many times to him when, she would explain, he had "just got on my nerves." Then she would add, "You kiss what I twist and I don't mean my wrist."

He would go to the bathroom first. He took the door at the side of the one through which the president had exited. A dark hallway, the door behind slamming shut as if it would never open again. He checked the handle. It did open. He closed it again. Then he bent over and stuck out his rear at the door, a symbol of Boye and Peters. He straightened up, turned and stuck out his tongue at the door. Again he turned around, bent over and pointed his rear at the door, this time shaking it back and forth and, lips pursed, made sputtering noises. He was doing this—wagging his rear at the door (Boye and Peters) and sputtering with his lips—when he caught the movement of shadows down the hall. Two legs; a waist; chest; neck; head. A man; one of the workers. Henry stood, started toward the employee, and his neck was now hotter than it had been all day.

"Doing some exercises," he said, forcing a smile, face twitching with embarrassment.

The man shrugged his shoulders, turned and began down the hall. Henry went after him.

"Some Christmas ceremony, huh?" He cupped his hands to his mouth. The man sped up, elbows held high. He turned a corner.

"What section are you working for?" yelled Henry, picking up speed, sliding past the turn, turning and running up the other hallway. Their footsteps echoed down the ceiling, down the walls. "Do you like working here?" he shouted, picking up speed. The man looked over his shoulder and turned left through another door. Henry followed. "Why are we doing this? Have you ever thought about that—what this all means?" His sentences were coming slower. Now the man, his jacket flung to the floor, was moving much faster. He came to a landing of steel stairs and went up them, his feet banging metallically against the stairs' edges. He didn't use the railing. Henry followed, yelling, "I bet you don't use your tools either, do you? Well, do you?" But when he got to the top of the landing and watched the fleeing employee scramble to his right through another door with the red EXIT sign above it, Henry slipped on the highest step and his knee banged against the cement landing; his ankle, the one injured on his first day of work, twisted. He grabbed it in pain, fell to a squat on the steps. The man slammed the door and the noise seemed to reverberate up

Henry's ankle. He stood and looked around, tried out his leg, the knee still stinging. He could walk. Where was he? He couldn't hear a thing. Even the banging and clamoring were gone. He cleared his throat. It echoed, seemingly going in two directions—down the steps and along the halls of the other floor, and up the steps, along the halls of the landing on which he stood, and even then splitting, going to the left and to the right. Immediately this divided repercussion settled into what seemed to Henry an eerie soundlessness. He limped toward the left hallway, deciding that the worker wouldn't speak to him even if he could catch the man. Another steel door, and again it closed as if it would never open again.

Another long hallway, but this one full of light, almost white, almost too much light, and Henry had to squint his eyes at the brightness. Also—he frowned—wasn't it cooler? Yes, there was no oppressive heat, and the coolness was stinging the perspiration on his arms and face. On his right was a door, but this one was wooden, normal-looking, with a brass knob. He stepped toward it. Voices, muffled.

". . . And that's what we have to do. It's the only way I can see it."

"But suppose he gets to the other workers before we can handle things?"

"He won't, we'll be sure of that. If you hadn't opened your big mouth, Boye, he never would have started thinking. This error in decision-making will adversely affect your promotional review coming up soon."

"That's how he got me to talking."

"What?"

"Never mind."

Henry sprang away from the door on his toes. His breath came irregularly. They—it sounded like Boye and Peters and another man—were definitely talking about him. They were planning something. They were suspicious of him. He forced himself to approach the door again.

". . . The other workers start thinking, it'll be a mess. We'll have a shitstorm on our hands. If it hits the fan—"

"I told you not to hire that bastard. He looked suspicious to me during the interview. I didn't like his teeth."

"He looked pretty dumb to me. It's Boye's fault."

Henry tiptoed away again. He got to the landing and eased down the steps, turned up a hallway. All the hallways looked the same, but somehow, as if in his frenzy to get back to the workroom he was possessed of an extradirectional ability, he was able to get back to the thick, heavy door (deliberately stepping on the jacket thrown down by the employee he had chased) that led to the auditorium. He opened it, and consciously not limping, headed for his desk. Glancing at Boye's office, he noticed the door was wide open. The other employees glanced at him and stared back at their work desks. Ten minutes later, after having sat at his desk transfixed, attempting to rearrange his psychological bearings, he rose with the other workers at the sound of the bell signaling the end of the workday.

6

IN THE TWILIGHT, by himself and away from the other workers, Henry Adams stopped to look up at the sky. It was dove-gray. How could he like that sky with its ripples of fading light? But standing in the entrance of a closed-up restaurant, he felt a kinship with it. There was nothing bright about it, nothing cheerful or communicative. It was distant, alone, somber; he was also. He wanted to be by himself, wanted to think things out and enjoy the odd pleasantness of his mood. It was good to feel bad. But he wasn't alone. Chimes, bells, loud voices, car horns, tambourines filled the streets and added to the usual turbulence. And recorded music scattering up the avenues. Pedestrians stumbled down the sidewalks with large boxes against their chests. And it wasn't until he saw the thin man in the Santa Claus suit across the street did he remember that Christmas was near. He liked that, too—that Christmas, season of gaiety and good tidings, was approaching, and he was feeling like a dog without its master. The pedestrians weren't smiling; no, they were still bumping into one another as he had always known them to do, and with the packages in their hands the crowdedness was increased, but still he could detect a bounce in the walks, a hopefulness in the faces. Henry felt weak. It seemed to him that a hole was left in his midsection where all spirit had flowed out, and there was no way he could ally himself with these people and their Christmas. Again he was glad of the hole, the void of feeling, for it gave him something to concentrate on, and he could nurse himself. The beautiful sense of dread. He could care about himself. He was infirm inside and ailing, and the sky with its allying drabness plus the spirit of the music and the voices with their conflicting cheerfulness—both elements allowed him to feed upon them. And he did. And felt more melancholy. His chest was hot and tight. But out of the despondency grew a therapeutic sense of overcoming, a hope that things would be better and that this funereal melancholy was only temporary.

Sure, he had been in these states before, and they seemed immutably keyed to certain music inexplainably part of his blood. So standing in front of the store, fists stuffed in his coat pockets, his mind drifted back, drifted. . . .

> *The day is done, night comes down,*
> *You are a long ways from home.*

Yeah, he liked that one. And what about

> *Woke up this morning, feeling sad and blue,*
> *Didn't have nobody to tell my troubles to.*

His father, almost flat broke and not a job in sight, taught him

> *Oh me, oh my*
> *Wonder what will become of poor me.*

Those were the songs he should be singing, he believed, not this mistletoe stuff. He decided to walk up the street and had taken only a half-dozen steps before he was hit in the head by a box attached to a pedestrian's shoulder. The pedestrian kept walking. At the corner Henry noticed a man selling Santa Claus balloons. Walking carefully across the street, and although bumped gratuitously he reached the pavement. All the stores were selling something related to Christmas. Henry stopped to examine a battery-powered tree that promised to disintegrate on New Year's Day. He saw a plastic tree-stand that could be converted into a chair after the holidays; re-usable cards coated with invisible ink for signature erasures; an electric Santa Claus guaranteed to climb down small chimneys; chimes, bells, tinsel wreaths, holly, lights ("with psychedelic yuletide colors"), artificial snow (that actually melted), candles, incense.

He would have to leave Home. Almost as if his mind had gone blank and somebody had slapped him, the thought hit Henry as he listened to the mournful lyrics of a Salvation Army band. He would have to; there were no two ways about it. They—Boye and Peters and who knows how many others—had a plan for him, and the only way to gain the advantage was to quit. Leave them. *Leave them.* They'll see me on television one day going back for a drive with *homer* written all over it, and I'll spring up from nowhere and snag it; then while I'm in the air, I'll be sure to smile right at the camera so they'll see me. Bastards.

But then what will I do? He was putting his earmuffs on, for the pandemonium of the streets, now that the end of the workday had come, was deafening. And he felt sorry for the band, fighting against the bellow of car horns and brakes, the vocal artillery of street merchants and the continuous thumping, clanging of construction machines. What *can* I do? Just get any old job until the Stars call me? He reached into his pants pocket, pulled out seven dollars. If he quit this week he'd have one day of pay coming to him and how long it would take to find another job to hold him over until . . . until they called him? And suppose they didn't? Just suppose they didn't and all that planning, all those dreams, all those evenings throwing the ball against the wall of their house; hitting stones in the field with a broom handle; throwing rocks at trees; practicing a slide in the middle of the road, dust seeping into his nostrils; suppose this—his entire life's plan—was all in vain?

He had never thought of doing anything else. And now, turning a corner just as the street lamp went on, he felt he knew how dreadful a fish stuck in the sand felt. Oh well, yes, he had almost finished high school, but he hadn't taken a college-prep course. He didn't know how to do *anything*—except work, and what did that mean, to work? He hadn't read a book in years. He wasn't interested in anything, really, remembering that for a week or so Little Stuff collected coins, then sold them all to pay for one meal for the entire family. And look, he told himself, lips moving in his silent monologue, nothing I can do can make me famous, known, or rich but baseball. If I can't do that . . . and maybe Beatrice will have to *work*. The air stung with cold but Henry's face perspired, and his hands were moist, and there was again that melting sensation around his heart, and he had a vision of that fish flapping on the sand, turning and jumping, pursed lips extended to a circle while bystanders stood, backs bent over. It wanted to get back to the water because it was there that it could breathe, live, *live*, and move. Henry could taste the sand on his lips. He didn't want to be a fish crawling in the sand. He dropped out of the crowd to lean against a light pole. He was breathing heavily.

Well, there was one approach he might try, he thought, breath coming easier now and the calm melancholy settling within him. I could write the Stars. I could write Stumpy and say that I need an answer and perhaps he had written the letter to me and the mailman had lost it. Henry's father would advise him against it. He would say that Henry was pushing and if the Lord wanted it— Yes! Of course! Naturally! Write them tonight. Get Beatrice—she had secretarial training—to compose a nice letter (his father would insist on its being a "nice" letter) to Stumpy. She was smart like that. Then—then he would have an answer. Then he could go barging into Boye's office, and when the supervisor stood up to protest Henry's indiscretion, Henry would throw down Stumpy's letter and say, "Read that," giving Boye *just* enough time to finish the letter, then snatch it up and stalk toward the door, turning as he was about to close it, saying calmly: "I quit." Boye's dandruff would be jumping, his pimples would burst.

And if Stumpy's letter wasn't affirmative, encouraging, positive? The smile—he hadn't realized his lips were parted—disappeared. He jumped away from the pole as a group of passers-by, faces hidden by boxes, aimed at him. The vision of his being a fish, gills scraping against the sand, loomed before him again. He would be destroyed if he had to flounder on the sand, and he would flounder if Stumpy didn't give him the nod. But why was he worried? Hell, he had demonstrated he could play, hadn't he? Why was he worried? They would treat him right, wouldn't they? Wouldn't they?

Back home, he thought, taking a turn at the corner, Sissy

Linda, Lil Stuff and Joe Boy were saving up their money to buy a present for Momma Lou and Daddy. They'd probably write him soon and ask Henry to send some money. He'd promised Stuff some alligator shoes, Joe Boy a bike, and Sissy an electric hair-dryer, for he had thought he'd be in the money now. They all were probably sitting around in the evenings and wondering what Henry and Beatrice were doing and why he had written them so seldom since he had left. This would be a nice time to see them, he thought, and if Stumpy would give him an answer before Christmas—what was it, two weeks away?—he could sign a contract and have some money and go down with presents for everybody. Two weeks away! Two weeks, and he had seven dollars and hadn't bought Beatrice a present yet. Jesus Christ, the noise. What can I get her? We should go to church.

The sky was darkening and the street lights were popping into brightness and the Christmas music, still fighting the hammering and banging throughout the streets, became louder. The noise seemed to seep into his bones. It was cold, but not uncomfortably so. Still, the stinging against his face helped to remind Henry that he was unstable, and his feet ached from the cold; and then suddenly, as if it was necessary for him to survey his entire body, he noticed that his fingers were bent from the cold, too. He stopped walking. Winding through his body was a heavy swell of loneliness, and it was coiling around his heart and his stomach. The drumfire of noise was concentrating on him, he felt. All the pedestrians were by design aiming themselves at him. It was too much for one man, he thought, certainly too much for him, and as a stream of images passed over his mind—the tryout, the truck accident, the train ride, the apartment's leaking, the soldiers—he stopped and leaned against a store window, felt dizzy. What was he to do?

> *Woke up this morning, feeling sad and blue,*
> *Didn't have nobody to tell my troubles to.*

He eased the lyrics over in his mind. But they were too accurate, seemed to point to his condition unmistakably, and before he could gather enough resolve to check himself he knew tears were filling his eyes. He sniffed and cleared his throat, and then, walking blindly up the street, body rubbing against the windows, he wiped his eyes with the sleeve of his coat. He coughed too.

Get yourself together, Henry, he told himself. Straighten up and fly right. Things get tight like that. Keep a song in your soul. You get a little down and out and then start crying like a baby. Suppose Beatrice had seen you? Don't be a whining boy. This is just temporary, that's all; just temporary. You can persevere, you can make it through if you try, just hold onto yourself. You'll be all right. But get a good grip on yourself, that's the secret.

Yes, hold on tight to yourself, he reiterated, rubbing a cold finger under his eyes, then blinking. After all, this is for Beatrice. I want it for her—everything, the simple, happy life. I can't break down now, especially since she's getting tired and frustrated herself. She's ready to call it quits; I saw it this morning in her eyes, heard it in her voice. I've got to hold onto my mind for her sake. I'm doing it all for her; everything is for her, Beatrice. He looked up in time to see the sign as he passed under it: FLOWER SHOP. He had never brought home any flowers to Beatrice. He entered the shop, and enjoying its warmth, decided to take his time choosing, finally picking out three red flowers and a yellow one from the glass case. Outside again, he stuck the package inside his coat and walked sideways to keep them safe. He decided to get some wine, too, and they would drink it in bed after dinner. He would put it in the refrigerator as soon as he got home. If he could sneak it in and then surprise her—no, she would go to the refrigerator before preparing dinner. They would have the lights out, too. He quickened his pace. Oh, it could be a beautiful night—and why couldn't they just talk? Why couldn't he just start and tell her about all the things that had happened to him from age six? Why couldn't he just do that? He'd wanted to since they'd been married. Tonight it could work, he thought, and his insides were relaxing now, for his mind was untumbling itself from the knot of confusion binding it just minutes ago. He knew he was smiling to himself. He realized too, that just as quickly as he had fallen into gloom, he had risen out of that gloom, and he accelerated his steps toward the liquor-store sign.

He bought a bottle of wine—"Christmas wine" on a special sale—and walking out of the store, promised himself he would cancel all thoughts of how he and Beatrice were to get along for the rest of the week with the few dollars he had left. He was trusting in some miraculous series of unforeseen events, a supernatural string of luck to bring him through what was clearly a crisis.

God, there must be thousands of things he hadn't talked to Beatrice about yet. They hadn't even decided how many children they should have. He wanted to explain to her how he could teach their son how to throw a baseball at age one. They must have a son. When he was seven years old, he had found a quarter under the rug one day and spent it all on candy, and his father had whipped him for a half-hour, after obtaining a confession at the dinner table by refusing to allow anyone to eat until "the thief" stood up. He would tell Beatrice that story. She'd like that, and with her strength insist probably that Henry should have held out a little longer—or gone without food. I'm going to talk to her all right, he promised himself, and we'll get high and make freakish love—on the kitchen table and leaning against the front door and—he bumped into a group of people and excused himself. Then he stopped. The muffled clanging in his ears grew uncontrollably louder with a new, terrifying thought. Beatrice would not be there when he arrived. He was perspiring again. He had no great reason to believe she would be there. In his mind, he saw an empty apartment. He would run down the halls shouting. And nobody would know anything. He had a vision of the Hurt girl giggling at him as he climbed the steps, knocked on the door—nothing. He could see Alvarez's dog lunging from behind the super's cracked door as Alvarez declared he "didn't know nothing." It would fit in, too, her disappearance, and seem almost naturally unnatural. Henry Adams picked up speed. He was taking a new route home, but he knew he was away from the outskirts and past the downtown area and should be fifteen minutes away from home.

He was slowed by a movie-house marquee glistening in the new darkness, its announcement—of burlesque women—jumping in the night. Henry was curious. Yes, he had to get home to his woman, but he felt a reckless sense of reluctance about

going straight home. Maybe just a peek. Again his insides felt
funny and active, as if he shouldn't be doing this, shouldn't be
advancing toward this theater with its wall-length photographs
on each side of the entrance of women clothed in strips of
transparent cloth. But he was walking faster, almost running
as if to flee from his voice inside him warning him not to go,
it wasn't right, go home. Or was it Leon Mark? His wrist slid
into the oval box-office opening; his other arm held the flowers
and the bottle of wine. He glanced around: nobody. In the
lobby he took a sharp incline of red Oriental carpeting up to
the ticket-taker. Henry glanced to the side, hummed to himself, tried to look bored, avoided the eyes of the ticket-taker
even after, pressing the torn half of the ticket in Henry's hand
until Henry had to look at him and his eyeglasses and mustache, black tie tucked within a dirty, white shirt collar, the
ticket-taker said, a sinister smile on his face as if he knew
every secret Henry had ever had: "You do have a nice time,
now."

Henry shook his head, grunted; then hearing the music, a
marchlike blast in waltz time, his heartbeat quickened, and
the realization that he was actually here, actually pushing
through the swinging doors when he should be home, when he
should be home with his wife, but was *here*, excited his insides.
This could be better than finding the apartment door of those
women living in back of him. Oh, God, what was he doing
here? What demon had driven him to this madness? But it was
exciting, hell. Wait until Joe Boy hears.

"Sidown."

He was inside the swinging door and had taken a half-dozen
blind steps down the middle aisle, then stopped to stare at the
women on stage. The voice was from the left. Henry froze. It
sounded like his father-in-law. Leon Mark here? With a rifle?
Should he run out?

"Sidown . . . sidown." Three or four other voices were
directed at him. They all sounded alike.

"Hey," said the woman in the middle of the stage lineup, at
the microphone now and pointing right at Henry, whose eyes
were accustoming themselves to the darkness of the theater,
"come on up here and sit in the front row. Plenty of seats. You
don't have to stand." The entire room laughing. He whirled

116

around to run out, but two men—he was sure he had seen them tackle a quarterback on television the previous weekend— blocked his way, then took him by his arms, almost crushing the flowers (the wrapping paper crackled), and guided him to a seat in the second row. Everybody applauded.

He turned to look at the audience. Suits. Briefcases or newspapers in their laps. Hats. Middle-aged, white. He looked ahead. Three men were in the orchestra pit: a trumpeter, drummer and bassist, stirring up a peal of melody that Henry knew he had heard before but couldn't quite place. Higher up the three women were facing the audience and performing a sideways dance step. Two, including the woman who had invited Henry to the front, seemed overweight, and the other was skinny; and her long, artificial eyelashes kept slipping so that she was out of step as she adjusted them. All three were white, but their faces, caked with makeup, had a pink tinge that was darker than the rest of their bodies. Their lips were redder than his flowers, Henry decided. The dance completed, Henry found himself clapping once more that day with those around him. They ran backstage on their tiptoes and returned to a slower melody, this time their pasties absent. A triangle of cloth tied around the hips was their only clothing. Whistles and foot-stomping.

Soon they were dancing again, the music had an Oriental flavor, and Henry noticed that the drummer was now playing the scarred grand piano. Their dancing reminded him of exercises. He concentrated on their bodies, looking for something that could stir him up, something memorable enough to tattoo on his mind and report to Joe Boy or Stuff. He wasn't interested in the faces, which were the faces of middle-aged women who had cried too much in their lives. Yet as he focused on their breasts, he found them disappointing also. The skinny girl's pair were the best of the group, but they were long and thin with only a slight, plumpy roundness at the end, reminding him of the legs of a Raggedy Ann doll one of Mom's employers had given her for Sissy. Plus, he decided, the nipples were too recessed.

The leader, the one in the middle, had the worst set, he felt now, for she had scars on her left breast.

Looking at the third girl, Henry kept thinking of both his

mother's water bag and her pancakes on Saturday mornings. He wanted to leave. They didn't even arouse him. From the side of his eye—he was sitting near the aisle—he could tell that the other men in his row were transfixed. They crossed and uncrossed their legs, the briefcases banging against each other. Several in his row were leaning forward, forearms on the seat backs in front of them. Maybe, Henry thought, he was missing something or wasn't looking at these women from the right perspective, so why not stay a little longer? Besides, the audience would probably shout and whistle at him if he stood to leave.

He appreciated a plumpness around the waist, especially Beatrice's slight swell where his wrist rested naturally during a slow dance. And below it the substantial contour of her behind. But these women—the closer he examined them, the more their excesses looked like swollen abscesses. Where were the sensuous protrusions? The waist of the girl in the middle looked like a life jacket of extra bouncing skin. There were streaks of fat splitting up and down her thighs, and when she turned around, exposing two wrinkled globes of behind, Henry closed his eyes. She was facing the audience again when he opened his eyes. She had the stage to herself now, the other two having fallen into the background and gyrating in accompaniment, and began pumping her torso out toward the audience and then back again. Henry was startled by a voice behind him yelling "Wow!" and he stared, fearful. Leon Mark? No. Was this man really excited, and was he too far back to see the sacklike stomach trembling on this woman as if she were beginning to show her pregnancy? Her hands were on the strings now, and the voices chanted, "Take it off, take it off." She did, and stood there fully naked now and globular, her arms, creased with fat, above her head, and the rings on her fingers flashing glints of light as the fingers snapped, and the inverted delta of pubic hair was as flat as if it had been pressed. Her associates had pulled their strings also and were standing behind the leader to each side, bracelets tingling. It wasn't until someone from the crowd had run up to claim the bikini bottom which had been thrown to the edge of the stage did Henry notice she was wearing white socks—anklets.

She bent backward and stuck a finger between her legs, began pumping her torso.

"Go, go. Whoowee." Hand-clapping and foot-stomping.

Henry jumped up and ran up the aisle, and he was relieved, standing in the back near the door, that nobody had noticed him leave. He told himself he didn't belong to this.

"Leaving already?" asked the usher.

"Yeah, gotta get home to the wife, you know," Henry answered, forcing a smile and certain that this was the perfect response.

"Sure," said the usher. "Well, it helps to get out, you know," moving toward Henry so that he had to stop. "Um . . . how about some telephone numbers?" He put his hands in his pockets.

Henry almost jumped at it. Hell, he needed some adventure. He still loved Beatrice, that wasn't even a problem. But a man likes to get out. Needs some adventure now and then. She's my woman, but I have to get out sometimes. He started to open his mouth but then recalled the trio of obesity he had just seen. Hell, he was going home to his Beatrice. "I'll drop back later on in the week to pick up something," he said and began moving around the usher.

Outside, the noise having died down somewhat, he buttoned his coat and breathed rapidly. Henry, you must be sick, he told himself. What's got into you, freaking out like this? How could you keep a beautiful black woman waiting for you while you congregate with a group of idiots? He took off his earmuffs. He felt a headache developing, a thick pulsing in the back of his head. If Mr. Mark could see me now, he'd shoot me. Let me get myself home before anything can happen.

Henry wanted to take the subway. It might be crowded—it would be because of the shopping—and perhaps . . . maybe he could get a nice position like the time he rode out to the stadium. He could keep moving his hand downward because he was trying to protect the flowers. A nice man bringing flowers to his wife wouldn't be suspected of trying to feel women. He was perspiring and nearing the subway, and the closer he got, the quicker he walked, stepping over a figure eight of dog manure and crashing into pedestrians. He might

even meet someone who would invite him to her apartment
. . . He stopped. His heart was beating fast, his wrists were
trembling, the pain in his head was moving toward the front.
He was dazed, not positive he had thought what he had
thought or that he was doing what he should be doing. A
terrible fear of everything. Would someone lead him? Would
somebody help him?

A clock outside a jewelry store told him it was eight. No
wonder he was so hungry. The moon was full and bright, surrounded by streaks of darkness, and as Henry walked up the
street that led to the bridge separating his part of town from
the industrial section, he had an extraordinary feeling of inert-
ness. On the rattling bridge it was much colder, and the wind
whistled through the spokes of the railing. His feet clobbered
over the cement. He turned around. No one was behind him.
He thought he had heard steps. He stopped and leaned on
the railing with his elbows. He heard a few cars pass by.
Below, the river, smelling of oil, reflected the buildings from
the left. A foghorn honked. Although he could see the moon
clearly, there was still a strip of yellow floating in the sky.
Also on the left, by the edge of the river, Henry saw the dump:
a pile of cars with wheels missing, fenders dented, doors
swung open. Farther up—he blinked his eyes—it looked like the
dump he had taken the fish to. It was. And it looked a mess,
with pyramid piles of cans and boxes. He couldn't see very
well, but it looked like garbage also: food, bottles, bags.

For an instant he had the urge to remain on the bridge and
just look. The nice, hypnotic lure of the water. And think. He
wanted to be by himself and just consider what his life had
been so far and what he could do with it. The water—it was
so still and dark. He wanted to review the day's happenings.
There was a message somewhere in those events, and perhaps
if he stayed here long enough and just thought it out he could
get an understanding.

Something caught his eye to the right, on the bridge, but
far enough away so he couldn't see it clearly, especially with
the circled glare of car headlights coming toward him. But he
thought he saw some pants legs dart behind a beam. He

pushed himself away from the railing and began walking to the other side.

First he would eat, then he would tell Beatrice about the letter to Stumpy, and they'd get that off. Then they'd have some wine. And then they'd make love for the rest of the evening. While resting he would talk to her and tell her all the little stories he had been meaning to tell her for over a year. He was within a block of the apartment and thinking about taking her to bed. A swift current of fear flowed through him. Suppose it didn't work for him again? He might come out of it again with the same dull incompleteness. Well, keep the faith, he told himself. Things will look up if you don't give up. Keep on pushing.

Soon he was on his own block, and he was both tired and refreshed to be this close to home again. He ran up the front steps, down the hallway, then up the cement stairs that led to his floor. Beatrice opened the door for him before he could knock.

"I had to work late," he said, coming out of his coat and handing her the bottle of wine and package of flowers. "These are for you, for waiting."

"Oh," she said, taking the packages, heading for the kitchen. "We've had heat all day."

"Good." That "Oh" got him. She was probably tickled pink, but she wouldn't allow herself to break down and skip around the room, jump up and down and kiss him, or insist that he shouldn't have. He heard her coughing in the kitchen. Then she called to him to come get his dinner, and she followed him out, her plate in her hand. He turned on the television. She coughed again. He noticed she was wearing the green dress with buttons down the front, and it reminded him of the many times he had tried to run his fingers down the seam—before they were married. She crossed her legs, and because she was sitting higher, on the foot of the bed, he could see her thighs up to her behind.

"What did you do all day, baby?" He chewed the hamburger and paced his words.

"I took a walk like I do every day," she said, and he loved

the tilting of her head to the side, and heard the announcement of a variety show on his left from the television set. "The rest of the day I looked at television and cleaned up, went to the laundry, you know." She bent forward to scratch her ankle, and Henry was thrilled to see her breasts press against her dress. He imagined his hands slipping over them later tonight. The right one was the larger—or was it the left one?

"I'm not going back to Home anymore. I have to look for another job until the Stars call me." He hadn't expected her to act surprised, but she was staring at him, he knew, as he half-concentrated on the television screen. The announcer had said something about a one-man band, and there was a man sitting at what looked like a giant piano with buttons, and the man had just pushed a button. A trumpet hanging on the side, up high on the piano, was sending out an up-tempo version of "Taps." "I'm not going back to that place." He scraped his plate with a fork.

"What's the matter?" she said, and she was sighing almost, her tone a smooth, caressing melody that made his heart stammer. Oh, God, I need her, he said to himself. Here I was running after those no-good hussies, looking for something, and it's here. He felt jittery inside. His life was clearing up already. Suddenly the fog ahead was lifting, there was no detour ahead, his mind was untangling itself, and although he was facing her, saw her lips separate and move as though she was saying something to him, he couldn't hear her. He was away again, backward in time, to an afternoon in October when his mother had used those same three words. Phil Beets had punched him in the stomach at recess. It was the sixth grade. A crowd had formed even before the pain had penetrated Henry's muscles. Somebody from behind had pushed Henry into Phil's fists, and Henry had closed his eyes and even now, thinking back, he winced at the remembrance of his stumbling and the pain of Phil's fists drumming against his lips and cheeks. He went home with one eye closed up, all strength spent, pants ripped at the knees which were scraped anyway, and when he got up to the doorway, saw his mother standing there, posed with apron and broom, he bawled. And she had asked him the same thing—used the exact three words that Beatrice had used—as his wife had just done, and then as now he had felt as if all of his worries had been flushed out of him, rinsed and drained away. "Tell me about it," she said, placing her plate on the other side of the bed, a napkin sweeping across her lips, yet calm and unruffled.

He wondered why he had procrastinated. He should have run straight home to Beatrice. There was no need to mope along the street like a dejected bum; no need to have gone to that disgusting show of physically deranged women; no need to have stopped on the bridge, feeling a companionship with the privacy of the moon, and contemplated strongly for an entire minute the temptation of jumping off. Yes, and now he felt that he had betrayed her by merely considering it. But she, Beatrice—he loved the name, too, and promised himself to whisper it repeatedly in her ear tonight—was here waiting for him, and what more could he ask for? Christ, if they didn't make love tonight—all night—

So he told her of his talk with Boye and of the Christmas singing and of trying to catch one of the workers. His voice was low, so he had to clear his throat frequently, kept glancing from her face to the television screen, although not comprehending any of it, just visually recording in his mind the man sitting and pushing buttons. When he told her about chasing the other employee, he spoke rapidly, desperately, emphasizing his unnervedness at the incident. But the scene of his overhearing them speak of him was relayed slowly, so at times he stuttered and searched for words, cleared his throat, scratched the top of his head.

She lifted his plate out of his hands while he talked, deposited it in the kitchen and came back, sat down. They looked at the television screen. A new act: a husband-and-wife team with a parrot perched on the rump of a Siamese cat.

"I'll write the letter, Henry," she said. "But I want to get out of here. I want to leave, Henry."

"But where can we go? What will we do? Beatrice, I can take care of you."

"I know you can, Henry. But it's so bad. I could hardly breathe today." Coughing.

He glanced at the television. The parrot was on the floor; it was shouting directions to the cat, who rolled over on its stomach, then meowed loudly. The audience applauded, the husband and wife took bows.

"Shall we have the wine now?" Beatrice asked. Her body was turned toward the kitchen, but her neck was twisted so that she was looking at Henry, and although he was staring at her large sepia eyes, he was able to glimpse the diagonal folds of her dress pressed against her behind. And the dress rose a few inches, so he enjoyed also the widening of the back of her thighs. "I'll be right back—" gone through the doorway to the kitchen with that bouncing step.

Henry concentrated on the television again. He rose to turn the channel, straining to hear the women in the apartment behind them. They must be out. It looked like a variety act, for two men were tap-dancing while facing each other and throwing their hats in the air.

Beatrice came back with two glasses, and she was moving slowly because the wine level dipped up and down from the top of the glasses, and Henry watched her hips navigate her safely to the couch. She flipped her slippers off, started humming.

"Remember that tune?"

"Do it again."

She rose, the glass in her hand, and twirled in a circle, moved toward the television and turned it off, still humming, then glided, one arm guiding an imaginary partner, toward the doorway and turned off the light. "I hate that television. There's never anything interesting on."

"It sounds familiar, what is it?"

"You don't know?" Her voice was by the doorway, but he couldn't make out the details of her figure clearly. "You don't know the name of that tune?"

"No," he said. "It's a beautiful piece. The words are lovely."

"When I was little, I wanted to write poetry, Henry." Her voice was moving toward him. It was just above a whisper. "But there was nobody to teach me, so I gave it up."

"You never told me that. Poetry is so hard to read."

"If I could write now, I would write us a poem so we could

get out of here. I'd write a poem about a clearing and we could run into it. There'd be trees and grass and watermelon and yams and grits and it would be quiet and full of sun. We could go into the poem, into the clearing and get away from here. We could get to know each other. We could be free. We need a clearing, Henry. We have to get out of here because there's no sun or trees, no peace or love."

He didn't understand her. Maybe it was the wine. She wasn't used to drinking.

He could see now the outline of her body, and she was close enough to wiggle her legs between his. He sat up and enclosed his arms around her hips, pressed the side of his face against her stomach. There was no place to go, she should know that. She wanted to get out of here? Okay, fine. Now where? No peace? Okay, where is it, where does it exist? He didn't even know his own wife. He didn't know she wanted to write poetry. Something was between them. If they went to this clearing, would he know her better? He'd like to get to know her. Oh, God, what was it between them? What perplexing, impalpable, stubborn block held them at arms' length? Couldn't they go back to a used to be? There definitely was one because he felt it. Maybe that was the clearing she meant. In his bones, in his memory, in a deep well of his mind, he felt that there was a place they had been lifted out of. Yes, a place, a time softer than the comfort of her stomach now, where there were no divisions, no interruptions, no maddening influences. No. None of that. A closeness. Peace. Trees and sun. Drums and flutes. Had they been captured out of this? If so, now what? Go back? Go back where? Stay here? And do what, look for the clearing? Shit.

"Tell me the name of that song you were humming."

"No. Never. It's a secret."

"Tell me," gritting his teeth, "or you'll never get out of here alive."

"I'll scream."

"I have a gun."

"I won't scream."

"You give up?"

"Yes. I'll do anything you tell me to."

125

"Okay." He turned to finish off his wine and threw the glass to the end of the couch. "Take off all your clothes and then take off mine."

"Beast. What about the name of the tune?" Drinking her wine.

"Who cares?"

"Well, I made it up." Throwing the glass to the end of the couch.

"Now, you see how far that got you?"

"Yes," she answered, stepping out of her dress which was now a lump of wool at her feet. He could still make out the distinctive patterns of her body, the concavities and convexities. She was standing there in front of him with her knees trembling against the inside of his thighs—buoyant and blooming before him. "Stand up," she said, and began undressing him, fiddling with his belt hook (tinkling as it fell), lifting his arms and pulling his shirt over his head, and next, leading him toward the bed. "Hold me, Henry," she whispered as they scrambled under the wool blanket. "Will you be with me forever?"

"Of course," he said, lying on his side kissing her nose, and the little light there was enabled him to catch the glimmer in her eyes. "Of course I'll be with you forever."

"I was thinking that if you left me or if we should be separated, I wouldn't know what to do with myself. I'm scared without you, Henry. I always feel something will happen when you're gone. It's all been so strange."

"Don't worry, baby," pulling her closer and enjoying the mildly sweet scent of her underarms. "I'll take care of you."

"Henry, will things get better? Do you think?" She coughed.

"Oh, sure," he said. His voice was almost hoarse and he had to clear his throat. But in answering he realized that she too had apprehensions; she, too, although establishing herself in his mind as an unwavering foundation of constancy and durability, was anxious, hesitant, had misgivings; she, too, had probably been filled with as much dread and fearfulness during the time they had lived in this city as he had felt earlier that cold evening in the street crowd, and all the time—*all the time*—had acted as if she were almost unaffected. Her strength had been so conspicuous he had never conceived of its being a mask, had never considered that she was acting. And Lord, how long—how long had she been parading like this, how long the cloaking and masking? Certainly she was doing it for him, to buttress him, but hadn't she been doing it before they met— for her father and mother when times had seemed unduly abusive and oppressive? Wasn't this a spirit that he was considering; an emotional makeup, a soul force whose bearing was as automatic as it was inexplicable, phantomlike in the vigor with which it sticks to one's bones, becomes a sixth sense; wasn't it—hell, wasn't it endowed or ancestral, this spirit, marching through the ages with the stride of an ineradicable heritage? Why, yes, he thought, and that's why it seemed so familiar—her aspect of it—because he had seen it, this disposition, this spirit, in his mother; in the old ladies, throats wrinkled, who sang in the choir at Bethany Baptist; in Beatrice's mother; in all the black women, especially the older ones, he had ever seen in his life. He must protect that spirit. "I'll protect you."

"Tell me about the first time you hit a home run. Tell me about your first girlfriend. Tell me about the first time your father beat you. Tell me everything, Henry. I want to know everything about you. We never get to talk. And do you know we haven't been to church since we came up North, Henry? You take me to church this week"—jabbing him in the side. "Do you want a girl or boy for our first baby? Will you teach them to play baseball? Why do you smell things all the time?"

Her words hit him with an urgency that, although roguish and sportive, seemed still to be directed by frenzy and panic, as if she were possessed of astrological foresight that determined this night, this moment, to be nonexpendable. And it frightened him a little, the feeling he had; for now, right now, he was about to talk with her as he had never before, and he was filled with the same sense of hesitancy he had experienced before the spending of his monthly allowance; he liked to stand outside the candy store for a while; and before that, walk up and down the block; turn the quarter over in his palm; think about saving it until the next month (he never did), and then rush in and point and buy and dash out with the paper bag and eat the candy before reaching home.

"Talk to me, Henry."

He smiled, turned over on his back, slipped his arm under her waist and began, but before he could finish his first sentence there was a knock on the door. Beatrice stiffened against him.

"Don't answer it," she whispered.

He didn't want to. It was late and his heart was skipping, thundering with fear, his imagination running even faster. But he couldn't let her know he was frightened. Perhaps somebody from Home? Maybe a telegram from Stumpy? Hell, suppose—could somebody have followed him from the burlesque? Alvarez?

"Don't worry," he said, clearing his throat, injecting a heaviness in the words and throwing the sheet and blanket off snappily, fully in command, "it's probably just Alvarez checking the heat. I'll be right back." He eased into his pants, put on his shirt and walked to the door. The knock came again. They were short, timid raps. He took a deep breath, unlocked and opened the door, glanced in at Beatrice who was entombed under the blanket. Little Betty Hurt stood, a note in her hands, a frown on her face, white-stockinged legs crisscrossed. "Betty, what are you doing up this time of night?"

"I thought you'd never answer," she said, smacking her lips at the end of the sentence. "Here, this is for you," handing the white, folded slip of paper up to his chest.

"Where'd you get this?"

She sprinted toward the stairway, giggled and ran down the hall, shouting, "A man—he's waiting for you."

He bent out the doorway to see her close the door to her apartment. Henry opened the note, dropped it, tried again.

> You have been drafted to help
> fight the war. We are waiting
> for you outside. Report
> immediately—right now.

He closed the door, and something very heavy was banging against the wall of his stomach. His fingers were moist.

"Who is it, Henry?"

He walked into the room, still reading the note, considering each word, his eyes sticking on the phrase "right now." Maybe Betty Hurt—no, she couldn't have typed this. He was sure it was for real.

"I've been drafted," he said, the words were mumbled and he wasn't even sure she had understood him. He was in a stupor standing there by the bed, seeing his wife sit up, the sheet falling and her breasts curved toward him, and it didn't mean anything to him now, not even the exotic shine of the dark brown ringing her nipples. "I'd better get ready," he said, and turned, not seeing anything, groping in the closet, picking up some pairs of socks, some pants; going to the dresser for underwear.

"Henry, you aren't going, are you? You aren't going to fight? Are you going to leave me?" She was shouting, standing right next to him as he knelt to pull out his shoes from the closet. He looked up in her face. Her eyes were large with wildness, her lips were trembling and her cheeks twitched, but he still was looking at her in a daze, moving away from her.

"I have to go fight, sweetie, they called on me. It's my duty."

"You don't have to fight nothing," grabbing him around the neck. "Henry, you don't have to fight. You might be killed. Don't go. Please don't leave me." Coughing over his shoulder.

"I have to fight for my country—it's our country. We live in it. How do you expect me to play ball for a team if they know I didn't want to help keep this country safe? I'm a man." He had thrown some clothes in a pillowcase. Then he moved over to the couch to change into his underwear.

"But what will I do?"

"You can take care of things while I'm gone. If Stumpy calls, tell him to hold the spot open for me until I return. I'll write you," moving to kiss her on the cheek, his pillowcase of clothes over his back, ready to leave.

She jumped away from him, and now he was beginning to focus on things more clearly and he realized that she was standing naked before him, and he easily could have lifted her to the bed—but he threw it out of his mind. The war was calling him.

"You're just like my father said you were, Henry Adams—just like all the black men in the world. Pack up and leave me here by myself." She was crying, fell to the couch, hands over her face. "I thought you loved me."

"I do, baby. I'll be back." His hand was on her shoulder, and he knew he never wanted to see her curled up shaking and crying like this ever again in his life. He turned and went toward the door. Before closing it he said, "Take care. I love you."

Down the steps, moving around the circle of saliva to another flight, finally reaching the first floor and walking down the hall. He heard footsteps tumbling behind him when he reached the front door. Beatrice, running naked down the hallway, breasts swinging and hair waving side to side, held out an arm toward him.

"Henry, wait."

"Get back upstairs, dammit," he whispered, and went outside. Standing on the steps, he saw the gray transport truck parked in front, motor idling, MILITARY printed on the canvas side; and the driver got out, looked up to Henry.

"Adams?"

"Yes. Yes, sir."

"Climb in the back." He turned, opened the door and gunned the motor.

He went down the steps as if he were pushing through waves on a beach. He knew he was moving, but wasn't quite sure where, only that this large gray mass was waiting for him and something heavy was on his back and he had to keep moving. A hand reached out from inside to pull him up from the street, and just as he was stepping down into the floor of the truck, he saw Beatrice stick half her body out of the apartment door. The tears on her face were sparkling from the night lamp, and she said, voice cracking with unsettledness: "I'm pregnant, Henry." And the truck motored off, he was thrown against a wooden bench seat, facing a line of men across from him, and her words were only words still unscrambled in his mind. He closed his eyes.

. . . I love you and Momma for all that you've done for me, but I can't go on like this. I want some control over my life. . . . I don't know precisely where I'll go with it, but I want it. . . . It's not your fault that I'm like this and that I have to write from the battlefield of Alaska while in some tank, and we're about to gun down some beautiful animals. But you, Daddy, would probably go along with it . . .

7

"GENTLEMEN, good morning, gentlemen, and welcome to Birthday Pass, Alaska, and welcome to Alaska, too. Gentlemen, I am your CO, call me captain, Captain Nevins. Gentlemen, we don't have time to train you. We're here to fight. For your information, gentlemen, the enemy is holed up in the Valley of the Willows and also in Lookout Ridge, and our mission is to kill the enemy or be killed. Gentlemen, our mission is to destroy these ginks, these sloop-eyes, or the next thing you know they'll be in our fuckeen backyards. Now, gentlemen, do you want that for your wives and children? Shit no.

"Gentlemen, may I take time to tell you how lucky you are? I am a graduate, gentlemen, of Officer Candidate School, and I know hundreds who would give their right ball to be in the situation we're in. We're where the action is, gentlemen, and this is a *beaucoup* assignment. You have the opportunity to make your wives and children proud, very proud of you, gentlemen, remember that, please. Gentlemen, may I repeat, we are here to waste and destroy the enemy. Finally, gentlemen, welcome to Company B, Third Battalion and so forth. I know you'll all be good troops. Oh, gentlemen, you will have noticed it's very cold up here. It will *be* very cold up here, gentlemen, so the sooner we waste and destroy these goddam sloops, the quicker we can get back to the states.

"Now, gentlemen, you are about to be processed. Print,

133

don't write, in the spaces allotted, then hand in your cards as soon as you can. After that, gentlemen, you will write to your old lady and tell her you are very happy up here and having a nice time and so forth. That's all, gentlemen, carry on."

He closed the door and there was a flurry of talk, and Henry began to put things together in his mind as if the captain's slamming the door had tripped a mental motor. He looked around him. He was sitting at one of the rows of wooden tables facing a wall of blackboards. Other soldiers talked among themselves while filling out the cards, but the one next to him, crewcut, was concentrating on his card, and Henry could see that he was young, probably as young as Joe Boy, and his eyes were blank, his writing hand was shaking and kept dropping the pencil. While the captain had spoken, Henry tried to remember where he had seen him before. He was short, had thin lips and big ears which jerked every time he said "gentlemen." His eyes were cold and gray and tiny, and it was that feature, the eyes of the captain, which kept Henry thinking, I've seen him before. The voice was squeaky, crisp, a soprano siren, and the words never trailed off at the end but stopped abruptly as if he was spitting out a period, too. I've seen him before, thought Henry, somewhere. And then, coming fully out of the daze which had kept him in its grip intermittently since he had climbed up into the transport truck, climbed down and boarded the plane and flown over the continual landscape of white until landing, he remembered that Beatrice had told him she was pregnant. God damn! No wonder she was so frightened at his leaving. How long? When was the baby due? He would pose those questions in his letter and tell her not to worry, he would be home soon. Just another obstacle.

"Gentlemen—" The captain was back, standing straddle-legged, boot tips peeking out from the bottom of the coat, and Henry could barely see his face because it was circled with fur, and the coat, a parka, seemed to impede his balance with its weight as he leaned from side to side while gesturing with his hands. "Gentlemen, we've got word of movement about one-fifty-four off Maybe Creek." His words came out hollow from inside the coat. Then Henry, staring at the eyes again, taking in the nuances of the voice, remembered where he had seen the captain before: in the movies. He reminded Henry of Bob Steele without the white horse and pistols. He smiled to himself and looked down the tables at the other men to wonder if they had caught the resemblance too, but their faces—a mixture˜of black and white—were vacant. "I want some men to take a chopper and get a sitrep and then vamoose back here. If we're lucky," smacking his giant mittens together and Henry could see the glare of his teeth for an instant—"we might have a firefight. We got plenty of gunbirds with mucho mikemike, grunts, so just sitrep and vamoose, and so forth. God, you mothers are lucky," shaking his head. "All right, you"—pointing at Henry, who had just signed his name to his letter—"be gunner; you, crew chief; you be the lieutenant. Suit up. Shit," shaking his head, "I know a dozen em-effs at the O.C.S.'d give their right ball and so forth for this kind of training." He walked out.

A flurry of chatter from the table of soldiers. Henry's knees shook, and he had to lean on the table to steady himself as he stood. He asked the crewcut to mail his letter and hand in the processing, and the crewcut swallowed and nodded, never looking Henry in the eye. Then Henry saw two other men rise, one white and the other black and tall with a toothpick tilted down from his lips, and he followed them to the prep room.

"The name's Mack," said the tall black man. The white boy's name was Alvin. "I'm also known as Runner Mack, Runnington Mack, Runner, and the Run. Where you from, bro? Let me have some power." They stood in line outside the equipment booth, the white boy in front.

"Henry Adams. Some what?"

"Some power, blood. Where you from?" He was busy, moving his feet back and forth and swinging his long arms, unable to keep still, Henry figured; like some batters he'd seen in the box, scooping dirt, knocking the bat against their cleats, hitching at their belts, tugging their cap fronts.

"Mississippi—except for the last year when—"

"Well, no wonder. Yawl ain't even voted for Lincoln yet," and he hooted with laughter, his eyes closing. "Look here," taking the hand of Henry, who was thinking that it wasn't so funny and forced a smile to be courteous, "when a brother ask for some power, you whip this handshake on him, dig?"

"Yeah, okay." They practiced it a few more times until Henry's name was called. He went up to the booth and gathered his gear and turned, but was stopped.

"Aren't you the gunner?" And before Henry could think— it reminded him of that split second of judgment he would need before running down a high fly ball—a large, frightful hunk of steel was pushed in his arms, on top of his coat and helmet and gloves and boots. "Here, take this. This is a sixty-millimeter machine gun. You should get a big body count."

He dropped his other gear and examined the sixty. He had only seen these in the movies. It was heavy. Holding it with the butt on the floor, it came up to his waist. There was a pipelike muzzle after the barrel, and the muzzle tapered off to a rod sticking out at the end. The handle was much too large for Henry's hand, and it had grooves for his fingers. And finally there was the opening for the clip of ammunition. This could blow somebody till kingdom come, he thought, remembering one of his mother's sayings. He carried everything— the sixty was sideways—with him into the other room to dress.

The white boy suited up without a word. Henry kept thinking of the sixty, that big, heavy machine gun—and he would be using it, would be carrying it, holding it at least—so it came to him that he didn't want to kill anybody with that gun; or with anything; didn't even want to have to hold that handgrip too tightly and push the butt against his shoulder and aim it at somebody.

"Were you cats drafted?" It was Runner Mack talking again and sticking his arm into the sleeve of his long parka, and he was moving again, bouncing on his toes, shaking his head up and down.

Henry heard Alvin grunt and nod his head, and he reminded Henry of a rookie in the dugout for the first time. He didn't seem to know where to go or what to do or if he should say anything. Henry was relieved. He was scared, too, almost frozen inside, not feeling anything but the trickly beat of his heart and the burning behind his eyeballs. Henry said that he had been drafted also.

"I guess we've all been drafted," said Runner Mack, tooth-pick sweeping across his mouth, big, white teeth catching Henry's eye, the head nodding knowingly. Henry noticed Mack's thick, shiny mustache. "Well, let's go out and work for John Wayne," grinning.

Henry, fully suited, stood and looked at the other two, who looked at him. He could hear the muffled noises coming from the other rooms, but it seemed as if this room at this time was the quietest he had ever been in, and he wanted to stay there, just stand there for hours and think about this.

"Let's go," said Mack. They followed him out, Henry in the middle, heavy mittens cradling the sixty-millimeter, fur-covered hood like horses' blinders, and the boots—they were so heavy he had to convince himself he wasn't climbing stairs.

Outside the chopper blades were whirling thirty yards from where they stood, and a soldier came running down from the ladder, shouting with cupped hands, "She's ready," and squirm-ing past them to get inside. The cold smacked Henry in the face and he staggered from it, then had to shake his head to the side because—he couldn't believe it—his eyelids had frozen shut. He had forgotten where he was, but then something clicked in his brain—Alaska—and he couldn't walk easily, had to lift one crunching, lead-heavy boot after the other, nearly walking sideways. His breath was freezing in front of him, and there was no feeling in his arms and legs; he was just moving forward, pushing through a screen of invisible frost. When he got to the chopper, Henry waited for Alvin to climb up, then he turned to look around.

Directly ahead, the two wooden headquarters buildings, like giant rectangular tents, rested against embankments of snow tinted pink from the sunlight. Wire fencing surrounding the grounds around the buildings. Two roads leading away from the main building, one going left, the other, right; both soon disappearing into the chain of jagged snow bluffs that composed the landscape. Snow bluffs every five feet, it seemed. He had never seen so much white before in his life—not even on the largest cotton field. And the snow glistened from the sunlight, which had a muted, early-morning hue as if it was straining to break out into a sparkling radiance.

"Beautiful, huh?" asked Runner Mack, his voice muffled because of the whirring of the copter blades. "I've heard of going up North, but this is ridiculous." Teeth reflecting the hue of the snow.

"Yeah. What's the temperature out here?" asked Henry, squinting his eyes because it pained him to move his mouth.

"Minus forty."

Henry laughed. "You must be kidding."

"I'm not bullshittin', bro. And it *will* get worse."

They climbed up into the chopper.

"Where'd you learn to fly these things?" Henry took the seat next to the pilot. Alvin in the back was shivering. His knees knocked against Henry's seat.

Runner Mack pulled a lever and the helicopter lurched upward, sending Henry's insides plunging to the bottom of his stomach. He was afraid to look down, and then suddenly the chopper sprang sideways and he fell against Runner Mack.

"I've never flown before in my life," said Runner Mack, looking straight at Henry Adams, who turned from him and looked at the roofs of the camp buildings.

"Well, watch where you're going, then," yelled Henry, clenching the barrel of his gun. They took a dive, then stood stationary, and Henry looked down. They were directly over the base. Runner Mack pulled another lever. They descended more. Henry could see the aluminum smokestack of the main building very clearly. "I think we'd better climb, Runner Mack." The Run pushed in a bar. The blades whirred louder but the chopper didn't move. "Do you know anything about—" said Henry, turning around to the other soldier, but his head was against the back of his seat, his mouth was open and his eyes closed. "Damn, he's fainted."

Runner Mack pulling and pushing and clicking knobs and levers, Henry Adams watching him and praying. They jerked forward; lunged backward; went up; came down; sputtered in a circle around the base; climbed diagonally; accelerated backward. But Runner Mack through it all never seemed to panic or lose control of himself, Henry observed. He frowned, Henry saw out of the corner of his eye (too petrified to move too much), but still his head was shaking as though he was enjoying it all, and the toothpick jutted in and out of his mouth.

"I've got it," he said after a half-hour of maneuvering, and the chopper groaned, then moved smoothly away from the base, rose in the sky. They were flying.

"Runner Mack," said Henry, shaking his head, not believing that he was in a helicopter in Alaska with a machine gun in his hands and the temperature was minus forty—up here in a helicopter flown by a man who must be mad—and his wife was miles away, pregnant, "you . . . you are fantastic."

"You can call me Mack, bro," was the reply. "Wake up Audie Murphy back there and tell him to read the instructions."

When Henry was able to wake up Alvin, they were heading toward a range of mountains that began on the left and continued as far as he could see out of the window to his right. It was a blue-white world of craggy ridges now, and there was no sun, so that as they flew deeper into the shadows of the mountains, it seemed twilight to Henry. The ridges were sprinkled with blotches of snow running from the tip and going down to the sides, and it was a constant landscape of these light patches tacked to the bluish sides of the ridges, the pattern reminding Henry of crayon designs he used to make in grade school.

"Wow," said Mack, "it's a beautiful place for a war, huh?"

Henry looked at him and saw that he was kidding, and said, "Yeah." Then, while Alvin was running off the names of creeks and ridges they were supposed to scout, they went higher and Henry saw just above the line of mountain tips a band of pink sunlight—hazy, soft, faint—resting, he thought, over the entire stretch of land. He had never seen a bare luminosity like that before and he thought there was something precious in the moment, so, while thinking that he must write Sissy Linda a special letter describing only the spray of light (and other letters to the rest of the family, who'd be surprised), and still not wanting to spoil it, he just nudged Mack on the shoulder and nodded ahead at the view. Mack nodded, grunted, shaking his head as if he couldn't believe it.

Then over another range and again approaching a similar shimmering band of sunlight, Henry lost all control and said, shaking his head as he had seen Mack do, "Good God, Mack, do you see that?" He was pointing.

"Goddam," said Mack. "Goddam." The white boy, Alvin, was reading a map.

Ahead of them were two cliffs, the diagonal of their sides stretching upward to form a V, and they were sprayed with sunlight so that their summits seemed to be capped with triangles of burnished pink. Henry could have looked at them all day, and again he didn't want to say anything, as if his words would dissolve the scene.

So they flew around looking at the designs the sunlight made on the arcs and ridges and pointed at sights that staggered their senses, were enjoying the beauty of the snow and rock and interruptions of grassland. And Henry felt that he was getting to know Runner Mack just from the way they laughed together and seemed to be in agreement about what the beautiful sights were. The man was likable. The man was vibrant, forceful, hard to ignore. Already he knew that. Henry even forgot they were in a war and that his wife was pregnant miles away. He was laughing with ease and freedom.

"Look," said Alvin, and Henry was startled by the voice behind him. He had almost forgotten the lieutenant of the crew. "What are they, moose?"

Mack swung the chopper around to get a better look. Moving north along a pass below them was a herd of caribou. Henry counted seventy of them. They moved easily, most of them, lifting their hoofs gracefully as if they were pawing at the snow. Others had stopped and had their noses dug into the snow. Mack took the chopper down closer, and those in the rear of the migration—afraid of the noise, Henry reasoned—hustled toward the middle of the pack. Henry had a good look at them now, and he thought he was much closer than he should be, as if he was intruding. They were dark brown and white, and their antlers were magnificent, the way they stretched outward and forward, the thinner branches sticking out like fingers on a cupped hand. Mack took another swing around them. Henry didn't want to say anything; he just

wanted to watch them lift their hoofs and tilt their antlers and
let them be peaceful. Finally the caribou got to a snow patch
on a mountainside and stopped, milling around; so now Henry
had a view of the patch dotted with animals and rocks and
small stretches of moss surrounding the patch.

"Let's get on back," said Mack, and they went up and
turned around.

Henry Adams had the muzzle of the gun in his hands, and
it wasn't until they were flying level that he thought of the out-
of-placeness of that gun. He was willing to fight for his country—he was supposed to, no questions, he was supposed to.
But where was the enemy? And what were they doing up here
in Alaska? Where did they come from? So far he had en-
countered a polar front that was too cold to think about and
a surfeit of beautiful scenes that had a mollifying effect on
the turmoil that had filled his mind lately. Here he had come
to fight a war, he thought, and strangely, he had never felt so
peaceful or been filled with so much composure as he had
during the past hours in the helicopter.

And Mack. The Run. Runnington. There he was flying this
chopper as if he had been doing it for years. Henry wanted
to check out carefully this strange, fascinating black man
with his thundering, intense voice and eyes that were deep
and flashing. The Run had been a lot of places and seen a
lot of things, Henry could tell, and he was certain of himself,
sure, positive, unhesitant—the way he walked.

"Where're you from, Mack?" He was testing. Maybe he
wasn't close enough yet to ask that.

"Some little town you never even heard of—out West."

"Oh. I haven't gotten out there yet." He wanted to talk but
he didn't know what to say. Everything coming to his mind
sounded ridiculous or unnecessary, and twice he turned to
Mack to ask something, his mouth just about to open, but
each time he held back and began to whistle, moving in his
seat to redistribute his weight. "Well, there's the base," he
said finally, not sure it was necessary for him to announce it.

Mack took it down like a professional. Henry was relaxed.
Alvin struck up a conversation. After they had landed and
jumped down from the cockpit, the captain stumbled toward

them. The sunlight was really bright now, and the gray of his eyes seemed to pierce through Henry as he addressed him.

"Well?"

"Sir?"

"Sir, hell! What's the sitrep? Oh, goddam, I forgot you just enlisted. What's the situation report, gunner? Make it snappy."

"Well, we got the chopper up finally, sir, and we saw some beautiful ranges and the sunlight was really nice. Other than that and some deer eating some moss, there's no situation to . . . to report, sir." Henry wanted to go inside. The cold stabbing him. He was certain it had dropped ten degrees since the trip. Mack was moving around in a circle and flapping his mittens against his thighs; Alvin stood on Henry's right, shivering.

"Other than that!" The captain turned in Runner's direction, but his left mitten was out sticking toward Henry's chest. "Did you hear that?" he said. "Other than that. Hell, what else do you want, and so forth? Deer! Shit, we'll blast the fuck out of them. Those sloop-eyes won't have shit to eat. Let's go get warmed up before we take out a platoon," turning and scuffling toward the base, Alvin rapidly behind him. Then stopping: "You didn't see any troop movement?" Henry and Mack hadn't moved yet. "Okay, good work, and so forth, grunts. Come on inside."

"John Wayne is crazy," said Mack, moving slowly toward the door the way Henry's father used to amble when they would take walks at night and his father would "explain" something to Henry.

"We have to go back and kill those deer, Mack?"

"Yeah, ain't that the craziest shit—killing those caribou because the enemy might eat them?"

"I don't want to go back there," said Henry, but he knew, opening the door to the main building for Mack, that he didn't have much choice.

". . . Use the sixties unless they start running, then we might have to call in some gunbirds." Captain Nevins was briefing the other troops. "The best place to hit them is in the head, above the eye, but if they start running together, aim for a leg to slow them down. Gentlemen, are there any questions? Okay then, we'll follow Adams' chopper. If we get a good body count, I might have a pleasant surprise for you grunts when we return."

So, hardly able to warm up, Henry found himself marching out the door again, this time coleading with Mack in front. Now the atmosphere had turned bright blue—aquamarine—so Henry was forced to squint his eyes from the reflected sunlight. And it was colder, much colder. Mack started the engine and Alvin took the back seat again, but this time he had two machine guns, one for him and one for Mack, and a box of ammunition in his lap. They took off.

I'm not going to shoot at these animals, Henry told himself. I have nothing against caribou. Beautiful creatures. I don't even have anything against the enemy. Who is the enemy? Where are they? Why are they our enemies; what did they do?

Mack's chopper was the first to go down behind the grazing patch. They landed in a valley below the cliff where the caribou still grazed. The other choppers—Henry counted ten—hovered over them and looked for a solid landing zone, and then Henry watched them come down one at a time, like birds searching for sturdy branches, until he couldn't look any longer because the purple sky was too bright for his eyes. So now his eyes were tearing from the luminescence of the sunlight and the tears were freezing on his lashes. He took a clip from Alvin and finally loaded his gun after dropping the clip three times, his mittens unable to grip it firmly. Nevins, gray eyeballs flashing, rounded up the troops. It looked like twenty-five to thirty soldiers crawling over the snow. He sent one regiment to climb directly up the ridge and wait for orders. He led another regiment—which Mack and Henry joined—around the pass to climb up the ridge on the other side.

This side of the ridge was drowned in blue shadow, and as they climbed up, sticking one precarious boot in an opening of rock after another, Henry behind Mack behind Nevins, their guns serving as crutches, Henry recalled how far he had traveled during the last year. Here he was—again he was

143

taking stock of his position, his situation, trying to keep a hold on his equilibrium—climbing up a mountainside for some four-legged, antlered animals.

He heard a thump and knew then that Nevins had reached the top and had thrown his rifle on the ground. Then the thump of Mack's gun, then Henry moved alongside him at the top of the ridge, and he looked down to see the line of soldiers, about fifteen or twenty, struggling up behind him. The caribou looked to be seventy yards away when he sighted them. They must have sensed the soldiers, for they stiffened and grunted, stopped eating to wave their antlers backward, and one, standing farthest outside the herd, seemed to be looking dead at Henry. Not moving. Foreleg poised. Frozen motion. At last the other soldiers took positions along the ridge. They aimed, then looked down past Henry to Nevins. He nodded.

The guns went off, beginning a continual chant of bullet chatter, and it seemed to Henry that the entire sky was filled with *rat-tat, rat-tat-tat*. He wasn't shooting, just aiming, and he took a second to glance at Mack. He wasn't shooting either. But the caribou, who had looked as if they were about to leap just before the gunfire started, dropped to the snow as if their legs had collapsed under them, falling on their sides, falling on each other. Several were able to reach the path beginning at their extreme left, but they bumped into each other trying to negotiate the thin avenue of escape, and the soldiers picked them off also. Finally, the entire herd lay heaped on the snow patch, and the only firing that could be heard was the sporadic two- and three-shot blasts aimed at caribou that had been wounded but not killed. Moving closer with the other soldiers, Henry turned away at the sight of the blood frozen now and sticking to the coarse hair of the animals. He looked at Runner Mack. They shook their heads.

"We must have wasted almost a hundred," Nevins said, kicking one antler as he moved around the animals. "They'll get no venison from these suckers," he said, "huh?"

The other soldiers shook their heads; they were looking at their victims; and Henry was looking at them, man for man, wondering if their silence meant anything. Immediately after a soldier took a body count ("Eighty-four, sir"), they headed for the descent down the ridge to the valley. It was then that Nevins reminded the soldiers of the treat he would surprise them with when they returned to the base.

Once more Henry and his crew, Mack piloting, led the tour —back to the base this time.

"What'd you think of that?" Mack asked Henry.

"Terrible, just bad," said Henry, the picture of the blood and hair and snow still before him. "I wouldn't have come if I had known it would be like this."

Mack looked directly at him. "You mean you would have refused to come?"

Henry considered that question. Why was Mack concerned? Anyway, he wasn't sure he would have refused. His father hadn't refused, had been in the Second World War and had a medal. He had relatives who had fought in the Civil War. Yes. There were pictures on Momma's mantel. A tradition, his father had called it, and this country—look what it did for us. So Henry, understanding that there was something he owed the country, wasn't positive he would have refused. "I don't know," he answered, and they flew the rest of the way in silence.

This time Nevins' chopper was the first to land. He was surrounded by the company when Henry and Mack reached the circle of soldiers.

"Gentlemen," he spoke, "for that *beaucoup* waste-and-destroy operation, I've got a surprise for you. Let's go inside." Everybody followed him in, Henry and Mack last. "Push the benches back against the wall." Henry helped, still in his ankle-length parka, the hood frozen stiff so that he couldn't push it back, and soon there was an open space in the briefing room, a space separating Nevins from the other soldiers. Nevins knocked some of the frost off his parka hood. Henry looked down at his boots, and now the tips were pointed up and sticking out from his coat. Silence: Henry and the other soldiers looking, staring at their captain on the other side of the room knocking frost off the arms and chest of his coat, stamping his boots on the wooden boards of the floor. "See this door?" said Nevins, his hand on the knob of a door Henry had not even noticed until now. None of the soldiers answered. Henry with Mack was in the thick of the group, and he stared, nodded his head with the others. "See it?" said Nevins, eyes widening. Again just a cumulative nod from the soldiers until—

"Yeah, we see it." It was Mack. All heads in his direction.

"Well, watch. Lieutenant, take charge." The officer who had earlier handed Henry the gear came from nowhere, it seemed, and he was fat, slacks belted around the cheeks of his behind. "Open the boom-boom room, lieutenant. Give the men a treat."

"Yessir." He opened the door, waddled through it. Footsteps as he bounced down the stairway. Nevins grinning and smacking his big mittens together, the soldiers restless. Then a stampede of light soles coming up the stairway. Giggling and tittering. The door swinging open wide, very wide, and two short women in slips, bras, high heels, came out and stood by each other, facing the soldiers. They grinned, stuck one leg forward in a model's pose. The one on Henry's left had two gold teeth in the lower row. Then two more came out, followed by the lieutenant, out of breath. The third swung a pocketbook on a string, cheeks and jaws and her entire face twitching as she chewed gum. The last one was the tallest. Her lipstick continued on one side to a dimple on her cheek. She twirled an umbrella above her head; her legs had scars.

"Madam Ahgook and her friends, gentlemen," said the captain, mitten stretched out in an introductory gesture. "How about a reah-ly big hand for the madam, huh? Let's hear it."

Everybody clapped. Whistles soaring. Henry noticed a few smiles, expanding into laughter; shouts, yells, real animation. Madam Ahgook bowed, smiling, and clicked her umbrella out and in.

"We've brought these natives in from Kilimantavi, gentlemen—lieutenant, you may leave now, thank you—for your benefit. Hell, a man can't fight all day without something to look forward to, right?" More cheers. "And we get a chance to help out the local economy." Laughter. "How much did we agree upon, madam?" She looked, puzzled, at the captain. "How much? Money . . . howww . . . much . . . cost . . . to pay . . . to pay . . . monee." The four women huddled, whispering among themselves, then staring at the soldiers, giggling, whispering again. Mack, next to Henry, sighing and shifting his weight. Madam Ahgook separated from the other three women and, umbrella twirling, took timid steps toward the captain.

"Twenty," she said, then held up a finger, "for one."

"Twenty dollars for one hour?"

She nodded her head quickly and repeatedly. "Yes, yes."

"Why, that's preposterous," said Nevins. Madam Ahgook frowned.

" 'Merican rich, got many monees."

"Yes," said Nevins, glancing at the soldiers, and Henry figured he was indicating he had things under control, "but so much . . . so much money. Twenty dollars for all of you. . . ."

"No, no. Twenty dollars for one. Four times twenty for all."

"Oh, Christ, madam. 'Merican soldiers tired, fought all day . . . shoot bang bang . . . kill, all day, tired . . . worn out . . . need woman." The madam shook her head. "Well, okay, twenty dollars. Go downstairs. Wait downstairs in boom-boom room."

She smiled, the other women smiled, then moved toward the door. The madam was the last one through it, and before she closed it she stuck her head through. " 'Merican men nice men," she said smiling, then fussed with her umbrella, which had been caught in the doorway.

"All right, men, four at a time. Don't worry about money, we'll take it out of your pay." Before he had completed his sentence, the soldiers had pushed and shoved, shouting, "Me, me, I'm first," toward the captain, until Henry couldn't see the captain at all. Some of the soldiers held back and were, like Henry and Mack, just trying to see who the lucky four would be.

Mack nudged Henry, then started toward the main door. Outside Mack said, "Let's tip over to the fence, bro." It was still cold, but very quiet, and there was just the crunch, crunch of their boots in the hard snow. Henry's arms hung at his sides, his head was down and he was walking fast to keep up with Mack. They leaned against a post. Their shadows stretched long before them, and the sunlight was now so mellow, the wooden boards of the two base buildings looked velvet bronze. Beyond the buildings were stumps, hillocks of ragged-edged, pointed, hard snow. Snow soldiers, thought Henry.

"Does the sun ever come out?" asked Henry. He was staring at Runner Mack, taking in his features that could be seen in the oblong of fur edging the hood. His nose was wide, and he was black, as dark as Henry, and the thick mustache shone.

"It's shining now," he answered, "but we can't see it this far north." Toothpick jumping in his mouth.

"Oh," said Henry.

"I should write a book about this shit," he said, shoulders shaking, and he kicked at some imaginary object. "But then all the critics would say it's not a novel, just propaganda; as if all art isn't propaganda, right?"

"Right," said Henry, and now he was more intrigued with Mack. He didn't know what the man was talking about; he hadn't read that many books in his life; he didn't know what propaganda was. And what was Mack going to write about, anyway? He didn't want to show his ignorance, so he thought he'd listen and agree.

"What do you think about the enemy?" His back was to Henry when he spoke, and the words were almost lost in the cold.

"Well, I don't know," Henry answered, "I guess we gotta . . . gotta get rid of them. They're fighting against our country. We gotta protect it, you know, I know things aren't right all the time with us, but it's still our country."

"Shee-it."

Henry Adams was uncomfortable. Runner Mack, standing a foot away from Henry leaning on the post, was looking out toward the horizon, and Henry feared that he couldn't relate to this man. But he wanted to. Still, the distance, a separation of their spirits—feeling it as he felt the cold. Mack seemed to know things, had things to say, and Henry was sure he could learn something from him. Henry imagined himself a rookie pitcher and Mack a catcher. Together perhaps they could be a battery, a combination of skills? But Henry, mind roaming

148

now, saw them frequently disagreeing on signals. Mack would call for a fast ball and Henry would want to throw a change-up. Perhaps he was right; perhaps the fast ball was the pitch to throw. Henry might be wrong. He might be wrong. Listen, anyway, find out what the man knows, what he has to say.

"Well," kicking his boot against the post, "you're up here fighting."

"Shee-it. Me? I'm not fighting for that John Wayne mutha-fuckah. The muhfuckah's sick just like the rest of the country. Out of his mind—do you hear me?"

Damn, the language. Why must he use such language? I could never take him down home. He'd be cursing in front of everybody. Reverend would usher us both to hell. Damn, a brute; rough and angry, bitter. But I want to relate to him, find out about him. He's different. Ornery, but smart. Has read some books. I've never met anyone like him. He wants to talk, too, but is testing me first. I haven't talked with anyone in so long.

"Why should I kill somebody that I don't dislike? I don't have anything against these people. Who are they? What did they do to me?"

Oh, yes. Now Henry relaxed a little. They might have something in common, for he had thought the same thing, had posed the same question to himself. But hell, who had all the answers? It was hard enough to come up with the questions. I don't know! I don't know. Can you help me, Mack?

"We better not stay out here too long. You'll miss your chance in the boom-boom room." He walked ahead.

A test. Henry understood the statement as a test. He remembered the subway. And he was ready: "I'm not going in there. I can't do it, Mack . . . those girls . . . I don't want any part of it. You go on."

Runner Mack stopped and turned around. "Me? Not me. Let the beasts enjoy themselves. I got me a fine black mamma back home." Walking back to the post. "How about you? Got anybody at the crib layin'?"

"Yeah, Beatrice. She's pregnant. We'll have a boy, I hope. Then he can play baseball, too."

"I thought I seen you somewhere. Didn't I see you on television last summer playing ball? Don't you play for a team?"

"No," Henry smiled, and a stream of cold rushed down his throat; he coughed, swallowed the chill. "I was about to be signed up, but I got drafted. The Stars were going to take me."

"No shit?"

"Yeah, really."

"Look, you must be playing a hellified game of baseball to get drafted by the Stars."

Henry smiled, shrugged his shoulders.

"Everything's all set, huh? How much bread they givin' you?"

"Well, everything's not really set yet." He stamped his boots. He couldn't feel anything below his ankle, it was all frozen, and he was wondering how long Mack would keep him out here. He wouldn't complain about the cold. He'd stay out here as long as Mack could. Where was he getting these questions?

"Then they must be bullshittin' you. Run it down and let me see."

Henry told Mack about his high-school days on the baseball team; how the scout came around; three years of semi-pro; the tryouts. Mack interrupted him during the last tryout.

"Tell me no more. Dude, can't you see they bullshittin' you? Obviously your shit is together, from what you say, but they don't want to give you a play. Seen it happen a million times. Same ol' same ol'. It's our history. Can't you see?" His eyes were dancing, focused directly on Henry's, and his mouth had a quizzical smile, he was still in one spot, not moving, just staring.

Something about this moment—the staring eyes, the question—galvanized Henry. It was dreamlike, hypnotic, this moment, as if he had gone through it before somewhere. It was familiar, and he could recognize it as familiar, but still, he couldn't make the acquaintance with it. A flashing, dizzying moment of reminiscence, like trying to remember a dream.

"Well—"

"Well, hell, my man. You'd better wake up." Then Mack

turned away from Henry, and arms flapping against his parka, stared beyond the fence. "So whatcha been doin' with your time while waitin' for those jive muthafuckahs to call you?"

Henry told him about the jobs he had, went into detail to explain his last one at Home. He hadn't spoken with anyone for so long about his jobs, not even Beatrice, and the tense, uncertain anxiety that had built up within him flowed outward as he explained it to Mack.

Runner Mack shook his head. "Now, *those* muthafuckahs are really out of their minds. How come you went for their shit so long? What's the matter with you, Adams, don't you use your head?"

Henry was confused. Mack seemed to have a judgment for everything Henry had ever done. And he had some answers hidden somewhere—had something. Seemed sure of himself. Seemed to know something. But what? Why was everything he said so confusing, yet attractive? Henry wanted to talk to Mack all evening. Perhaps he had explanations? Of course! Mack, help me, will you? Talk to me. And let me talk to you.

"I use my head," he said, and immediately knew that he had rarely sounded more childish.

"Yeah, I'm hip," said Mack, walking away. "Look here, let's get out of this goddam freezing shit." Henry caught up with him. "I'm gonna take a nap. Let's rap tomorrow after breakfast. You got time?" His back was to Henry and he was taking those long steps toward the other building.

"Yeah, okay," said Henry, standing, watching Mack move in the sunlight, shadow stretching long. He waited for Mack to turn and wave, or say good-by or nod, and he was still waiting as Mack opened the door to the wooden barracks and leaned in and closed the door.

8

HENRY NODDED to Mack. There they are now, forming a semicircle. Beautiful things! Why do we have to kill them? Now that was a rhetorical question. Because they're mad, gone insane, unable to function with reason. Mack, you are fantastic! Three months rapping with you—or three weeks, something like that. Mack, where have you been all my life? Hell, that sounds like a damn love song. . . .

Beatrice, why hasn't she written me back? If anything has happened to her . . . I'll kill them. . . . Who? Them!

Minus fifty degrees. It can't be. Nowhere no way can be that cold. I don't feel anything. Just burning. It's so cold, the sky is purple. When will the sun come out? Come out, sun, dammit, you sucker, come out. Easy, now, easy. Remember what Mack said: Don't let them drive you as mad as they are; don't get yourself contaminated by the filth of their idiocy. A nice phrase, that one—the filth of their idiocy. Mack, you are fantastic. The mind you have. You got it. I've been asleep all my life, a slumbering giant. I didn't know what was wrong with me and you came along and named it.

Must we use eighty-one mortars on these animals? Oh, hell, I keep forgetting. Everything is explained, everything is explained now. It's clear. Adjust my seat. Hard to even sit comfortably in this big-assed parka, but I wouldn't take it off. The sunlight is so bright; it's treacherous, too. At least they gave us shades. Who made this tank, anyway? It's got enough steel for an office building. God, tanks all around . . . let's see . . . eleven . . . twelve . . . thirteen. And John Wayne's going to call in the gunbirds too, says they need practice. Mack's a gas. When the colonel came in for inspection, Mack called him Gary Cooper. Static; somebody on the radio? No, just static. Probably the enemy.

Where are they? Around. I don't mind not shooting at the animals, but the enemy is shooting at us. Mack's on the case again, though—just aiming at nothing, the sky. And some other soldiers are doing the same thing. Mack's an organizer. We don't have any reason to be shooting, killing. But still, we get killed. When are we going to see the enemy? I just want to see them. How can I explain to Joe Boy and Stuff that I never even saw what the enemy looked like? Static again. Must be the gunbirds over the ridge.

"Roger, Pineapple Four. Into you, seven five. Good business, weather is fine but cold, and you should have clear flying this afternoon. What's lineup?"

We keep getting killed and they keep sending more men to reinforce us. How long, how long? Well, Mack and I won't be around. God, Alvin. In the blizzard last week. Never had too much to say to the cracker, and he wasn't going down with the group anyway—but to see him dead like that. Leg shot off and lying in the snow away from him and the blood bright and splurting in the snow, more snow falling into it and freezing over it. There was nothing we could do for him but put him on a stretcher, the leg left in the snow. I may die like that. I don't want to die. Not now, God, please. Let me live, please. Take a leg or an arm, but let me live, please.

"Roger. Swell, target is a K.E.L. off Liberator Lake and about two hundred meters off the money at one-fifty into the ridge. You got a beaucoup *clean shot. . . .*

God, please let me live. Mack and I had a dilly about that. How did it start? Let's see. . . . We were smoking one night, getting down nicely by the fence, pretending to dig the violet sunlight, and my head was reeling, I was seeing double, could hardly stand up, wow, it was nice. . . .

"Make this one fifteen meters at six o'clock. Start your mike-mike."

153

I didn't even know what I was saying. It was all nonsense, and his words were bouncing off my forehead; I could see them bouncing off and splitting off into Technicolor letters, and the letters were floating in the air: *l*'s, *p*'s, *r*'s. Mack was running it down about how we've been brainwashed, but his words were clear and loud (that's his voice: loud, very loud), and mine were slow, stumbling out of my mouth so slowly I wanted to bring them back and rearrange them.

"Another good one right on the money. Roger that, Pineapple."

And Mack had said, "Another one of our problems is Christianity. We been believing in their God and the golden rule all our lives while Chuck has been laughing at us and acting like a beast. What's it done for us, Henry? Huh? Can you answer me that with your black self? Can you tell me why we still listen to that jive dogma while whitey acts the mad hypocrite? We can't follow them anymore, Henry. They've fucked up everything, they've killed and mangled and transgressed all their lives, and we can't become a part of it. We must remain humane and spiritual within this madness. Our heroes must be different, Henry. Can you get to that? Was Jesse James black? Was Booth? Was Custer? Was Capone? Have we bombed any churches with little white girls in them? Have we leisurely cut the balls off of white men? Are there any famous black murderers, assassins, kidnappers, bank robbers, swindlers? We're decent folks, Henry. But thanks to Christianity, meek as hell. We don't need their God."

Me thinking, the nigger is mad. He said that they were trying to drive us crazy and he's on his way. If Reverend Fuller heard him talk, he'd tune up to faint.

"What we need, Henry, is our own God. Somebody who looks like us and thinks like us and loves us more than any other people. Do Chinese have a white God? Hell, no. Do Mexicans? No way. Indians? Wake up, Henry, that's what I've been trying to get you to do since I met you. I know it's hard. You been brainwashed all your life and now you start to think about everything you've been taught and it's hard for you. But you have to grow, Negro. You have to wake up, like every black man in this country. Check it out. Is Christianity for us?"

154

"Hell, Mack, I'm trying to grow; I've listened to everything you've said, but this— All my life I've gone to church. We've always been close to the Lord. Who's looked out for us all these years? You're asking me to give it up? I met Beatrice in church. I can remember sermons, I can remember hymns, I can remember Sunday school. Weren't no white people involved in that. Mack, I don't know. God, the sermons . . . Reverend Fuller. . . .

He's callin' and ah be a long time talkin' 'bout Jubilee so won't you listen to me please won't you listen to Him callin' you ooh doncha see no sinner can't hide uhmm don't care if you run to the rock uhmm don't care if you run to the church uhmm don't care if you run to the mountain uhmm don't care if you run to the sea uhmm you can't hide, He's everywhere, can't hide, He's everywhere, can't hide, He's everywhere, He's everywhere, He's everywhere ooh ah everywhere yes . . ."

"Roger, Apple. Ready for the B.D.A. It looks like six bunkers, a sustained fire and one one-twenty-three near the red ball. . . ."

No, Mack, I just don't know. Really. I have to think. But look, at least I'm thinking, right? You just can't go out and pick up another God just like that, hell.

"Roger, Pineapple. A one-twenty-three? You got a one-twenty-three? Incredible!"

"Turn it off, Henry, that shit's worse than television. Worse than Hollywood, too."

Television is a bitch—part of the national insanity, says Mack, and I believe him. When we get back home I'm going to kick the screen in with this boot I'm wearing right now. Mack, how can you see so much? Or, how come I haven't noticed anything? Oh, yeah, I know—I've been sleeping. Hell, how many people are there like me? Sleeping. Damn, Mack says there are people all over the country who are like I was. They don't have the slightest idea of what's happening, and don't even want to know. Little old ladies in Idaho and Pennsylvania, too, and husbands working at a million Home Manufacturing companies and not understanding anything. Ho-hum, Mabel, bring me another beer, and how's the war going, and did you send in the payment to Sears and what, me worried? This is the greatest country in the world, I just saw the President on TV, he told me, and Mabel, what about a vacation at Disneyland this year, and aren't those Miss America gals cute —look at the trampolinist. People like that all over.

My father—I have to break from him—is something like that, now I understand. But how can I reach him? How can I explain to him that his way is not *the* way, that we can't afford anymore to be passive and back-bowing, grinning and kind. Mack says we must overcome or die trying to overcome. He says to die for the revolution is nothing. Should I write Daddy a letter? I love you and Momma for all that you've done for me, but I can't go on like this. I want some control over my life. I don't know exactly what I'll do with it, but I want it. I don't know precisely where I'll go with it, but I want it. I may not be any different when I get it, but I want it. It's not your fault that I'm like this and that I have to write from the battlefield of Alaska while in some tank, and we're about to gun down some beautiful animals. But you, Daddy, would probably go along with it just as you went along with Stuff's dog being killed and when you didn't find out about the social security. We can't have any of that. I don't want you to feel bad, it's just the way you've been brought up. But for God's sake, hold your tongue and let them think, let Sissy and Little Stuff and Joe Boy have their heads. Please don't tell them that your way is the right way. I love you both. But your way won't work anymore. You never questioned. I want my sister and my brothers always to question.

What's the use? He'll just tear up the letter and call me a lost son. Maybe I should write Sissy Linda? She's the strongest, she could influence Joe Boy and Stuff. Oh, I should write Leon Mark. I'll tell him that now I see why he was so worried about his daughter. Hell, we haven't been treating them right. Beautiful black women sustaining us all these years and we not appreciating their worth. Their movements; the way they twist, smiling; their voices; the soft, uplifting tenor; and the strength, the strength, all these years. And we running around like a collection of madmen, trying to imitate the general lunacy. Mark, I'll take care of your daughter, believe me, please. Wait till I get home, I'll take care of her.

Careful, Mack, as you wind your way to the edge of the tank. Remember the knee. You and me both have injuries to protect. My ankle still gives me a little trouble when I run fast. That's how we got talking about the movement, wasn't it? A three-quarter moon, bright orange up against a dark-purple sky the night we were on duty. A growling about fifty meters outside the fence. I froze. Crunching in the snow, behind one of the frozen banks. Then we saw the eyes sparkling. My hand tightened on the M-16. Was this the enemy? Were we up here actually to fight animals (it must be an animal—the growl) without being told? Nobody said the enemy was human. Nevins (John Wayne) just calls them ginks, sloop-eyes. Those eyes look a little slanted, too. Don't tell me the enemy is not human . . . all this time we've been fighting against . . . no, that can't be. . . .

"It's a bear," whispered Mack, "a polar bear." And it was. As if it had been beckoned by Mack's words, it came out from behind the bluff of snow, stood on two legs, and I was weak at the knees with fear. "Don't shoot." He was standing, tottering on two legs as if he had been wound up. Paws together as if he were praying. Snout in the air, toward the night sky. Sniffing for us? His hair was pink from the orange moon. And straight and smooth as if it had been groomed. I backed up. "He won't bother us," Mack said. Oh no? I took another step backward. Mack—Christ, Mack, are you crazy? He lifted one leg over the wire fence, another one, holding on to the post, and he was beyond the fence. Rifle thrown behind him, bent over, stumbling through the snow toward the polar bear.

"Mack, come on back here, you fool!" I said. "He'll kill you." I should have jumped over the fence too, but . . . but . . . that big bear . . . seven feet tall, it seemed. The bear turned sideways, eyeing Mack curiously out of the corner of his eye, and me thinking that he's about to start attacking. Then Mack stood up, beat his hands on his chest and growled. The bear fell to all fours and began running into the night. Mack running after the bear and growling; the bear skirting around the snow bluffs. But Mack was falling about seventy meters away and for a second I thought he had been hit, but the bear was too far away, disappearing toward the range.

I climbed over the fence. Took my rifle with me, though. Boots (my socks were wet and soaking when I reached him) too big for me, causing me to lose my balance as I hustled, going in a zigzag around the bluffs to where Mack was curled up in an opening between the banks. Parka pushed up to his waist. The white polar bear—the first one I had seen in my life—was in the middle of the moon and running into it. His head and shoulders were up against the edges of the moon, and then he was going downhill and I couldn't see him. I was on my knees.

"Trick knee," says Mack. His voice was still clear and strong, but he was out of breath, the smoke from his mouth freezing against the net of his face mask. Standing, leaning on one leg. "Kick my knee." You must be out of your mind. You must have fallen and hit your head against a hard snow bank. I'm not going to kick you. Hysterical?

"I'm not going to kick you. I can't kick you. Run. Get yourself together."

"Kick my muthafuckin' knee, dammit, so it'll straighten out. Come on and stop bullshittin'. Kick it! Kick it!"

He must know what he's talking about, so I kicked it, tapped it, tapped my boot lightly against his knee. He was standing on one leg, the good one, holding the ends of his parka up.

"Don't play pittypat. Kick it. Hard! Come on!"

I kicked it hard. He straightened up. "Thanks," he said. "The goddam thing gets out of whack if I run too fast. You have to kick it, Adams, it's the only way. Where's the muthafuckin' polar bear? Did I chase his ass away?"

"He's gone, but let's get back to the other side of the fence." I picked up my rifle. "You must be crazy, chasing polar bears." Sometimes I think the dude is crazy—well, just off a little, different.

I thought he was crazy when he pulled my coat. Came out of the barracks one morning and Mack's in a crowd of soldiers, he's in the middle, the tallest of them all. What's going on? They glance over their shoulders. A football huddle? Into a

158

deep whisper session. I scoot by as if I don't see them. They break up. Mack catches up with me. Walking alongside me as I make it to guard duty.

"So where you at?" He never says hello or good-by but breaks right into it. I like that, doesn't waste time. But different, very different. Plus you never know where he's coming from. What does he mean, "Where you at?"

"Whatcha mean, where I am?"

"I mean, what kind of move are you going to make? Man, I thought you had your head together until I saw you out there whipping on those seals."

Another mission. The war had gotten to me. I was tail-end Charlie on a cordon-and-search and we ran into a family of seals. A lot of us had said we wouldn't aim at animals, just shoot like we'll do today, over their heads. But John Wayne had armed us with clubs. We had to go to the edge of the water and club the seals. Against their necks, and on the tops of their heads. They flapped around and tried to fly, but we were too much for them. They were barking and honking, we were clubbing them . . . thump . . . thump . . . thump. The captain was watching, so I had to do something. I thought I'd tap them on their tails lightly. But I was enjoying it. I wanted to hit them on their noses and short foreheads. It felt good to me. What have they done to me, Lord? I was whipping, swinging my club, biting my lip, my teeth were tight. I hated those seals. Brown, slinky things. I was the last one to stop. We got them all. I was out of breath at the end. I wanted to hear them cry. I was hurting them for something . . . I wanted to hurt them for something . . . for something . . . brand them with my club . . . something urging me to be a *killer* . . . something. I didn't try to explain to the Run.

"I lost my head," I said.

"How old are you?" he asked—he's like that, going on to another point right away, but don't think he isn't digesting what you said before.

"Twenty, going on twenty-one."

"That's a good age. I got ten years on you, but when I was your age I didn't know shit, Adams. Look here, somethin's going down, let me pull your coat." I looked at him as he bopped and shuffled along with me. We were going beyond the fence. We stopped at a snowbank that came to my waist. "I been sounding cats since we been up here. About ready to make a move. I want you in on it. I don't know you too tough, Adams, but I think I dig where you comin' from. Understand?" How could I understand? What are you talking about, Mack?

I said, "Yeah, what's happening?"

He put his head in the air. Toothpick straight up, twirling around his mouth. I knew it was going to be big . . . but this big? "Dig. The muthafuckahs have fucked up the whole goddam country. We gon' take it over and get it back together." He was looking right through me. He was serious.

"Say this again?"

"We're takin' over the muthafuckin' country, goddammit. We gonna save it before those crazy muthafuckahs drive us all crazy. I want you in on it. Be my road partner."

"Mack . . . uh . . . I don't get it." It sounded weird at first. Naturally. I knew the dude was heavy, but I didn't think his shit was that official. Damn, he's got me talking and cussing just like him. "Who are these people you talking about?"

Blowing and sighing. "Goddam, Adams. Free schools and dumb niggers. I been rappin' to you about this shit for months now, and you gonna come up shaky? Look, I been planning this shit for ages. I got followers all over the country who are ready to go down now. It's time to organize."

"Well, look, don't count me out, I just wanna know what the score is, Run. Who . . . who . . . what's the plan?"

"All right, dig. We're going to bomb the White House. After that, we take over. Simple as that. I got blueprints of the White House. It's all mapped out. All we have to do is break out of here and make some contacts. Then the shit is on."

"Wait a minute. Did—did you say the White House? Did you say bomb it?"

"Well, what the fuck did you think we were going to bomb, a doghouse?"

Everything inside is melting. An unpleasant urge. "Wait a minute."

"Where you goin', Henry Adams?"

"Keep talking. I have to go to the bathroom. Come on."

"Look, I got muthafuckahs all over the country layin' for the signal. This is it, Adams. Black dudes and white dudes. We can't do anything without the paddies, they got the bread and resources. After we take over, then we can start getting our own black thing together. But we can't do nothing the way this country is now, right?"

"Yeah. I guess so, Run." I'm squatting in the barracks latrine. Couldn't hardly get my parka off fast enough. "But do we have to bomb? Can't we talk to them?"

"There can be no revolution without violence. Never has been, never will be. Hurry up and finish."

Outside I say, "But Mack, is it that serious? Is that all we have?"

"Look, Henry Adams, I'm asking you to go down with us. I'm asking you to understand that you are the new black man. Your life has been shit and you don't want to realize it and yet you want to cry on my shoulder. Cryin' is over. You have to wake up, Henry, and understand where you been and where you must go. You must go with me. Scope yourself, Henry; scope your history and understand why you went through all that shit you told me about. Don't be like your father. Be a new black man. Wake up. Act. Go down with me, Henry Adams. I'm asking you plain, no bullshit, if you will."

"But suppose it doesn't work?"

"Can it be any worse?"

"Well, let me think about it, anyway."

"Let me know tonight and I'll hip you to the plans. Easy."

Well, it's got to work. And even if it doesn't, Mack's right: What's worse than this? They've got me killing seals with a club, shooting at the enemy nobody's seen, working in a crazy plant, following women . . . Christ. I could get killed. We had a man part of the movement the other day when it was minus sixty who just fell down dead from the cold. You don't even have to be shot to die up here. Over on Lookout Ridge during a storm, the winds whistling at thirty miles an hour, and we couldn't see in front of us. We formed a line, going in single file. Falling in the snow. I held onto the coat of Mack in front of me. Faded whiteness everywhere. Couldn't even see the sky. So three or four fell down from white-outs. They couldn't see anything. My mittens wet and cold, snow running down my neck . . . Christ. Frost on my nose.

No bluffs or ridges out there. It's all flat snow, barely disturbed by the wind. I count fifteen of them. Look at the legs on them, like stumps of bone. They look like they might fall over from no support.

"Have you ever seen musk oxen before?" Mack coming around the top of the tank.

"No, look at those little legs." They're forming a semicircle. They know we're out here. The short curves of horns coming out of their ears. Nose and mouth white, and white hair at the top of their heads, as if they're wearing caps. Don't even look like they're cold. There's one with real shaggy hair coming up to join the rest. Suppose they charge us?

One of the tanks over there at the top of the valley is aiming. Nevins must be ready.

"Better get set," Mack says. "Aim just above their heads."

"Right." When you have all this power in front of you, you know that war is serious business. All this steel designed to kill people. I'm almost glad we haven't seen the enemy. How does it feel to kill? I got sick after we clubbed the seals. Suppose I had to shoot them?

They've started. Almost scared me, the beginning rounds. Poor oxen are running in circles. God, everybody in Alaska must be able to hear this commotion. There's one down on his side. They're just running on those short legs in no direction. There's nowhere for them to go in this valley, with gunfire surrounding them. Tearing up the snow. I hear the gunbirds. Oh, Christ, they're using Willy Peter. "Mack, they're using Willy Peter." The white phosphorus is coming down in smoke streams, falling all over the oxen. They're running in circles. One is hit. Flames over his back, jumping all over his body. He's burning up.

"Take cover, take cover, Henry. They're firing at us!"

I can see the flashes of gunfire coming . . . coming from where? Just fire and noise. Now pinging against the tank. Hell, that was close. I've never heard so much noise.

"Henry, get down here in the hatch, dammit! Get down!"

I'm scared. I'm scared to move. They'll get me if I move.

They're after me anyway. For clubbing those seals. I can't take my hands off the artillery. I can't see nothing but dots and circles of red flashes. God, the noise, the noise. The banging and popping.

"Motherfucker, will you get down from that motherfuckin' tank and take cover?"

I'm frozen. My hands won't move. My heart has stopped, Mack. Please come up and get me, Mack. Can't you hear me? Please come up and get me. I'm afraid to move. My feet won't act. I can't turn around. I can't get up. Chills all over. All I can see is white noise.

"Oh, God, I'm hit! Mack, save me, I'm hit! Mack, please don't leave me, I'm hit."

"What? Oh, Christ, he's hurt. Henry, hold on. Jesus, look at the blood, it's all over him. He's got a hole . . . MEDIVAC . . . MEDIVAC. . . ."

"Oh . . . God, I can't stand it, Mack. It's going through me. Mack, do something, please do something."

"Hold on, brother, we got a chopper coming for you. It don't look too bad. We get you out of here . . . MEDIVAC . . . MEDIVAC . . . multiple frags. . . ."

"Watch his arm . . . okay, lift . . . he needs blood . . . not too serious . . . keep your eye on the pipper . . . take her up . . . easy . . . seals . . . clubbed seals . . . good troop . . . we'll call you . . . we'll call you . . . do you steal? . . . hey, dig my white shoelaces . . . don't worry about the enemy . . . boom-boom room . . . shall we sing? . . . can I get an amen? . . . take care of my daughter . . . what are the tools for? . . . new black man . . . buzz, buzz . . . where's the social security office? . . . Buzz, buzz . . . Steppin Fetchit, stop it. . . ." I'm going to die. I'm going to die. No! You got the wrong man. I'm Henry Adams, not me. Not me. Don't you understand? I'M HENRY ADAMS. It's not my time. Not yet. I'm too young. There must be a mistake. Check. Please check. Look into it some more. Not now. Mack needs me. I'm the new . . . I represent something . . . my history . . . I'm an example . . . waking up. I just woke up, dammit, you can't take me. No. No, no, no. Hell, no. No way in the world I'm supposed to die. I'll bet you a fat man. I want to talk to someone. Please, there's a mistake. Are you sure? Can't be. No way. I can't die now. Look, give me a chance to explain who I am. You don't want me. Shit, no. You got the wrong man. This is me. Look at me. Can't you see who I am? LOOK AT ME! It's not my time yet. I got things to do. Get somebody else. Plenty of cats who should be dying before me. No way I should be dying. A mistake . . . mistake. . . .

If I wasn't black, I wouldn't be dying. Not like this. Why can't you help us, Lord? Why can't you be on my side this time, just this once? I haven't done a damn thing. Asshole John Wayne. If we hadn't been shooting at some damned animals I never would have been hit. What am I fighting for? Hell, if Beatrice had any sense she would never let me come up here. Here we are trying to protect our black women, trying to make things better for them, and they pushing you out to war. All it would have taken is some begging on your part for me not to go. Daddy ain't no better. All his life holding back and shucking and jiving, trying, making me think and act just like him and now what—I have to die for it. Lord, won't you even give us a little more life? What kind of justice is this? You just put us here to get accustomed to things, and then you sweep us away. If I could get my hands on Boye, that bastard. Just let me see him before I die so I can tell him he's the fool. And Stumpy. I wouldn't play for that Mickey Rooney if he begged me now. I'm gonna die before I even got to play one damn game in that stadium. . . .

Fuckit. Ain't no sense in getting mad. Maybe I haven't been the model husband. All right. Maybe I haven't done this and done that. I'm willing to change. Christ, give me a chance. Don't take me now, give me a chance. Everybody deserves a chance. That's the least I should have to ask for. Who hasn't done something wrong in his life? But does that make him a sinner permanently? No. I got years ahead of me to make up for shit. I need another chance. That's all I'm asking for, a chance . . . a chance . . . What can I do? There must be something I can do . . . something . . . ?

Poor kids. Poor Joe Boy and Stuff and Linda. They were counting on me. The whole family was. What will they do now? And Beatrice. Her smile and hips—I'll never see them

again. I'll never see her again. She trusted me. Earrings twirling. Had so much faith. Wanted to work for me. All of our
lives changed now. Momma won't come to the funeral. I never
told Sissy I stole her Yo-Yo that time. What will they do? Who
will take over? God, why are you doing this to them? To us?
We need each other. . . .

I'm floating now. I'm dying. I'm alone and it's dark and I
can't feel a thing. I know now I have to die. It's just my time,
that's all. Where is this place, death? There's nothing to be
afraid of. It will be very peaceful, wherever it is. Something
quiet, I know. It will be black and peaceful. Nothing to be
afraid about. No need to rage and shout. Take it easy. Accept
it. Can't fight it. Has anyone succeeded in fighting it? No way.
Be strong and float on in quietly. It'll be nice and dark and
quiet and peaceful. Nobody but me. Like being high and
being serious about it. I can hear the choir. Hum with them.
Is that the reverend's voice? Do I hear his voice? Rev, I hear
you. I'm coming. I know it'll be all right. Got to go, I understand. You can't fight it. It just comes like this. Some design is
there, but how are we to figure it out? Just take it. There's no
answer to this but yes. It's easier if you answer. I feel so free
and relaxed now. I'm floating. My answer is yes, I'm ready to
die. I'm ready now. I'm dying and I've given my answer. It's
beautiful and calm somewhere out there, and I'm glad to go.
Yes. I'm ready to die. I accept the call. Take me. I'm ready to
die right now. . . .

"Henry. Stop talking to yourself."

"He's delirious."

"Henry, you'll be all right . . . can you hear me? It's Mack."

"Better not aggravate—"

"But he's moving—"

"Still in shock—"

"But he's—"

"Still in—"

"But—"

"Still—"

"Nurse—"

"Bu—"

"Sti—"

9

MACK GOT UP from the table. He had nudged
Henry on the knee. He went over to the wall and pulled
down his parka and slipped into it. Henry watched him glance
around the chow room. Tinkle of silverware against plates
and low murmurings. He went down to the door. Went out
the door.

Henry took another forkful of beans. Wiped his mouth.
Pushed his stool back. Took quick glances around him. Then
went over to pull his parka down from its hook, and fingers
straining from its weight, held it up and slipped one, then
both arms into it. Hood over his head. Zipping up. Walking
out the door and hoping that no one was watching him or
even thinking about him for that matter. Outside, the haze
of twilight. He stood with his back against the door. Nobody
was coming.

"Pssst."

Henry turned. A cone of fur, bouncing near the top of a
snow bluff. A forehead. And just at the top line of the bluff,
two eyes. Henry put his mitten to his heart, then touched his
hip, then put his mitten to his right ear. The top of Mack's
parka disappeared behind the bluff. Henry looked around
again: not a soul. Then went running over the hard snow
until he came to the bluff, and threw himself behind it. He
nodded to Mack. Mack nodded back. He had grown under
Mack's influence. Before he would have said hello and so

forth, coughing out a series of greetings. Now he understood better the hip communication of a nod, a grunt, a twitch of the mouth, a movement of the eyes. "What's happening?" he said, sitting next to Mack, back against the hard bluff, mellow yellow twilight reaching out from him to the horizon.

"We gotta do something about those signals of yours. Takes too much time."

"Whatcha mean?" He knew but wanted to fall into the confidential terseness of Mack's way of speaking. He knew he had made too many movements.

"All that touching your heart and your hip and your ear. Why don't you just do *one* of those?"

"Solid," he said, not bothering to explain to Mack that those were baseball signals he had used in hundreds of games. "Touch the heart from now on?"

"Boss. How's the shoulder?"

"Just a scratch. I'm in good shape."

"All right. We make our move tonight. Just before dinner. A chopper will pick us up just outside the gate. Are you still game?"

"Better believe it."

"Shoulder's cool?"

"Sure . . . but you know what, Mack?"

"What?" he said, and Henry was staring right at his profile, staring at the thick lips guiding the toothpick.

"I was scared to death. I thought I was going to die. I don't ever want to go through that shit again."

"Just shock. Next time you get hit you won't even think about it."

"Maybe. But I've been thinking about it for the past week. What do you think death is?"

"We're almost dead now, so it can't be much worse, if any."

"Yeah, maybe. But I was almost there. I could feel it. My feet were going in. It was like wading into the sea; you go farther and the water gets higher on you . . . I was almost there, Mack, and it wasn't scary or anything. But it was strange as hell, you know?"

"Goddam. We gettin' ready to start a revolution and this dude's talkin' about death. Why don't you wait until you die?"

"Because I'll know then. But I'm interested now. You're the one who told me to think. Well, I'm thinking about death. What is it, and what does it mean?"

"First, it's the end for you and anybody else, brother. Second, it means you ain't living no more; you ain't walkin', you ain't talkin' and you ain't eatin'. What else you wanna know? Should I tell you when you gonna die so you can buy your plot?"

His voice had gotten louder, ringing, and his eyes were flashing. He stood, bent-backed, and peeped over the bluff, the bottom of his parka sweeping over the snow.

"What's it look like?"

"Still clear." Henry watched him sit down again. His legs were out straight and he was shaking them, and his head was nodding up and down. "The password is 'MacAdams.' When you see me leave the mess hall just as everybody is sitting down, give me five minutes outside, then follow. Be ready to smoke." He got up, peeped over the bluff, kicked Henry lightly on his parka: "Better get back inside. You go first."

Henry walked toward the barracks slowly, watching his shadow on the side. He was not frightened, there wasn't an ounce of fear within him, and he was not sure why. He told himself he was only coming in from the bullpen to protect a lead in the top of the ninth during the seventh game of a World Series, and as he came into the infield the fans flooded his ears with cheers. He tipped his hat. His head was down and he walked slowly, taking long, smooth strides of determination. His glove was tucked under his left arm, and he was chewing on three packs' worth of gum. Now he was coming across the infield grass and he stopped to greet the pitcher who had been hit. The pitcher looked up at him as dogs had that Henry had met on the Mississippi roads: they slunk along the edge of the road with their noses close to the ground, eyes shooting to the side in Henry's direction. The pitcher had a case of pencils on his hip. It was Boye.

"Take a shower, motherfucker," Henry muttered, barely moving his lips, and as if they had heard him speak, the crowd cheered Henry again. He came up to the mound. A half-dozen white figures, and he didn't even look at their faces but bent to pick up the rosin and pick holes with his cleats. The manager—it was Stumpy with shades on, his voice trembling with anxiety—gave Henry the ball. "Move out," Henry interrupted him. "I'm taking over. You've fucked up the game, so get your asses out of here and let me straighten out this shit." The crowd cheered him again as he smelled the rosin. He shrugged his shoulders and tipped his hat and hitched up his pants and smoothed his socks.

No, he wasn't a bit frightened, and he thought back with embarrassment at the scenes of dread and dismay that had been his unwanted road partners for so long. He was about to make history, about to be something in history, and the great couldn't stoop to fear. He would punch Alvarez in the mouth and kick his dog, too. Spank that little Betty Hurt, and bang on the walls of his apartment and ask—no, demand —quiet. And they would take over the Home Manufacturing Company too. Get that straight. He would loud-mouth the next sick woman who rubbed against him in the subway.

He had stopped and was bending over, hands in back of his parka, eyes focused down the mound at the catcher's signal. A soldier came out of the barracks door, hesitated, stared at Henry Adams. They locked eyes. Henry was unsure of what to say, what to do, still bending over. He straightened up, cleared his throat, tried to look innocent.

"MacAdams," said the soldier, then moved away from Henry, who understood now that the soldier was part of the movement.

He heard Mack's footsteps coming up behind him, put his hand on the knob and went through the door. Nevins' voice carried from the ready room. He walked down to the room, and standing in the doorway, could see the top of Nevins' forehead moving in front of the blackboard.

The squeaky, whining voice: ". . . Now we've already talked about the AR 15, gentlemen, which is *beaucoup* deadly because when it hits the enemy's flesh, it tumbles and turns end over end, gentlemen, then tears its way out, leaving a damage cone of about three to four inches in diameter, gentlemen. In other words, gentlemen, the goddam enemy's body is so fucked up, especially if you hit him in the stomach, that the meds will have to cut him all up just to evaluate the muscle and tissue damage around the wound and so forth. This cutting takes time, gentlemen, and time can only be on our side.

"Gentlemen, will you kindly allow me to end this discussion of new antipersonnel weapons we'll be using with a brief mention of Puff, the Magic Dragon. Lieutenant, the pointer, please. Thank you. Gentlemen, Puff delivers eighteen thousand rounds a minute. It consists of three Gatling-type miniguns that you'll be shooting from your choppers. Mostly at night, gentlemen. Puff circles an outpost and in three seconds can cover an area the size of a football field at a density of one bullet per square foot. Gentlemen, nobody will escape Puff. May I repeat, *nobody* will escape as Puff circles overhead and probes, searches, then flings bullets down on those fucking ginks. They won't be so tough then, gentlemen. Are there any questions? Gentlemen, may I go on to instruct you in torture procedures. Question? Remember, gentlemen, these weapons are costly but you're Americans, and nothing's too good for our troops."

Henry saw a hand go up in the middle of the group.

"Captain, sir, when will we see the enemy, sir, to use these torture techniques?"

Henry heard the pointer slam against the floor. Nevins was on his toes, for Henry could see the flashing, glinting of gray eyeballs. And the short, crisp command, so quick that Henry wasn't sure he had heard it all.

"One hour of stationary double time for you, soldier. On the double."

Then there was a shuffling of feet and turning of shoulders and bending of heads that seemed to move through the soldiers' ranks like a current as the trooper who had been sentenced eased his way out of the room toward the door. When he reached the spot near the back where Henry Adams was standing, Henry looked into his face. It was boyish, clean, thin. He was trying to grow a mustache but it wasn't working, and there was fuzz on the upper part of his cheek. His Adam's apple was slipping up and down his throat when he stopped directly in front of Henry, and taking his hand, squeezing his arm, said "MacAdams, brother," then slid past him. And a satisfying sense of fullness swept over Henry as the boy's hand slipped out of his. He was a symbol for this young, black boy of seventeen or eighteen, just as he was a symbol for Joe Boy and Stuff, and it occurred to him that this boy by joining the movement was really a man, much more of a man than the captain.

". . . Wearing down their resistance is the main thing, gentlemen, and if you ever think that these procedures are inhumane, remember that they're treating our POWs worse. Remember, gentlemen, we're Americans. We're Americans and nobody can fuck with us. . . ."

Mack eased alongside Henry but didn't look at him.

". . . So be sure, before you hang them up by their feet, that their hands are tied securely behind them, gentlemen. . . ."

"You must have gotten everybody in the company on our side," Henry whispered to Mack.

"Almost."

". . . One of the concoctions we can make them drink contains powdered lime, gentlemen, but keep your fingers away from it. . . ."

"I'm not even scared, Mack. I'm ready to go now."

". . . These electrical wires can be applied to the prisoner's ears, nipples and balls for best effects, gentlemen. . . ."

"Just lay low until dinnertime."

". . . Are there any questions? Class dismissed."

Henry and Mack were the first outside. They leaned against the wall just to the side of the door, and Henry, looking straight ahead, could from the corner of his eye see Mack's face turn slightly in his direction. The other soldiers were filing out of the barracks and splitting up in groups of twos and threes, walking to get exercise. Mack nodded forward, slapped Henry against the hip with his mitten, and started walking slowly to the left. In a space between two groups of soldiers, Henry saw two figures moving toward him. They had white armbands on their parkas: MP. One moved to the left in Mack's direction and the other, a nightstick in his hand, was coming toward Henry. Henry's knees were weakening, his wrists were perspiring. He started walking slowly to the right, along the wall of the barracks and his breathing was coming hard as he tried to restrain himself from running, tried to walk as unconcernedly as he could. Footsteps behind him, coming faster. He quickened his pace. Now he was past the barracks and in the open, approaching the series of bluffs and banks dotting the back field of the base beyond the wire fence. As if he were starting his sprint from first to second on a steal, Henry ran for the fence, jumped over it and headed for a bluff that was chest-high.

"Stop!"

Kneeling behind the bluff, he peeped over it. The MP, his rifle in the air and one leg half over the fence, had his parka stuck in the wire. He was kicking and twisting himself and puffs of frost were coming from his mouth, hiding his face. Henry ran farther out behind another bluff. He peeped out on the side. The MP was over the fence. Standing, his shoulders heaving, clouds of frost surrounding his face which jerked sideways, surveying the landscape. Henry was scared now, and he wasn't even aware of the cold. His forehead was hot, very hot.

"Come out. I just want to talk to you."

He was standing with his rifle diagonal against his chest. Then swiftly, rifle aimed ahead, bayonet, Henry imagined, pointed at his nose, the shoulder advanced forward, straight toward Henry. Henry looked up to discover that his breathing was giving off smoke signals: the frost from his breath revealed his position. Henry rose to turn and slipped on a slick stretch of ice. He got up, and running in a zigzag pattern, fell behind a bluff thirty yards away.

It seemed now that the bluffs were spaced like fat trees in a forest. He couldn't see or hear the MP, but he watched the east-west movement of the stream of frost signaling the MP's progress through the maze of bluffs. Then there was no more of it. Henry peeped to the side. He inched to the other side and eased half of his face out to peep: no stream of frost. Was he holding his breath? He stood up and looked over the top of the bluff: nothing. His imagination stirred. Maybe the

MP was on the other side of the bluff, about to shoot him? Perhaps he had somehow sneaked around and was aiming *right now* at Henry from behind? He whirled around. Nothing but the wintry bright sunlight and more bluffs. He sat down, trying to control his shivering. Where was Mack? Why had the MPs come after them? Had somebody squealed? And if so, did that mean the escape was off? He was still perspiring, but the warmth had left him. Now he felt the cold nipping and pinching his face. He kept turning it, but the cold followed it as if, he imagined, it was angry with him. His body started quaking and he knew it was dangerous for him to keep still like this, that soon he wouldn't be able to move at all and already the sunlight, the soft yellow sunlight, was becoming indistinct and all ahead was a screen of white-blue nothingness. He knew he should move but was afraid and too cold to do anything, his back against the bluff, his legs outstretched and bumping against each other, the keen spurts of frigid air biting his face. What? Footsteps. The distinct sound of footsteps, more than one man's, thumping and scraping toward him. He was falling asleep, however, and there was no choice for him. He was falling . . . falling asleep, drugged into senselessness . . . couldn't possibly call up the strength to get up and fight . . . let him come.

"There he is!"

"Damn, he's almost frozen, look at his lips."

Henry opened his eyes. Soldiers, face masks coated with thin drips of ice. They had their hands on him and were picking him up, slapping his face.

"MacAdams," said one. "Everything's okay. The Run's in the barracks, asleep. Everything is everything. We took care of the MPs, brother. Can you make it back to the barracks by yourself? We don't want to start any suspicion."

Henry opened his eyes; life was returning to his limbs. The soldier was white. Mack had gotten everybody in on it, damn. "I'll be all right," he said, losing his balance, then straightening himself up. "I can make it," moving around them and walking around the bluff, and it wasn't until he was climbing the fence did he realize that he hadn't even thanked them.

Still shaken up, he passed the young soldier who was pumping his legs, doing stationary double time, and nodded at him, then trudged toward the barracks. No one in the yard seemed to notice him.

Mack was lying on a bunk, propped up on his elbows. "Somebody blew," he said as Henry entered the room. "As soon as they find the MPs missing, the shit will be tighter than Dick's hatband."

The warm air hit Henry in the face and he wanted to put his face all in it. He threw off his coat, undressed and carried his clothing over to the bunk. His wool socks were wet. His legs still had the shakes and he couldn't steady his knees. He fell on the bunk and sighed loudly, deliberately holding back his words because he knew that was how Mack would have operated. "What happened to the MPs?" He crossed one leg over the other, his head rested on the pillow.

"They offed them."

Henry swallowed. He would have to get used to violence, he knew, but always when confronting it, when thinking about it, when seeing it, he suffered a feeble melting sensation in his stomach. This time it was more pronounced than usual, for the violence had been close to him—he had been the cause of it. He saw himself swinging with short, choppy blows at the seals and imagined the soldiers working on the MPs like that, the flat-sounding thuds of their weapons against the MPs' bodies lost in the cold air. God, wasn't there any other way? *Never was, never will be.* He turned over on his side, away from Mack.

"You all right?"

"Yeah," he said.

"Try to get some sleep then."

Mack is fantastic, he thought. He can actually sleep through this, knowing that in a few hours the whole thing may be over. In a few hours it's do or die. In a few hours he would be on his way to being closer to Beatrice. He wouldn't talk at all, just grab her and steady himself and slide his arms around her and squeeze her and squeeze her. There would be no trouble this time, he knew it, because his mind was clear, defogged. He was liberated, in the best psychological state

174

of his life, and nothing could keep him from concentrating on making love to his wife. If things went right he would have a chance to see Joe Boy and the rest. They might even be part of the movement. Yeah, maybe. He had never even thought of that before. There were sympathizers throughout the country. Ask Mack. He looked over to Runner Mack. The Run was asleep in his underwear, mouth open, toothpick sticking up. Henry stared at the triangles and rectangles of light on the floor. He looked across the room to the window. Through it he could see nothing but bright whiteness. He was anxious and restless and knew he couldn't possibly sleep. He was reminded of so many Christmas Eves, when, knowing there would be no more than some used clothing from the state under the tree, he would twist and turn sleeplessly all night. But this was worse than Christmas Eve because there was no tree, no guarantee of anything at all. Not a thing. So, warmth filling his body and much of the fear melting away from him, he turned and twisted his body, stared at every corner of the barracks until he heard the whistle for chow and knew it was time. He looked over at Mack. He was still asleep, arms outstretched horizontally across the bed in a perfect swan-dive position, fingers dangling near the floor.

"Run, it's time. The chow bell just went off."

Mack jumped up. "What time is it?" Rubbing his eyes. Nose sniffing.

Henry didn't answer, began dressing. He watched Mack begin to dress, too, and for a crazy instant was hoping the Run would say that it was all off.

"Let's go," said Runner Mack, and his face was hidden in the tangle of his parka as he heaved into it. He was at the door already.

Was this it? Where were they to get food? What about clothing? Henry had never asked about that. In fact, he hadn't asked about anything. Where were they going? For how long? When would they blow up the White House? Hell, it was too late now. Mack had the door open and was jostling his shoulders and moving his feet, waiting for Henry to zip up. He would have to get these answers in the chopper. "I'm with you all the way," he said.

Outside, a blizzard. Mack walking sideways toward the other base building and Henry following and wondering why he hadn't seen the blizzard from inside. Nobody on the grounds. The wind sighing and the snow gusts tipping down their backs. Henry couldn't see anything now but the occasional flickering of the lights in the barracks. It wasn't nightfall, he knew, but everything before them was hoary, metallic in its dullness and cloudiness. This is the way it would have to be, he thought. Nothing easy. Just another difficulty to add to the catalog. Chopper probably won't want to come anywhere near this place. "Not so fast, Run." Henry was hit heavily in the chest by a fresh gust and then he saw Mack lose his balance, toppling to the side while he, Henry, was spun around sideways, suddenly finding himself on his heels with his arms flailing in the air for balance, for a pole or tree that wasn't there. He pushed against the wall of wind until he was able to straighten himself up and turn again toward the base building. Mack too, he saw, had regained his balance after tottering on one leg as if he were climbing a bluff.

They rushed through the door, hung their parkas on the wall hooks and sat down opposite each other. The bulbs flickered from the ceiling, throwing the large hall into intermittent darkness. Henry was hungry but he couldn't eat. His stomach was tight and jittery, and the strong, spicy odor of the beans was at odds with their appearance, he thought. So he was mashing the beans slowly in his mouth while glancing at the other soldiers and wondering who, which one of them was trying to blow it, blow everything. The two on either side of Mack appeared solemn and very serious, and when their eyes met Henry's there was a relaxed, soft blankness in their stares. Mack looked up at the clock in back of Henry. And in a split second of darkness as the lights flickered, Henry was positive he saw one of the soldiers near the other end of the table rise hastily and vanish—through the wall, a door, a window? He wasn't sure. Mack rose. He had finished his dinner that quickly. Walked rapidly to the coat hooks. Was outside. Henry's heart was thumping, blood was pressing against his temples, and in a dizzying fit of impulse he pushed his stool back and hustled for his coat. He saw it hanging on the hook, an amoeba-shaped pool of melted snow forming on the floor-boards below it. He was walking and walking and it seemed to move farther and farther away from him, and he was reaching out for it and it wasn't there and he heard somebody call his name just as he pulled the wet mittens out of the pocket but he wasn't looking back and he threw the parka over his shoulders—didn't even notice its weight—and slid into it and went for the door and pushed into the growl of the blizzard. Mack was right there, moving his arms in dog-paddle fashion, trying to see.

"Now!"

Mack started. Henry was right behind him, thinking that his whole life was in this run and suddenly nothing mattered, nothing was on his mind but running, running. Mack was pushed to the side by the wind, screaming and churning up the snow, and already Henry felt his heart working hard; it was thundering within him, like the thumping he had experienced running up the seats in the hometown baseball stadium; but this time there was no stopping for breath, no rest period, he knew. Mack, three feet in front, was stumbling, staggering against the wind with his arms wide for balance, and Henry was almost kneeling, bent low, crouching as he too was pushed and shoved by the wind. He couldn't see anything but the unsteady bent figure of Mack, turning now and seemingly fully aware of his direction.

A crack. A snapping fissure in the air behind them. Henry turned—half as fast as he had intended because his shoulder was slammed sideways by the wind—and saw the red-yellow pea flashes in the distance. Another crack. They were firing blindly, he thought, they can't possibly see us. He turned to see that Mack had gone ahead without stopping and was over the fence, gesturing with his arms. Henry, fighting the wind, twice falling just as his leg was perfectly horizontal with the fence, finally sprang over it. He heard the whir of the chopper blades but couldn't see anything but the streaks of snow currents and Mack's solitary dark figure against the broad screen of snow.

Mack stumbled and Henry fell on top of him. Henry Adams rose. Runner Mack lay in the snow. He was holding his knee.

Henry tried to pull him up but understood when, kneeling close to Mack's face, he heard the Run scream out, "The knee, it's the goddam trick knee again." Flashes of crackling yellow. Whir of the blades. Howl of the snow. "Kick it, dammit. Kick it."

Henry lifted his leg to kick it but was caught off-balance standing on one leg and fell before he could swing his leg. He got to his feet again and kicked Runner Mack's knee twice with short, hard efforts. Mack jumped up and bumped into Henry, then made for the sound of the copter.

His heart was going to stop, he was sure. He wasn't running now, they were just jogging from tiredness, arms down at their sides, heads bobbing left and right, and Henry was spitting and swallowing, trying to discharge the dryness from his mouth, and his nostrils were wet and burning, his knees and thighs cramped with soreness. He could see the helicopter. It was only thirty yards away, he guessed, wiping the sleet from his eyes, and both he and Mack were walking almost. Red, small bulbs of light on the side of the pear-shaped chopper, squatting. Then another series of cracks and this time . . . he wasn't positive, it could be the excitement . . . but it came clearer this time . . . growls? Had to be the wind, he thought. But there were many of them, and he had heard them before in the middle of the many nights he had spent up here (and how long had that been?). No mistake. Wolves. They had wolves after them. Mack was approaching the chopper, was at the door, and Henry stopped dead. He turned. Small, very small beady eyes way off but moving distinctly closer. He looked in Mack's direction. Mack was beckoning, waving his arms, and Henry caught snatches of his faraway voice. He couldn't move.

The snarls were separate and louder and he couldn't move. Mack kept beckoning. He was in a cold trance, unsure of where he was or what he should do. He should run toward this man who was jumping up and down and waving his arms. His feet wouldn't go and the scream of the wind now had a fascinating, attractive quality about it, and he thought he could listen to it for a while. The wolves, they were just like dogs anyway and he might pet them. Beautiful teeth. The beautiful metallic gray of the snow. . . .

"Come on, dammit." Mack grabbed him by the shoulder and spun him around and pushed him toward the chopper. Henry moved automatically. They got to the chopper. Mack climbed up to the cockpit. Henry turned in the direction of the wolf snarls and caught a flash of sleet down his neck. Mack opened the cabin door. He was on his knees and looking down at Henry. "Help me get this dude out of here."

"What's the matter?" cupping his hands up to Mack.

"The muhfuckah," out of breath and spacing his words, "the . . . muhfuckah's . . . dead. He froze to death. Pull his legs."

Henry watched the body of the pilot fall stiffly to the ground and it lay there as if at attention. Henry climbed up. Mack had already pushed back the hood of his parka and was pulling some levers, and the entire scene looked comfortably familiar to Henry, who had already put the back of his head against the seat and was trying to recover from what he was sure must have been a minor heart attack.

They were going up. He wanted to smile, laugh, chuckle, snort, giggle, roar. They were going up, and he looked over at Runner Mack and couldn't believe it. Mack had a toothpick in his mouth.

"Run . . . Run, you are fantastic, man."

"Right on time," he said.

And as they moved over the mountains and left the storm behind them, they descended on the other side of the range and saw a small, ice-littered lake. At the far edge of the lake were three rays: red, yellow and green, rising upward and curving away from the mountains. Henry had little to say about it. He just nudged Mack and Runner Mack nodded that he saw it, too, and Henry decided that the first thing he would tell Beatrice about Alaska was not the cold or the animals or the war, but the shimmering, stunning rainbow.

10

"WHERE ARE WE GOING, Mack? We aren't go-
ing straight to the White House, are we?" Henry had just
awakened and had been staring down through the convex
glass of the helicopter cockpit to the ground. They didn't
have much altitude, so he could see the unmistakable streaks
of roads running through the landscape below them. He could
see everything clearly: the squares of green and brown, the
odd-shaped tops of houses and a blue-green river.

"We should be over Oregon now," Runner Mack said. He
was out of his parka and had his shirt unbuttoned to his
chest, and the side of his face had the short, scattered hairs of
a beginning beard.

Then Henry, perspiring, squirmed out of his parka and
threw it in the back. "How long have I been asleep?"

"About four hours," shouting over the whir of the propellers.

"Well, we made it, huh, Mack?"

"Yeah, but this is only the beginning, bro."

"What are the plans? I don't even know all the plans, Mack."

"We slide to the East and lay until the time is right, and
then"—toothpick flipping upward—"and then . . . boom."

"Uhm . . . uh . . . we aren't flying to the East in this
helicopter, are we?" asked Henry, hoping that his questions
weren't irritating Mack, but he had to know something.

"No, man. We go by train. It's all worked out. Plus, we have to make some contacts along the way. We can't get across the country in this thing. They'll be all over us. It was a bitch just getting into Oregon."

"How'd we do it?" asked Henry, looking away from Mack, looking out the window to give the impression that he wasn't worried, that this was just a routine question. He could tell that Mack was facing him now, for the answer came louder than his other sentences.

"Contacts. Contacts, baby. I've been compiling a list of contacts from the jumps, since I started this movement a couple of years ago. We got contacts in the White House."

"Where?" asked Henry, turning to stare at Mack.

"In the kitchen, where else? One of the cooks is a member. He spits on the food every day."

"Damn," said Henry.

"And not only that, dig this. The last time I rapped with the brother, he said that the more he spits, the more often he gets complimented." Mack raised his eyebrows and pursed his lips, and Henry took his cue.

"Ain't that a bitch."

"Can you get to that? Aren't those muthafuckahs crazy, Henry Adams?"

"Got to be, Mack. We're up against some strange shit," Henry answered, then thinking that he had better tone down his language because since they were going East he would have a chance to see Beatrice.

"Somebody blew the whole story, Henry, so we have to be extra careful. I think that's the field down there." Mack tilted the chopper and began the descent.

Henry looked down as they tilted, and it seemed as if he was lying flat on his stomach for a moment. He didn't see a landing field, though. To his left were tops and more tops of trees, and to his left was a lake. But they were going down, and sideways, he thought.

"Who do you think it was, Mack? McNewby, Bronson, Sloan?"

"Hard to tell, Henry," shouting and shaking his head left and right before the glass. "The best way is to assume that anyone is capable of betraying you. You know? Where is the damned landing strip?" He took the chopper up another two hundred feet.

Henry looked straight ahead—they were flying level—and stared and felt a weakening sensation capture his insides. He was staring at the sky and the dark tops of the trees, but the blue of one and the green of the other were just blurs. He wasn't sure. Was he staring at the sky and the trees and not searching for Mack's meaning? Mack saying he did not trust him, Henry? And should not Henry trust him, Mack? Did he think Henry had squealed?

"What do you mean?" Henry asked, but Mack's answer was interrupted when he saw the open patch of trees and concentrated on taking down the chopper. They landed in a stretch of dirt, a circular stretch surrounded by trees whose branches and leaves were waving, bending from the propellers' draft. Directly ahead in front of them was a path. Mack jumped down and Henry followed. The dust stirred up from the road hung in the air, and soon Henry was coughing and his eyes were tearing. It was a pleasant day, the sun high but unobtrusive, birds whistling deep in the trees beyond them. He wasn't sure what season it was, having lost track of time in Alaska, but the calm brightness of the day reminded him of spring back home. It was a perfect day, he thought.

He watched Runner Mack walk around the chopper and look up at the trees. His hands were on his hips, toothpick jiggling in his mouth, and he was walking in what Henry had in his own terminology called that boppety-bop way—big hands (dark, and his palms were pallid) down by his legs which sprang with each step, and head nodding forward.

"Mack," he began—because he had to have answers, had to know where he stood and what was going on, and what Mack, this mysterious, fascinating man who had taken him from the cold of Alaska to this beautiful, secluded spot in Oregon, thought of him, Henry, and what . . . just what was the story —"Mack, what did you mean by anyone is capable of betraying you?" He knew nothing about this man except that Mack had been the most influential person in his life. In the short time of their acquaintance, he had listened to all and agreed to almost everything Mack had said to him, and yet he knew nothing about Mack, really. He had told Runner his entire story, his life history, but in balancing the conversations now in this stretch of land in Oregon, Henry realized that Mack had told him little of his life. Maybe he didn't trust Henry? Henry didn't know anything about Mack's early life; nothing about his friends, enemies, bosses, lovers, wives, landlords. Where had he lived? Where had he learned all that he knew? Did he go to college? But wait, he told himself, now you're becoming suspicious. Don't you trust the Run?

"Are you listening, man?"

"Yeah, Mack."

"Oh. The way you were staring out in space, I didn't know. Dig, I trust you and I hope you trust me, but what does that mean? We're road partners and ace-boon coons, main men, but does that mean nothing would come between us? I don't know. I've seen it happen so many times, Henry, and in this business, the way we operate, anything can go wrong. Look at our escape. We almost didn't make it. We've got to be careful, that's all I'm saying."

"I trust you, Mack," Henry said.

"I trust you too, man, but just remember we both may change. Shit, I hope not. Who knows what we'll do, Henry?"

They were yards apart at this moment and alternately looking at each other and looking away, and Henry had the strangest feeling when Mack had finished of incompleteness and uncertainty, and it was an awkward feeling to stand there in the shade, the sun overhead and the birds hidden around them, because there was no place to go and nothing to do and he couldn't think of anything to say. Again, Runner was too often coming up with statements to which he had no answer, and again, here, they were standing, scratching their heads and moving their feet to nowhere and unfolding and folding their arms—doing this and Henry was lost, feeling that he wasn't equipped somehow to overcome this clumsy bridge in their conversation. So he turned away, swinging his arms and whistling, after nodding to Mack that he understood. Mack was too much for him. His mind was quick and alert, acute and finished, and Henry had been looking upon himself as the Run's pupil, as someone unlettered and unlearned who should tie himself to Mack's attainments in order to improve what Henry knew to be his own shortcomings. Yes, Mack had changed his life, opened his eyes, brought him around to *thinking*, and although he didn't believe everything, he was positive that there was a shared destiny of some sort between them. They had to stay together; that was their future. And they had to trust each other, because if they didn't. . . . But he couldn't translate these thoughts to words and it frustrated him, not being able yet to communicate with Mack. Well, Mack would guide him, and Henry would learn to stand toe to toe with the man.

"You're probably right, Mack," he said over his head, then turned to look down the road. A car was coming. Dust stirring up on both sides, bathing the trees, a fender throwing flashes of sunlight, the front grille rising up and down like a boat fighting waves. It was black and long and shiny and the motor was ticking easily, very quietly, and that's all Henry could hear as he and Mack stood on either side waiting for the car to stop. It was a limousine, like the one the governor had come in one day to visit Henry's hometown after a flood. The windows were up, and Henry saw that the hood still shone despite the new thin layer of dust covering the whole car. The driver opened the door and Henry jumped back from it and watched as two long legs turned outward and eased toward the ground, black shoes shining. Well-pressed black slacks. A round, firm waist. The driver's head bent and curved outward, too, and he was wearing a black stingy-brim. Now he was out completely, standing in front of Henry, who looked upward and thought that this was the tallest man he had ever seen. He was black, wore dark glasses; face covered with hair: a mustache, a full beard. A pink shirt, black tie, black suit jacket. Frowning down at Henry.

"MacAdams?" A whiff of after-shave lotion.

"Right," said Henry, and stuck out his hand. From the corner of his eye, he saw Mack walking over to them. His hand was still out as Mack stood by his side. He realized that the driver was not going to shake his hand, so he dropped his down easily.

"MacAdams," said Runner Mack, head bobbing, toothpick jumping.

The driver shook his head at Mack, then turned to the back of the car and signaled with a clenched fist. Henry saw a head pop up in the back seat, then the door opened, and he was surprised to see a woman in slacks and a blouse, climb out of the back.

"Hey, sister," said Mack, voice, thought Henry, too loud for the circumstances. She nodded, stood with her hands at her sides, and Henry could see she was nervous as she bit her lip; and bent fingers fidgeting, looked vacantly toward the trees.

"Take up the chopper, Melba. You know what to do after that."

And she was moving between the three men—fresh scent of perfume pleasing—excusing herself, and as Henry watched the cheeks of her behind flutter and wondered if she was wearing panties, he knew that his companions were watching, too, and it wasn't until she was in the cockpit and waving at them did they turn quickly to face each other.

"That's not bad at all," said Mack.

"Nope," said Henry, but he had a vision already of Beatrice even as he said it.

"She's all right," said the driver, turning his back and reaching down for the door handle. "Let's go. Take the back seat."

Henry went in first, and as his fingers slid over the soft grain of the leather upholstery, his legs and arms seemed to be ridding themselves of the accumulation of aches and pains that had been his companions during his—how long had he been in Alaska, anyway? The glass partition between the seats went up. The driver was waving at Melba, who had started the engine of the chopper, and with a few fingers of his left hand, was steering the car around and back toward the road. Henry sniffed in the clean, leathery richness of the interior and leaned back, crossed his legs. Even the carpeting was richer than anything he had ever seen back in Mississippi, and he had already counted three ashtrays, and there was a telephone attached to the cabinet built into the back of the front seat. He knew they were riding up a bumpy road, but he wasn't shaken, so he closed his eyes and floated with the motion.

"How'd it go?"

Henry jerked forward and turned around to search for the metallic voice. It had come out of the rear window. He saw two speakers.

"Not bad at all. We got a lot of cats in the movement up there. They'll be trickling out one by one."

Mack's voice was relayed to the front of the limousine in a hollow, squeaky tone, and Henry remembered some gangster movies he had seen in which two men cradling shotguns, hats turned down over their eyes, sat in the back seat. It was always Humphrey Bogart who gave the orders, and he always wore a carnation and carried a pistol that never ran out of bullets, and now Henry was thinking that he was Humphrey Bogart this time, riding in the back, about to make history that his son—it would have to be a boy—would read about.

"I bet it was cold up there, huh?"

"It was a little chilly. You know."

How far were they from Mississippi? He wouldn't ask that, but suppose he could drive past the house like this and wave at his parents. Suppose they could drive up to the one-room, white-shingled city hall and call the sheriff out, and when he got to the car Henry would say, "We're about to take over the country and you're the first to go, red-necked bastard"—tires squealing up dust in his face which was pink even hours after he shaved, and dust settling on his tan shoes with the hole cut out on the side for the corn on his little toe. But the thing would be if he could see Boye. He'd pull up to the curb and call Boye over, make him bend down, and he'd say, "We're taking over, muhfuh, and you just hold on until I check something." He'd reach back into the car for a slide rule, work on it, pulling the middle rod out and in, out and in, then report, "I'm sorry, you have to go." After that, smack the slide rule in his palm, push the button for the window, scoot off.

"This is just like the movies, Run," he said, tilting his head in Runner Mack's direction but not looking at him.

"Yeah, we might be in a movie, for all we know," was the

answer. "Except for one thing. Did you ever see any black gangsters in the movies?" And that was all, Henry knew. Mack wouldn't say anything else, would give Henry time to digest his statement, and in every instance, as in this one, Henry would be speechless, for there was nothing to say. Mack could capsulize history like that in a sentence, and Henry would be befuddled, because Mack was *always* doing this. And then: "This reminds me of a novel, you know, about a cat who iced a gray bitch and stuck her body in the furnace. But before that, he was riding in a limousine with her. Remember that one?"

"Uh, no, I don't think I read it," said Henry, once more feeling that he hadn't read anything and Mack had read all, everything, and that this was the absolute strength of Mack, that he had consumed the written word voraciously, like a tiger, and the ideas, the concepts were boiling within him. He knew about things—theories, doctrines, points of view—and Henry understood now after a hundred conversations with Runnington Mack that he had found a contradiction between what he called the values of those ideas and the reality of what he saw every day, which was an absence of those values. It had been heavy stuff when Mack had begun to run it down to him, for Henry's vocabulary had not fashioned the meaning of words like *values, reality, principles, ideals.* Now he wished —no, since he met Runner Mack he had begun wishing—that he had taken school more seriously, for there were thousands of books he was going to read after the shit was over, and he knew that his mind would be far behind the pace of his eyes over the words, and he would have to go back over pages; it would be agonizing. But he wanted to be able to talk about these things with Mack, Beatrice, maybe even Sissy—with somebody, anybody. He glanced out the window to see the trees, a tall green fence, still lining the road.

"So what's the story?" asked Mack.

"We got your clothes in the trunk. You take a train across the States, but you have to make a stop before you go all the way East to make some final contacts. When you get East, there's a final meeting before . . . boom."

"How's our man at the capitol? Still on the case?"

"Yeah," saying this with a half-laugh, surprising Henry, who looked upon the driver as a man who would throw a stone at a hearse (Joe Boy used to say that about Reverend Fuller). "You know that dude almost fucked us all up?"

"What?"

"No shit," said Henry, for the first time to anyone other than Mack, and he kept his eyes on the driver's head to test his response.

"Where'd you get this cat from?" said the driver, looking at Henry through the rearview mirror, the eyeglasses black and shiny. "Sounds like he's from the South."

"He is," said Mack. "So what happened?"

"The dude got caught spitting in the President's turtle soup, man."

"You must be jivin' me."

"Square business, man."

"So?"

"Yeah, so what happened?" asked Henry, thinking that they would drag it out for an hour.

"So they asked him why he wanted to spit in the President's turtle soup."

"Yeah?"

"He said he didn't want to, then he started sneezing and made like he had an attack of asthma and they said cool, now we know why we thought you had spit on purpose."

"Ain't that a bitch. And he's still there?"

"Still working for us. You'll get the blueprints when you get East."

He drove onto a paved road, but there were still trees on both sides, and it was quiet and a quick glance backward assured Henry that no one was behind them and there wasn't a car coming in their direction. Soon the driver pulled over to a shaded parking area. Henry saw a picnic bench and a trash can. He got out with Mack and the driver and followed them to the back of the car. The driver opened the trunk. Inside were two suitcases and a cafeteria of food: a watermelon, pretzels, sandwiches, apples, bags of candy scattered over the trunk.

188

"You cats go get changed"—pointing to the woods—"and I'll put the food on the table and keep a lookout."

Henry lifted a suitcase and followed Mack to the woods. He opened it. He watched Mack open his and immediately begin digging through it, then stopping to stare at Henry and say, "Hurry up, man, whatcha waitin' for?"

Henry changed his pants first. For his military fatigues he saw that they—whoever they were—had given him a pair of formal trousers with a silk stripe down the pant sides, and he already had the feeling that he would be dressed as he had been that night with Beatrice in the Come On Inn. And he was right, he told himself, as he spotted a cummerbund, a red-and-green-plaid bow tie, a stiff formal shirt, a package of stays, pearl cuff links, silk knee-length socks and a green formal jacket with NATIONAL RAILROAD printed on the shoulder emblem. Mack was snapping his bow tie as Henry slid into his jacket, and it felt like paper compared to the parka he had been wearing for months. Then he watched Mack bend over, and when he looked at Runner Mack it was from an unaccustomed angle, as if Mack had fallen instead of merely bent. As a matter of fact, he thought, the trees seemed to be—. "Hey, Mack," he said, hesitating a moment, until finally, "are these . . . these are elevator shoes, aren't they?"

And Mack, way below him it seemed, looked upward, said, "You got it."

So he had elevator shoes. Clever. Very clever. And what else besides this suit? A dark-red wig. A red Vandyke beard. A mole, which he stuck on the left side of his neck. He wished for a mirror. "How do I look," patting the curly wig on his head, "with this on?"

"Not bad at all," said Mack, now wearing a pair of black horn-rimmed glasses.

Henry put his old military outfit in the suitcase, closed it and followed Mack up the incline to the small picnic area. The driver was sitting at the picnic bench, which was occupied this time with paper plates and cups and food. Henry and Mack put their suitcases in the trunk, and just as they turned, Henry anxious to bite into some of the food, he saw the driver collecting the plates and food, saying, "Well, the picnic's over," and folding everything in the tablecloth and tying the ends of the cloth together.

"Aren't we going to eat any of that?" asked Henry, swallowing the last word because his stomach had begun to fidget. "At least cut the watermelon." He watched the driver heave the bundle of tablecloth over his shoulder.

"This is just to fool people into thinking we're having a picnic," he said, and his stingy-brim was tipped to the side while his neck tilted off-center, so he was looking at Henry at an angle, as if he were dodging a punch Henry had thrown.

"Well, if we eat some of it, it'll still fool them, won't it?"

So the driver unraveled the picnic and they sat down at the table and Henry was so hungry he lost all contact with the uneasy and frequent pangs of fear he had been experiencing since climbing out of the copter. He felt the mayonnaise drip on his beard as his teeth galloped over a sandwich, but he didn't care, just as he ignored their complaints about smacking his lips. The sandwich was so good, each bite tasted like he wanted more. Occasionally he would look up to stare at the dark glasses of the driver and this would remind him of the magnitude of their mission, but his mind was in a temporary stupor and all that he could concentrate on was fulfilling his hunger. After he drank his fourth cup of juice, he felt bloated and wasn't sure he could stand up. He wiped his napkin over his mouth, then stood unsteadily and headed for the limousine after looking down at Mack's plate and belching relief out of his stomach and getting a disappointing response from Mack to his question, "Can you eat all of your watermelon, Mack? Need any help?" So he got in the car, stumbling in his new shoes and bumping his head against the top of the door. He was full. But he was also tired. Could stand a nap. Soon he was nodding, his eyes catching glimpses of the sunlight filtering through the front window and his ears picking up the vacillating strains of bird calls. He couldn't hold on any longer.

He dreamed about a train coming through his living room and picking up him and Beatrice. It dropped them off in front of the White House, and during the entire trip he kept shiver-

190

ing and talking about how cold it was. Beatrice was in the train naked and white men kept coming by and feeling her toes, and once a fat one with a cigar as long as a broom bent to tickle Beatrice's baby toe and Henry slapped him, and suddenly there were a dozen soldiers surrounding him and Beatrice, and they were pointing M-1 rifles at Henry's forehead and he started perspiring and then he was afraid of dying and began crying. He wiped the tears away with his fingers and woke up with wet eyes.

"What are you crying for, man?"

At first Henry didn't know where he was, but it came back to him and he reconstructed what had happened. He had gotten into the car. Had fallen asleep. Had dreamed. Had a nightmare. A daymare. Meanwhile the limousine was moving, and that's where he was now, in the back seat of the limousine, crying, Mack asking him why.

"Just a dream," he said. "Didn't even make sense."

They slowed down. Henry looked over the seat and through the front window. They were coming to a train station and it seemed, as they pulled into the parking area, that it had been designed exactly like the one in Mississippi. Henry looked at the crisscross sign, the dirty, capped, red warning light, the old wooden wagons of suitcases. And the faint tinkle of the arrival bell even sounded the same. He counted three or four waiting passengers.

"There's another suitcase waiting for you in roomette six," said the driver, his arm along the top of his seat, voice still being transmitted from the speakers in the back. "Don't talk to too many of the waiters. Here she comes now."

Henry again felt excitement and fear creeping over his bones when he saw the train bursting toward the platform. They nodded to the driver after the train had stopped and the passengers had boarded, and soon they were striding toward one of the aluminum stepways. Henry couldn't move as fast as Mack and he hadn't yet accustomed himself to his new height, so he knew he must have appeared a giant with new shoes to anyone looking from the windows of the train.

"It's so nice and quiet out here, you wouldn't even think it was part of America," said Mack, pushing the door to the dining car. "But I bet they're just as crazy out here as the rest of them."

The train lurched forward, sending Henry against the side of the entrance, knocking his beard off-balance. Mack was through the door. Henry hurriedly adjusted his beard, then pushed with two hands the heavy door to the dining car.

All the tables were filled with diners. As Henry walked straddle-legged down the thin aisle, the train's uneven movement sending him left and right, he kept his eyes on the back of Mack, who was just ahead, making his way carefully. Henry heard a blurred, buzzing commotion of voices and silverware and glasses on either side, and he wanted to keep it like that, just wanted the blur to stay there until he could get past it. But just as Mack was going through the door at the end of the car and Henry was about to thank the Lord for getting him through yet one more crisis—his fingers were reaching for the metal, horizontal strip of door handle—he heard a voice behind him. It was high, cutting through the hollow, low tone of the blurred clicking, and it sliced through, pierced Henry's consciousness, stabbed him in the back.

"Waiter."

Mack was gone through the door now and Henry had to act for himself. He saw Mack, framed in the door's window, turn on the platform, and Henry waved a signal for him to wait. Henry Adams turned around carefully because the train was making a turn and the glasses were sliding around on the tables. A single braceleted arm in the air about the middle of the car, fingers vibrating. He was on his own now, he thought, as he started down the aisle, sliding along in what he knew must be the clumsiest shoes ever made. They were swimming on his feet and his head was too high. He approached the woman's table and turned to face her. She was young, wore purple lipstick and had a dimple on her right cheek. Her companion was behind a newspaper, but Henry could see his balding head.

"I'll have a cup of coffee, please, and a Danish."

"Yes, ma'am," he said, feeling that the movement depended on him right there and that it was no time to act like a revolutionary. "Will there be anything else, ma'am?" Now who would ever guess that he was about to blow up the White House? Had she any idea that he was about to destroy things as they were?

"Christ, Helen," her companion jerked down his paper, "did you read this? What are we coming to?"

Not much, thought Henry, and suddenly he was enjoying it all. He was about to give them an answer and they themselves were wondering what the answer was. They were sitting right there in front of him wondering, and *he had the answer*. He! And they were ignoring him, as if his mind couldn't possibly approach or appreciate or even rebel against the enormity of it all. He was a waiter, a black waiter at that; and that was all. He didn't even count. Sure, they would take care of it all—sitting there exclaiming. He watched her grab one end of the paper.

"I don't believe it," she said. "It's terrible, Marshall, just terrible. What's happening to this country?"

"Just wait," said Henry, and he tried to send his tongue after the words as soon as they were out. I've blown it all, he thought as he collected their stares; and then, without any idea of how he had thought of it, he added, "Just wait until I bring back this coffee, ma'am. It's the best in the West." With relief he saw them nod and go back to the newspaper and he straddled his way down the aisle, the rattle of voices louder now, but he didn't care if they all ordered something. He was too smart for them and he could handle them all. He went through the door. Mack must have kept his eyes on him.

"How'd it go?"

"Okay, but she wants some coffee and a Danish."

"Fuckit."

"But suppose she pitches a bitch and says the waiter with the red hair didn't serve her and then they start looking for the waiter with the red hair?"

Mack's toothpick jumped. "Yeah," he said, "you're right on time. Let's go get some coffee and a Danish, but don't take no more damn orders."

They pushed through the other door and walked down the aisle of parlor seats, and at the end of that one was the small booth of a kitchen. The attendant gave Henry the tray of coffee and Danish without a word, and later Henry wanted to pat himself on the back, for just four steps away from the booth he heard the attendant ask, "How's the kids, Morgan?" It took him a split second to guess that he was disguised as Morgan.

"Coming along fine, thanks," he said, squeezing through the door held open by Mack. In the platform space before the door leading to the dining car, Henry shook his head in relief and his mustache fell in the coffee. He dipped his fingers into the coffee, retrieved the mustache, shook it out, and had it stuck on before he was stepping down the aisle again. The passengers paid him for the coffee and Danish and he went back to the end of the car and through the door to the dividing platform, having stopped momentarily to glance at a little boy with a baseball glove, thinking that maybe when everything was straight, when the movement had gotten the country back where it should be, he would be able to play. He put the plastic tray against a wall and asked Mack what should be done with the three quarters the lady had given him.

"Keep it," said Mack, advancing this time through the other door and adding, "let's find the roomette."

He tipped behind Mack, past the booth of a kitchen and through the parlor car and onto another platform division and through another heavy steel door. Now the aisle was much narrower than those in the other cars as they made their way, Henry's shoulders bumping against the walls of the sleeping berths. A conductor, a black man who looked uncommonly familiar to Henry, was advancing toward them, half of his face bobbing left and right over Mack's shoulder.

"Looking for roomette six?" he asked, and even the voice, disturbed by the rattling click of the train wheels, sounded distantly familiar to Henry, so he moved closer to Mack and peered over his shoulder. It was the same conductor! It was the same conductor who had been on the subway going to Star Stadium. "Follow me, MacAdams," turning, spinning around and suddenly pushing through another door to his side. Henry, dipping his head, entered the roomette with the two men. The conductor pulled the shade down and then shook the hands of Henry and Runner Mack. Henry stared at his eyes; he wanted the conductor to remember him, to assure him that indeed they had met, however casually, before. But the conductor had looked away from Henry's stare after pumping his hand and twisting it symbolically, and at this point he was working like the sleight-of-hand artist who had tricked Henry out of ten dollars one night after a dance at the Tip In Inn. He lifted up his cap and pulled two wallets out of his hair. Jingling his ring of keys, he reached into his pants pocket and pulled out two slips of paper and gave them both to Runner. Finally, Henry watched him lift a pants leg and pull a pencil out of his sock. "Your clothes are in that bag," he said, pointing to it lying in a corner. "Leave these things"—pointing to Henry's waiter uniform—"in that bag." He swung out of the door and slammed it shut.

Henry looked at Mack and they both sat down. He was tired now, and as he looked at Mack sitting across from him and at the steel gray walls of the roomette, he thought of all the stories he had heard of prisons. It reminded him of a prison cell. He sent the shade up. Trees, only a frieze of trees blurring past the rectangular, cracked, dirty window. Mack tore up the two pieces of paper.

"We have to get a truck at a rock festival to get the final plans," he said, standing to take his disguise off, and soon he was only in his underwear. Henry watched Runner Mack change into a blue denim suit with a sign on the back sewn in red, announcing SUPREME MAINTENANCE CO. Henry changed, too, stuffed his elevator shoes and the rest of his old outfit into the bag, then sat down to look through his wallet.

It is like a jail cell, he told himself, and we have to break out of here or suffer for the rest of our lives. In the billfold section of the wallet he found some fives and tens and twenties, and he stopped counting at five hundred, telling himself that this was the break-out money. Also there was an identification card with his photograph on it, but the photograph looked like the one taken in his senior year at high school, and he discovered a piece of paper with phone numbers written in tiny print. So these were his tools, he told himself. And when he had been staring at his card for a while, he realized that the name wasn't Henry Adams, but Paul

Williams. These were his tools for breaking out of here, he repeated to himself, and he would be a new man, a new black man; awakened, sore, angry, strong. He couldn't think of himself as Henry Adams anymore, he was convincing himself, enjoying the smell of the wallet's new leather. Of course, his family was part of that old life and so was Beatrice, but everything else connected to it, everything that had annoyed and perplexed and suffocated him in the past, was canceled out of his memory. He was canceling them out right now. He would leave them all here in this gray, impotent little swaying room and burst out in a subversive and demolitionary act of rebellion. He and Mack. When they left this room he would say, so long, Boye; so long, Stumpy; so long, Nevins, and so long to all the delirious shit I've had to encounter. It's all, all over; very, very much over, folks. Things will never be the same anymore. And Daddy, try—at least *try* to understand what I'm doing.

11

TWO DAYS LATER Henry woke up to the long, hoarse yelling of the train's horn. They were slowing down. Mack was already dressed, had the shade up and was peeking out, a slash of sunlight jumping on his cheek.

"This is it," he said.

Henry dressed quickly, folded up his bed, and he couldn't drink the coffee or finish the roll that Mack had saved for him. The jittery feeling was still there in the bottom of his stomach, but he was not afraid, just anxious. Since leaving the war, he had been feeling like a pinch-hitter just brought up from the minors. He knew it was a test, knew he could perform, yet the awful magnitude of the task, of the expectation—that it was up to him—kept him on edge. But he was not afraid. And Mack, how did he feel? Was he ever nervous? Did his knees sometimes tremble and did his mouth go dry at times? He never showed it, never showed anything. A very unusual cat, and Henry still knew very little about him. But he did know this about himself: regardless of what happened over the next several days, because of Runnington Mack, he would never be the same person he was before he had met this man. *I didn't know what was wrong with me, and you came along and named it.*

He closed the door behind him and followed Mack through the aisle again as the clanging of the train bell and the squeaking of the wheels filled his ears, and then he was behind Mack, whose hands were supporting his weight as he stood in front of the entranceway, the door open. Faces passing by slowly, trees and bright sunlight behind them.

"Hat up," said Mack, and jumped off the train. Henry went right after him this time, his feet thumping against the hard sand, palms scraping against it, too, as he tried to soften his fall, and as his knees hit the ground hard, the memories of his being hit by a truck and of standing petrified in the snow as they had broken for the helicopter flashed before him. "You all right?" asked Mack, toothpick in his mouth, rising from the ground.

"Sure," he answered, turning to see the caboose clatter past them.

They walked to the other side of the train station as the passengers milled around the Pullman cars, the train now stopped. Henry saw the truck first and pointed it out to Mack. The driver was stepping down from the cab, and Mack gave Henry the signal to walk to the parking lot. The driver, white, met them halfway. He had long hair, red; a beard; wire-rimmed eyeglasses, and his uniform was similar to Henry's and Mack's.

"MacAdams," he said, and after they had returned the greeting he pointed with his thumb over his shoulder. "We're parked over there, man, let's go."

Henry noticed the sign on the van: SUPREME MAINTENANCE Co. He sat by the driver and Mack took shotgun. He kept his legs together because space in the cab was tight, and he knew from having ridden in his father's pickup that the gearshift would knock against his knee. Backing up. Driving carefully out of the lot and finally onto a two-lane blacktop, Mack and the driver looking to the rear frequently.

"So you guys are making the big hit, huh?" asked the driver, turning to look at Henry and Mack but not really looking at them, now chewing gum. Henry nodded with Mack. "Oh, by the way, my name's Luther," holding his arm sideways. "So how do you like the Midwest? Listen, it's just as bad as the rest of the shit, it just looks cleaner. It's a mess, man. It's a mess all over, you know? That's why, when I heard about the movement, you know, I said, this is it, you know? This is the only thing that can save us, you know, man. I mean, like it's not only a white thing, it's white and black—it affects all of us. So when I heard that there were blacks in the movement, I felt better. We got to work together, you know."

"Yeah, for a while," Mack said. "Who's the contact man at this festival?"

"I don't know his name, man, but he'll be in the soda booth behind the stage all night. You'll really flip over the festival, man. We have some very groovy vibrations, like the Unreasonable Resonance, the Real Bad Mothers, Slick, and we think the Fluorescent Oriental Rug will show. Very freaky and very acid, you know. It should be a fantastic scene, man."

"Wow!" said Mack, and when Henry glanced at him out of the corner of his eye, he knew Mack had meant something else, for his toothpick wasn't even jumping and his voice was low. "It sounds . . . freaky . . . very . . . freaky. Who's on drum's, Buddy Rich?"

They were off the highway, taking an incline now and the road was soft and dusty and the driver, Luther, slowed to fifteen, Henry saw, and the dust was stirring up and covering the windshield and soon had all of them coughing and smarting as it settled in the cab. They put up the windows. Luther turned off the dirt road to a large stretch of grassland that seemed to Henry was the size of two large outfields. He stopped, pulled the emergency brake and they got out.

"We go up there, man," Luther said, pointing to a slope at the top of which Henry could see a wooden fence that seemed to curve into the sky. So they followed Luther, sometimes losing their footing on the slippery grass, and it occurred to Henry that since he had met Mack he had been climbing and running and dodging and he would be glad it was to be over soon. At the top they stopped to regain their breath. Henry, chest heaving, saw the top of an orange tent with flags above it far to their right inside the fence. Ten yards away was the entrance, and a dozen policemen were talking among themselves on one side of the gate.

"Everything's cool," Luther said, "just follow me." And when they reached the gate he said, "We're here to check the wiring," and they were inside the gate, Henry having fought a great urge to glance at the police. "I'll catch you cats later," Luther said, leaving them, and over his shoulder added, "the stage is down there."

Ahead of them were scattered groups of young, bearded men and women dressed in shawls, capes, gowns, long dresses, lying on the grass. The stage was at the bottom of the plane formed by the slight decline of the field, and Henry saw the orange canvas of a roof come to a cone shape in the middle. Flags along the roof. He didn't see many black faces as they made their way between the groups toward the stage. The sun was dying behind the stage, so when they reached it they were walking in shade. Behind the stage, a soda booth, and a young man with the sleeves of his T-shirt rolled up to his shoulders.

"MacAdams," said Runner, and the greeting was returned.

"You cats take off in the maintenance truck just before tonight's concert ends. You'll be driven to the big city." He stopped to fill a glass of soda for a customer, waited until they were once more alone. "Last big organization meeting tomorrow night under the guise of a union meeting. So everybody will know what to do the following day. That day, day after tomorrow, you'll be flown to the capital. Then the shit is on."

Mack nodded.

"Here's something to loosen you up," he said, handing Henry a small plastic bag. He took it and thanked the man, and felt a new surge of excitement run through him. The man had given *him* the bag. He was just as important as Runner Mack now.

"What is it?" he asked.

"Some smoke and papers."

He started for the other side of the stage, leading this time, going up to the spectator field, Mack behind him at first and then walking along. They sat down about sixty yards from the stage, and Henry looked around them at the bunches of young people. Some were about his age, he decided, but many of them seemed younger than he, about the age of the teenager who had been assigned stationary double time in Alaska. They were all smoking, giggling; some lying on their backs staring

200

at the film of rusty haze settling in the sky behind the stage. On his left Henry saw a cluster of youths kneeling in a circle, three bottles of wine propped on their blanket.

"Are most of them with us?" he asked Mack, who was already lighting a joint.

"I guess so," he said, spitting out his toothpick, "but we won't be working with them after the shit goes down, man."

"Why not?" turning to look for hip boots and goggles and not seeing any on the field at all.

"Because they're white and we're black. Our interests are the same now, but they won't always be. We have to get our own movement together, bro, but we can't make a move until the air is clear, you dig?"

"Yeah, I can understand that, Run, but why didn't we just do this with all black brothers and sisters?"

"Because we don't have enough bread, we don't have enough contacts, and half the niggers wouldn't follow us anyway unless they thought a white man was somewhere in the background."

"So we break from them after the bombing?" Henry had finished his joint and was reaching for another. His head was light and his brain was stinging, it seemed, with questions and statements, but he couldn't form the sentences as fast as he wanted and he felt them rise up within his mind and he would try to grab at one but the others would slip away, and then the question that he wanted to ask, the one that he had grabbed at originally, would slip away; and then another series of questions and statements would form.

"We have to, Henry. We have to. Can't you dig what I've been trying to tell you all along? We have to look out for ourselves because nobody else will. And the only way we can do that is organize, bro. That's why I keep talking to you about our history. We ain't never been together. Look at Du Bois and Garvey, beautiful black brothers fighting between themselves. We can't afford that."

His words kept getting louder and louder, then softer and softer, as if he was alternately speaking out of a bullhorn and then whispering, and Henry was nodding to keep up with his arguments. Some of Mack's words were booming against

Henry's ears; others buzzed by him like passing mosquitos. Then the loud words had colors—dark blues and greens—while the soft words had musical tones. Henry looked to his right at some of the kids. They were sitting upside down.

"But Mack, look," he began, pushing the words in a wheelbarrow up a slope, then slowing down because the words were heavy and they were falling out of the wheelbarrow, so that he had to stop, lean over and pick them up, start over again. "Is . . . is there hope for us? . . . I mean, you've read more history than I . . . than I have . . . you've read more . . . I mean, I'll go down with you because I . . . it's important . . . but . . . Mack . . . what are we supposed to do? . . . How can it mean anything? . . . Suppose we die tomorrow? . . . You see? . . . Will anybody know or care? Will the world stop, Mack? . . . Will Beatrice have our baby? . . . Mack, I want some answers . . . you have them . . . who are we . . . what does this blackness mean, Mack? . . . What am I here for, anyway? . . . Why are we sitting right here right now, Mack?" And then the wheelbarrow was too heavy for him and he dropped it and watched the words spill out, and he fell on his back and closed his eyes, clutched the grass with his fingers to keep from falling out of the boat he was riding.

"Damn," he heard Mack say, the word and the world booming all over Henry's head and he was sure everybody in the world could hear it. "You are really bombed, brother. Look, I don't know, Henry. We might be characters in a book or something, for all I know. But we . . . look, I've been working on this for five years, man. If we can't get it together this time, I may go insane with the rest of these suckers. Henry, we want a change. That's what it's all about. That's why you're so important, because our minds have to be changed like yours was. We have to wake up and understand what's happening to us, and then we can move on, dig?"

"So . . . so—" Henry was lifting himself up on his elbows—"we change the country first and then get our black thing together." He opened his eyes. Two girls were dancing to a portable radio in front of him and Mack, and he couldn't control his laughter. They were dancing. It was the most hilarious scene he could imagine. His shoulders were shaking and his stomach was aching and tears filled his eyes, he was laughing so hard.

"That's right," he heard Mack say.

"Well"—he stifled his laughter—"why can't we get our black thing together first, then change the country?"

"Good question, Adams. But we can't get our shit off under these conditions. Simple as that. Get rid of Stumpy, then you can play ball. Who's this?"

Henry stared down at the stage. Movement of figures in leather vests, guitars swinging. A young man at the microphone, announcing the group; the haze of the sun gone completely; suddenly, the entire front of the field filled with hand-clappers; the music starting, electric in its first chords of guitar melodies, and then it was overwhelmingly loud for Henry as the sound system was synchronized and the blaring, driving rhythm was shooting at his ears from every loudspeaker surrounding the field. He checked out Mack, found him nodding his head, eyes red and wild in the mild blue-gray of the twilight. It was driving Henry dizzy, the swelling, stunning, tin sound of the guitars squealing and plucking right in his ears, and he tried to stand up but the ground swayed on him and hit him squarely on the side of his face and he lay there dazed, watching the twisting legs of a group of dancers in front of him. One of the guitarists was singing now, but Henry couldn't catch the words; it seemed as if he was growling and moaning like the wolves who had chased Henry and Mack during the last stages of their escape from Birthday Pass. Then it was funny, too, the kids leaning with the rhythm of this noise and the singer groaning and Mack sitting on the grass, knees up and his head nodding. So Henry started giggling again, then laughing loudly, and everything was very, very funny; very, very funny.

He was useless, weak and delirious with laughter like that for most of the show. Rolling in the grass and unable to stand, watching half the audience dance and clap; and they were yelling also, right in his ear, all of them, with their hands over their heads, bottles in some of the hands. But Henry heard the music die down at the same time his head was clearing. The figures on the stage were discernible now as they closed their number; no longer were they blurred and out of focus as if he were looking through foggy binoculars at them. He stood up, still feeling mellow, but he was in control of himself and knew where he was and what he was doing. The group was leaving the stage and everyone was clapping.

"Mack, you all right?" Leaning down to his ear.

"Yeah . . . I'm all right," he said, but his eyes still had a serene, dopey blankness and he didn't look at Henry but stared ahead. Henry heard them announce another group and look down to see two musicians setting up drums. "Wow . . . I was bombed . . . I was bombed for a while, man . . . straight out to lunch . . . phew. . . ." Shaking his head.

Henry blinked his eyes. He still had a buzz in his head but he wasn't floating, he was master of himself. "What kind of smoke was that, man?"

Before the Run could respond, Henry heard the blare of the new group fall upon his ears. This one had bongos and a xylophone, and Henry thought he caught four or five disparate rhythms. Someone grabbed his arm. Panicky, he turned.

"Wanna dance, man?" Dark, tiny shades, lenses almost black. Hips twisting in faded blue jeans, a multicolored cloth belt. And her breasts. They were sliding up and down and he could see the points pressing against her white T-shirt. She took his hands and led him to her circle, and when he turned in the Run's direction, he saw that Mack too was being led by one of the girls. Her hands were soft and white, fingers thin. *Like Beatrice's. Like Beatrice's.* The whole group was dancing and laughing. Henry moved with the girl and now Mack was beside him and dancing with the one who had pulled him up, and then Henry couldn't take his eyes off the girl's breasts. He tried to compare their size to Beatrice's, but he wasn't sure, it had been so long. He looked over at Mack. He had a toothpick in his mouth and was shaking his arms, his face was serious.

Her smile seemed perpetual. It worried him until he decided that she must be high—they all must be high—and then his mind guiltily convinced him that he could probably score, that she probably wanted him to make a move anyway. Her tongue moved over her lips and she kept taking steps that brought her closer to him until one time, for an instant, the dull, plain odor of perspiration around her, she pressed her stomach and breasts against him. He looked over at Mack. Mack had his arms around his girl's waist and her head was nestled against his chest, her hair wild over her shoulders. Then Henry's girl was moving closer to Henry again and this time he had resolved to fondle the round bulge of her breasts if she pressed them against him, but before he could lift his hands one of the boys in the group said, "Let's go in the woods."

They shot out in single file, each male pulling a girl with him, and Henry was dragged along, Mack behind him. They pranced down the slope to the left of the main field and then trampled through a path littered with stones and branches until they got to a small opening. It was getting darker and most of the kids were shadows to Henry. They started dancing again. The girl had taken off her glasses as they ran down the path. To their left, a commotion. Two of the couples had taken off their clothes, thrown them on the ground and were dancing around. Then there were more. Henry strained to see. Then he rubbed his eyes. Some had formed a circle but Henry could see that on the ground was a couple and he was on top of her and those above the couple were clapping. But he was distracted. His girl and Mack's—they were closest to the slope —began peeling off their clothes and stood white, pale and naked before them, then turned to run to the circle, running sideways and beckoning Henry and Mack, and it wasn't until he looked at Mack with his maintenance suit did he realize that they were the only ones wearing clothes. It was wild and strange, and he wanted to run down, and yet something was pulling him back. The girls were waving for them.

"Let's get out of here, Mack," he said, not knowing where his resolve, his sudden sense of determination, his feeling of disaffiliation had come from. "This is not us."

"Right on," said Mack. "These muhfuckahs are ca-ra-zee, Henry. We don't belong here," climbing up the slope on fours.

The second band was still playing when they got to the back of the stage and received the signal from the soda vendor that the truck was ready. When they got to the gate Henry was filled with the fear that Mack was still high, for he left Henry and walked over to one of the policemen and whispered something in his ear, then they both looked at Henry. The policeman told a detail to follow him and went through the gate.

"I told them some kids were starting fires and running around naked," Mack said, reaching Henry, and they both laughed, then made their way carefully down the incline to the parking lot and ran for the maintenance truck. The motor was running and the driver was a brother, and he nodded to them, gave the signal and took off double-shifting.

For Henry, the drive to the East was a groggy nightmare, a chilling journey of uncomfortableness and toll booths, roadside cafés, long stretches of trees, motels and some mountains, inclines, sharp turns, bumps, quick stops. His eyes were open half the time and even then his lids were heavy and he wasn't sure whether he was dreaming or not; knew that it was an ordeal, that he had gone through an anthology of traveling episodes and that this would be the last long trip for him and Mack, but especially for him. And how long had Runner Mack, the Run, endured these scenes? Now there was a man who would make history, this Runnington Mack, and Henry loved him, would go down with him forever, this strong black man asleep, head against the window and the ever-present toothpick steady. He would see Beatrice soon and explain everything to her and assure her that it was all over—the nightmare would be awakened away—and their child would make it. Somehow he had changed up: had left her as a man asleep and would return bursting with wakefulness. Quick sense of terror: suppose . . . no, nothing could happen to her, she was too strong . . . but he hadn't received a letter from her . . . suppose they . . . whoever they were. . . .

They were breaking into the dawn now, and Mack stirred. He frowned and wiped his mouth. The daylight rising soft, muted, like the many early mornings Henry had arisen to go to school. Yawning as the window turned gray and rolling away from it, especially in the winter, trying to bury his head in the pillow. He heard Mack grunt. Then the driver, who hadn't said anything during the entire trip, and whom Henry had inexplicably dismissed from his memory as if the truck were rolling along by remote control, said, "We should be there in a half-hour." Heart beating fast again, but he knew he couldn't be frightened of anything, ever in his life. The fear had been frightened out of him. The unclean, uncoordinated feeling of waking up was about him. His eyes didn't feel up to their capacity yet. His mouth was dry. His face felt ashy. Mack strangely quiet, but fully awake.

"Anybody follow us?" he asked.

The driver shook his head.

"The shit's been almost too easy," he said, looking straight ahead.

"We've been planning for years," said the driver. "It should be smooth."

Mack said to Henry, "God, I hate this place sometimes. I'd like to leave it. Just split."

"Where would you go, Mack?"

"Where is there to go? There's no place to go, you can't escape."

"Africa?" Henry suggested. "What about Africa?"

"I was born in America," Mack said, "and I'm staying here. I don't talk like an African, don't dance like an African, don't walk like an African. Anyway, the Europeans are trying to drive them crazy."

Over a bridge. The city on the other side. Stone walls sticking above the haze. Bad smell of the river. Then the truck coming off the bridge and rumbling down the expressway to downtown, and there was little traffic, and Henry admitted to a strange feeling of nostalgia and—was it really gladness? Curving around the end of the expressway. "I used to work there," said Henry, pointing to rectangles of gray brick. "Home Manufacturing."

"Nice," said the driver, pulling off the expressway and onto a pothole-filled street. Henry saw the familiar bridge. Down by the waterfront. The automobile junkyard. "Here we are," he said, stopping. Then, as Henry followed Mack out, "It's all up to you." Speeding off.

So they were there. Henry stood with Mack and looked around. Rusting cars piled on top of each other; wheels missing, windows smashed, fenders dented. Farther from them, by the river, a tall woden box peeked out from among the rubbish of metal, and Henry, moving to the side, read the white painted letters above the door of the box: CUSTODIAN. He saw a man in overalls come out the door, and he was quickly reminded of Leon Mark's outhouse. The man had a pipe. He beckoned.

"Mack—" Henry interrupted Runner as he started for the custodian's house. "Do you need me for a while? I live close by and—"

"Go ahead, man. But be careful. Try to get back before noon, okay?" Moving toward the wooden box.

Henry balanced himself with his arms outstretched as he stepped over the obstacle course of burned tin cans, exhaust pipes, bald tires. He made it to the sidewalk. There was little traffic and few pedestrians. It was very early. Still the sky was pale and thick with haze, and this was one of the few mornings during the last months that he had not seen the sunlight clearly. He passed a dog lifting its leg on a fire hydrant; and another one, his hair scraggier than any wolf's Henry had seen in Alaska, was squatting on the curb, his owner looking away. Henry's nose was clogged now and his eyes—he tried to blink away the burning of his eyeballs. He knew he had one more block to go, but he hadn't noticed before that there were so many abandoned buildings, their brick fronts caked with dust, windows streaked with brown mildew. He turned finally to his street. The garbage cans were lined up on the sidewalk; a black cat jumped out of one near Henry. The same street signs; the cars parked as they had been when he left; even the few roaming dogs, noses skimming the ground, looked familiar. He ran.

Up the cement steps, bursting through the door, down the hall with its same rancid smell, turning and pounding up the stairway, then stopping in front of his door. "Beatrice. Beatrice." He pushed the door open. She was sitting on the couch. She jumped up and ran toward him. He embraced her, and every part of her body was comfortably the same: warm, agreeable, soft, shivering. But she started to whimper on his shoulder and then her body shook against his and he felt the tears on his neck, heard her whine; her fingernails were digging into his back. They stood holding each other. She smelled as though she had just bathed. "Let's go sit down," he said, leading her to the couch, and her hand went up to her mouth as she choked out her cries. On the television a bikinied lady was lying on the roof of a brand-new car, but there was no sound.

"Everything's going to be all right," he said, sitting beside her, his arm around her shoulder, kissing her on the neck and cheeks. "God. I missed you so much. But I'm going to take care of you, baby. Just relax. Did you get my letters?" She was still crying but she was taking deep breaths to steady herself. "Did you get my letters, Beatrice?" She was looking at him now. "Beatrice, the letters . . . did you get them?" Her eyes were strange—red and puffed from crying—but still strange, as if they didn't see him.

"I can't hear you, Henry," she said. She shook her head.

"You want me to speak louder?" Her eyes were innocent again. "Beatrice, can you hear me? Can you hear me?"

"Henry. I'm deaf. The noise outside . . . all that noise . . . I . . . it got quieter and quieter until . . . I can't hear anything." Tears again.

Sharp pang of anger. He couldn't move and he couldn't see —the room was spinning. He stood up. "Deaf? Deaf?" He was whispering to himself. "Deaf?" Yes, she was deaf, of course! Oh my God, my God. His head was swimming with anger. He glanced at the television. He walked over, grabbing without looking at something to throw at it, and smashed in the screen. Then he kicked it and bent down to pull out the cord and moved to the front again and kicked at wires and tubes until it was steaming and crackling. Beatrice ran to the bathroom.

She's deaf, he thought, staring at the bedspread. My wife is deaf and she didn't even do anything. All that banging and shouting and buzzing—and now she's deaf and who cares? They'll just go on. God, Mack, we have to end it. "I'll be right back, Beatrice," he said, and ran out the door, down the steps, through the hall, outside, and he was almost knocked down by the change. People were on the street now. Cars were easing down also, horns honking, and it was the same scene. The city had awakened and it was crowded, noisy, dirty, and he pushed his way down the street, bumping against the shoulders of the pedestrians, pushing them out of his way. When he got to a corner he stopped to look at the tangle of steel and bodies zigzagging through the haze and clamor and he wanted to yell, "Stop it! Stop it! Please! My wife is deaf, stop it!" Then across the street and along the avenue to the junkyard.

He found Mack waiting outside the wooden cubicle with his hands on his hips, face skyward. "Look at this shit, Henry. They've really fucked up this city good," he said. "I can hardly hear myself. You can't even see the sky, man. It stinks."

Then Henry remembered that he had told Beatrice he would be back soon, but she hadn't heard him. She *couldn't* have heard him. Well, she would be safe until he returned tomorrow. If he hadn't left right then, he might never have been able to. God, what else could happen to her? "I know, Mack. You know what I just did, Mack? I kicked in the television screen."

"Good move. Damn good move. How's your people?"

Henry squinted his mouth and turned away from Mack. "Should we be getting up?"

"Yeah," said Mack, checking his watch. "We can lay in the coliseum until the meeting starts. We have a couple of hours."

Again through the discard of the junkyard, the full pandemonium of the city swelling their ears. Airplanes, derricks, tugboats, construction machinery, car horns, whistles, shouts, fire engines. Squeezing and pushing through the streets. Eyes smarting from the mantle of eerie, rust smoke hovering over the buildings. Coughing and out of breath from lack of air, they reached the building, its sign in neon, UNION HALL.

"MacAdams," said the porter, and his round face was smiling and the shoulders of his uniform were spotted with specks of incinerator ash. They followed him down the hall to the auditorium and then behind the stage to a dressing room. They sat down on two cloth chairs.

Henry didn't know what they said to each other after that or how they had fallen asleep, only that he had, and Mack had too, and now he was waking up. Mack jumped up and peeked outside.

"They're coming in," he said. "We'll wait until the place is filled. We've got dudes coming in from all over the country,

Henry. You know how long I've been working on this shit? This is it. Damn, I don't even have my speech ready."

Henry looked over Mack's shoulder. Three men sat in the auditorium; one in the rear, two on the right side. He sat down again. They waited without speaking, Henry tense, anxious. Thirty minutes later, he followed Mack to the door and looked out again. Five people were in the auditorium, one sitting in the front row and picking his nose.

"Aren't they supposed to be here by now, Mack?"

"Yeah," said Mack.

"What's happening?" Something was disintegrating in his stomach. "Do you think they got caught? Mack, suppose we've been—"

"Be cool, Henry."

Twenty minutes later. Henry looked out by himself. He counted seven, and a woman was walking in to make eight. He told Mack. He watched the Run smack a fist in his palm, turn his head and walk to a corner of the room.

"They've bullshitted us," he said, voice so low Henry could hardly hear him.

"What?"

"They don't care, Henry, that's all. The shit's broken down. Out of the whole movement, only eight dudes who aren't bullshittin', Henry. Damn." His back was bent as he sat backwards now in a chair in the corner.

"We can start all over, then. Postpone the bombing until—"

"I can't do it anymore, Henry."

"Mack, that's the only answer—"

"There are no answers, Henry, that's the whole problem. I just figured it out. There are no answers. We just keep trying and planning and it doesn't mean anything. History keeps going and we keep trying and nothing happens and somebody else says, 'I'll do it,' and they try and nothing really changes. There are no answers, Henry. We just keep going on and on, hoping it will make sense, but it never does, does it?"

"But it has to, Mack. Otherwise, what's the use?"

"Exactly. What's the use if it's just the same shit over and over again?"

"Mack, I think we have to go on—"

"Well, you organize it then. I've had it."

Henry watched him walk out the side door. He followed, then stopped at the door, watched him walk down the hall to the men's room, and there was no bop to his walk, and as he turned to push in the door, Henry noticed that there was no toothpick in his mouth, either. He sat down in the dressing room. There has to be an answer, he told himself. He couldn't give up, not after all this. It has to make sense, but only if we keep trying. I don't care about that history stuff just being over and over again. So what? That was no reason to stop. Mack's just talking, a little upset. He'll be all right. We'll get it together. We can't give up. Maybe he should go down and talk it over with Mack? Yes, he was just down in the dumps. They could still bomb the White House, couldn't they? Then maybe the people in the movement would care. He pushed the door open, his shoes echoing against the tile.

"Mack?" Voice hollow. "Mack?"

He stood under the stalls. Nothing. Had he left? Wait. He heard a strange, flat knocking in one of the stalls. But nobody was in there. He walked down to it. Still the knocking. Each tap lighter and further apart than the other. He looked under the stall. Couldn't see a thing. He pulled on the handle. It was locked. Finally, he lifted himself, hands on the top of the stall's door, and looked in.

"Oh, Jesus," he said, and fell down on the floor and sat there. He started crying. His body shook, wrists, knees, heart trembling. Then he jumped up, feet slipping on the tiles, ran toward the door, pulled it open, brushed past a man, and hustled down the hall. He didn't know where he was going, but he knew he had to run, because it was rapidly making little sense and he knew that if he was still for a minute to digest everything he would have to give up. He knew if he had stayed in that bathroom and begun to contemplate what Runner Mack's hanging himself had meant to him, Runner, then he, Henry, would be drained. And he couldn't be drained. He had to run, search, look, fight—but more than anything, not give up. So through the lobby, over the rubber mat and out, crashing his arm against the handle of the glass door, onto

212

the sidewalk, picking up speed, running, barely hearing a voice screaming, "Look out, look out for that—" He saw the white line in the middle of the street and his knees were still going high. Again, "Look—watch it—" He glanced to his right and saw the truck bearing down on him, the shiny rectangles of a grille, the two figures in the cab, the pumpkin-sized glass headlamps, the engine groaning, and the mouth of a fender smiling at him, smiling at him . . . smiling.